Praise for the Davis Way Crime Caper Series

DOUBLE STRIKE (#3)

"*Double Strike* is special—funny, unique, and I love Davis."
– Janet Evanovich

"Delightful and hilarious...this novel shines with its resilient and reliably acerbic heroine, and the mystery is at its strongest when it highlights and exposes the fascinating details behind gambling, casinos, and the domination of social media. This is an extremely fun and entertaining third entry."
– *Kings River Life Magazine*

"Fasten your seat belts: Davis Way, the superspy of Southern casino gambling, is back (after *Double Dip*) for her third wild caper."
– *Publishers Weekly*

DOUBLE DIP (#2)

"A smart, snappy writer who hits your funny bone!"
– Janet Evanovich

"Archer's bright and silly humor makes this a pleasure to read. Fans of Janet Evanovich's Stephanie Plum will absolutely adore Davis Way and her many mishaps."
– *RT Book Reviews*

"Slot tournament season at the Bellissimo Resort and Casino in Biloxi, Miss., provides the backdrop for Archer's enjoyable sequel to *Double Whammy*...Credible characters and plenty of Gulf Coast local color help make this a winner."
– *Publishers Weekly*

"Snappy, wise cracking, and fast-paced."
–*New York Journal of Books*

D1104474

"Hilarious, action-packed, with a touch of home-sweet-home and a ton of glitz and glam. I'm booking my next vacation at the Bellissimo!"

"Take a gamble and read *Double Dip*! Five stars out of five."

"Davis and her associates, in particular Fantasy and No Hair, are back in this sophomore drama by Ms. Archer that does not disappoint in delivering delightfully charming and amusing adventures from the halls of the Bellissimo."

DOUBLE WHAMMY (#1)

"If Scout Finch and Carl Hiaasen had a baby, it would be Davis (Way). *Double Whammy* is filled with humor and fresh, endearing characters. It's that rarest of books: a beautifully written page-turner. It's a winner!"

"Archer navigates a satisfyingly complex plot and injects plenty of humor as she goes. This madcap debut is a winning hand for fans of Janet Evanovich and Deborah Coonts."

"Fast-paced, snarky action set in a compelling, southern glitz-and-glamour locale. A loveable, hapless heroine Jane Jameson would be proud to know. Utterly un-put-down-able."

DOUBLE
MINT

**The Davis Way Crime Caper Series
by Gretchen Archer**

DOUBLE WHAMMY (#1)
DOUBLE DIP (#2)
DOUBLE STRIKE (#3)
DOUBLE MINT (#4)

DOUBLE MINT

A DAVIS WAY CRIME CAPER

Gretchen Archer

HENERY PRESS

DOUBLE MINT
A Davis Way Crime Caper
Part of the Henery Press Mystery Collection

First Edition
Trade paperback edition | July 2015

Henery Press
www.henerypress.com

Copyright © 2015 by Gretchen Archer
Author photograph by Garrett Nudd
Bently photograph by Kenneth Munoz

ISBN-13: 978-1-941962-77-0

Printed in the United States of America

For Bently

ACKNOWLEDGMENTS

Thank you Deke Castleman, Claire McKinney, Larissa Ackerman, Cheryl Green, Stephany Evans, and Kendel Lynn.

ONE

Jeep USA rewarded the top fifty Jeep dealerships in North America by sending the franchise owners and their families to Lahaina, Maui, Hawaii, where they spent two glorious weeks in private villas with names like Kamaole Estates, Hula Paniau, and Wailea Beach. Sixteen-year-old Kiki Logan, whose father owned the Jeep dealership in Jackson, Mississippi, hooked up with seventeen-year-old Austin Griffith, whose father owned the Jeep dealership in Hattiesburg, Mississippi. They lied to their parents in general, but specifically about sneaking out to meet the other. They hid on a strip of secluded beach beside a shallow saltwater lagoon and drank spiked Hawaiian Punch for most of the second week. Fast-forward eight months, and it's Hele Mai 'Oe I Ko Maua Male 'Ana! (We're Getting Hitched!) and Hāpai Kaikamahine! (It's a Girl!) at the Bellissimo Resort and Casino in Biloxi, Mississippi.

Where I work.

My name is Davis Way Cole. I'm a redhead, a newlywed, and lead investigator on an undercover team for the casino, which is to say I, along with my partners Fantasy Erb and Baylor (just Baylor, like Batman) perform workplace duties no sane person would ever agree to. Tonight's impossible task? The Hawaiian Jeep wedding.

The families were bitter rivals and sworn enemies from way back who couldn't agree on anything, much less a wedding venue, so the wedding was booked on our neutral ground. Huge wedding. The $100,000 package. It was all so Romeo and Juliet.

The mother of the bride and the mother of the groom raised all kinds of hell in the weeks leading up to the wedding, which was nothing compared to the fits they pitched when they checked in and began tearing it up in person. Our special events coordinator, Holder Darby—mid-fifties, '80s big hair, wears Birkenstock clogs every single day of the year—who'd been with the Bellissimo booking, organizing, and being paid very well for coordinating every wedding, reunion, and conference since 1996, walked off the job. She didn't show up for work Wednesday or Thursday, and finally on Friday, the day of the rehearsal dinner, Human Resources tracked her down. Holder told them she would never set foot in the Bellissimo again, ever, she'd had it with being bullied, threatened, and strong-armed, send her last paycheck via the United States Postal Service, and don't call back. All because of a Hello Kitty cake.

The wedding parties checked in on Tuesday. Groom's Mother arrived first. She burst into Holder Darby's office to have a word about the bride's cake. It got ugly, and Holder had to call security. Groom's Mother, who housekeeping reported "ate rocks for breakfast" and was "mean as a snake," incensed at having been kicked out of Holder's office, decided to give it another go. She laid in wait, then followed the wedding coordinator out of the employee parking garage all the way to her Sunkist Country Club Road home. Groom's Mother angled her Jeep Laredo E against the back bumper of Special Events Coordinator's Audi S8 sedan, then climbed out of the car, dragged poor Holder out of hers, and put her in a headlock. She told Holder if she heard the words "Hello" or "Kitty" one more time in regard to her only son's wedding, she would take that cake and shove it so far up Holder, she'd have Hello Kitty coming out her ears for six months. Holder didn't even clean out her desk, she just stopped coming to work.

Until she could be replaced, Holder's job fell in my lap. Starting with the Hawaiian wedding. Mission? To keep the Jeep people from killing each other over a Hello Kitty cake. Here's how stupid this fight is: The groom's cake is a towering Minecraft number garnished with diamond, emerald, and eyeball cupcakes.

The ballroom was split down the middle. The families marked

their territories with two completely different decors, menus, and live entertainment. This marriage was doomed.

We made it through dinner without incident, the Hello Kitty cake was cut and served without bloodshed, and it looked like we were home free when the very pregnant bride propped her swollen feet in a chair and the older Jeep guests began nodding off. It was the dance bands who started the war. The Groom's band began playing Van Morrison's "Crazy Love" before Bride's band finished the last few measures of Frank Sinatra's "Fly Me to the Moon." A contractual infraction. The lead singers began arguing from their respective stages over headset microphones. Ugly things about each other's questionable paternity. F-bombs all over the place. In the blink of an eye, twenty musicians were off those stages and in a pile on the dance floor, fists and bass guitars flying. Every wedding guest under the age of sixty hit the dance floor and joined in.

Fantasy and I, on opposite sides of the brawl, spoke via earpieces.

"Where's Baylor?" I asked. "He needs to get in there and break it up." A man's shoe flew in front of my face. Then a bridesmaid's bouquet.

"Need some help over here, Davis."

I hopped on a chair and spotted Fantasy across the ballroom. She was wrestling a fire extinguisher away from a wedding guest who was trying to run out on the dance floor with it.

Good idea. I pulled my phone from my pocket, hacked the Bellissimo's building management control system, and turned on the sprinklers. Five alarm, full blast, make it rain. The fighting stopped, but the rain didn't. I managed to turn the sprinklers on and in the process, drowned my phone, so I couldn't turn them off.

It took until midnight to get the soggy guests sorted and disposed of. Thirteen were hauled off to jail, including five from the Top Forty band, two from the Jazzy Lounge band, and just the one Groom's Mother. The other guests were sent to their hotel rooms, with the bride and her family traveling via ambulance to Biloxi Regional Medical Center where she delivered a seven-pound five-ounce baby girl. The whole time, a cleaning crew pushed industrial wet-dry vacs through the ballroom. The groom was finally located in a guest room with a Hello Kitty bridesmaid, dry as a bone.

I didn't get home until one in the morning, and when I did, I woke up my husband.

"Bradley." I climbed into the warm bed. "You have to call Holder Darby and make her come back to work."

He pulled me into a hug and kissed my forehead. "You have frosting in your hair."

*   *   *

The problem wasn't Hello Kitty; the problem was summer.

Summer, with its fireworks, flip-flops, and SPF fifty, is the least welcome of the four seasons in casino land. From June through August, it's a madhouse. Diehard gamblers stay home and wait it out.

That we're on the Gulf doesn't help a bit, because the humidity stays at equator rainforest sauna levels. You can't step outside without being attacked by swarms of love bugs, plus red tide rolls in, unpacks, and gets comfy.

It isn't any better inside.

For one, the bell just rang, so it's a playground of hot sticky children and their hot sticky parents. ("I will wear every last one of you out right here and right now, I mean it. Shut up and stop hitting each other. Get down from there. I am not playing around.") (This is before they even have a room key.) Families are notoriously unprofitable for casinos, because they spend their vacations chasing themselves up and down the halls and around the pool, logging at least five hours a day at Plenty, our new buffet, and standing in line at Lost and Found to pick up the kids they've misplaced. They're everywhere but in the casino.

Then there are the weddings. Wedding parties spend their time and money at photo shoots, spa parties, all-day golf and fishing excursions, bridal luncheons, and tux fittings. Weddings keep the hotel, catering, floral, the salon, all eight bars, and in the case of the Hello Kitty, local police, fire house, and hospitals busy, but they don't get anywhere near the casino.

So Holder Darby, to offset all this unprofitability and keep the marketing people off her back, spent her winters booking summer conventions. Trade shows. Professionals Behaving Badly. Holder booked and planned the conferences singlehandedly and in my three years, there'd never been a bleep on the conference radar. The Bellissimo loved summer conferences for the warm body and bottom line contributions, and until now, by all accounts, the Bellissimo had loved Holder Darby. Because if it weren't for the Tiki Torch Researchers of New England, Ostrich Farmers United, and Flavored Dental Floss Reps of America, this place would go flat broke, and all because of summer. She had the summer packed out with fraternity, family, and Friends of Fleetwood Mac reunions, twelve conferences, countless weddings, then ran off and left it with me.

*　*　*

By noon Sunday I'd (shampooed the frosting out of my hair) taken fifteen Holder Darby calls and put out fifteen Holder Darby fires, including ordering $28,000 in replacement wedding banquet chairs and tracking down a wayward load of lobster. Is this what she did on her day off? No wonder she quit.

Half of the people checking in for the next conference didn't like their rooms. (What's not to like? It's a five-star resort on the beach.) The Massey-Ortiz wedding planner and her team arrived to prep for next weekend's nuptials and they weren't happy about the soggy reception hall. (I got chewed out in rapid-fire Spanish when I suggested we move the wedding to the outdoor pavilion. "*¡Los insectos del amor!*")

The Wagner Family Reunion needed a pediatrician, or four, because half of the Wagner preschoolers woke up with an odd purple rash on their feet, and the other half had bacterial swimmer's ear. (Take them home.) So at one o'clock on my day off, a day Bradley and I try to spend being married, the only day of the week he doesn't work twelve straight hours, I called Holder Darby myself. I didn't care what it took, we needed her back.

At three, when she still hadn't answered, I walked out my front door, hopped into my car, and drove to her house. My front door is on the twenty-ninth floor of the Bellissimo. My car is four elevator rides and a long dark walk through a tunnel away. And driving to Holder's Sunkist Country Club Road home didn't do me any good, because she was gone.

The house, a white brick and stucco Mediterranean with a circular drive and a professionally-decorated lawn, was pretty. Maybe ten years old, one level, big square windows all across the front, on a wide lot in a nice quiet neighborhood. I parked in the circle and eyed the newspapers strewn around the front porch. I marched up three porch steps and rang the bell. I heard an insane scream coming from inside.

I beat on the door. "Holder! Holder! Are you in there?"

More insane screaming.

I dodged azalea bushes on my way around the house, tried the door that led to the garage, a car inside, but it was locked. I pushed through a white waist-high gate to the backyard, nice infinity pool, long and skinny with a stone fountain on one end, and hopped across round terracotta stepping stones to the back porch. I pounded on the French doors.

"Holder? Holder!"

I ducked out of sight when I heard the screaming round the corner and head my way. I peeked. It was a cat. A fat, yellow, flat-faced cat, with a long thick tail, bared teeth, and terrific lungs. I could see down its throat. I don't speak cat, but the cat's dining room was on Holder's kitchen counter, a fish-shaped rubber mat, and it was obvious what the yelling was about. Two silver bowls were tipped over, both empty. I shook the doorknobs; the cat shrieked.

"Hold on, cat." I dug in my Super Secret Spy bag—think doctor bag, full of tools I need for my trade, but much nicer, because Michael Kors made mine. The cat, screaming bloody murder and racing back and forth against the French doors, was making me nervous. I dumped out my spy bag on a patio table. From the pile, I grabbed my new gun, a G42, the brand new .38mm and the smallest Glock pistol ever made, and my Quik-Piks, a set of universal bump keys. The only doors I can't get in with my Quik-Piks are cockpit, White House, and my mother's. (She's on to me.) Where did I get this amazing tool? Amazon.

I wiggled past the lock, stepped into Holder Darby's kitchen, and the cat began weaving in, around, and through my legs, still breaking the sound barrier with its asylum noises. With my eyes and gun everywhere, I inched to what looked like a pantry, reached in, blindly grabbed a box, then dumped a small hill of cat crunchies on the counter. The cat hopped up and, thank goodness, shut up. I filled a coffee cup with water from the kitchen sink and put it beside the crunchies. "Chew your food, cat." That cat had absolutely no use for me now that it had food. "You're welcome," I whispered. "Where's Holder?"

Leaving my shoes in the kitchen, I cleared Holder's home room by room (nice master with patio that led to the pool, closet large enough for four QVC-addicted women), and Holder Darby was not here. Odd lights were on—nightstand, front hall, patio—so she'd probably left at night. An assortment of prescription bottles were lined up, smallest to largest, along the bathroom vanity. Wherever she'd gone, she hadn't packed, and she had high blood pressure, something I completely understood, because the woman had the world's worst job. And she'd left in the middle of a movie. I sat on the first of three steps that led down to a media room, where a Blu-ray logo swam across the television screen and a full glass of wine on a small table beside a lounger had been collecting fruit flies, another fun summer Gulf amenity.

I called my husband. "Bradley. Holder Darby's gone. Poof. Absolutely gone."

"Davis, get back here," he said. "The vault has been robbed."

TWO

Cats don't like cars.

And I never knew cats were so vocal. Or that they moved at the speed of light. I drive a black Volkswagen Bug, and the cat, when it wasn't hanging upside down from the headliner by its claws, hurled itself face first at the passenger window, which could be why it's face is so flat.

"The window is *closed*, cat. You can't get out."

I didn't grow up with pets, cats or dogs, but I thought they loved riding in cars, sticking their heads out the window. The longest eight-mile drive of my life from Holder Darby's to the Bellissimo, and never again.

Fantasy answered on the first ring. "Are you murdering someone?"

"I'm trying to get a cat in my spy bag."

Dead silence.

"Fantasy, can you come in to work?"

"It's my day off, Davis," she said. "I'm catching up on my stories."

"Just an hour. I promise." Where'd that cat go? This isn't a big car. "And would you stop by Cats R Us on the way in?"

"For what?"

"A cat care package. A cat starter kit. I don't know. Ask the cat people what cats need and bring one of each. But no mice."

Kneeling on the hot pavement, I lured the cat out from under the passenger seat with a red Gummy Bear I found in the floorboard. It finally slinked out, then launched itself through the air, landing on and latching into my head. I tried to peel it off—dancing, gushing blood, shrieking—which only encouraged the cat to sink its claws in deeper. After five minutes of going round and round with the cat on my head in the vendor parking lot, behind the Bellissimo, on a blazing hot Sunday, love bugs everywhere, I got a grip. I stopped fighting the cat and stood there, catching my breath. As soon as I calmed down, so did the cat. I reached up and patted it; I spoke in very soothing tones. "Good kitty. Get off my head, you psycho kitty."

To reward it for letting go of my scalp I gave it the Gummy Bear, which immediately glued its front teeth together, quieting it down and keeping it busy.

Shopping list: Gummy Bears.

Hiding behind sunglasses the size of Frisbees, I entered the building. I had the hair of someone who'd been electrocuted, a few scratches, and a cat tucked under my arm. The cat whipped its absurdly large tail back and forth and slung its head around trying to lose the Gummy. We caught an elevator.

A lady asked, "Is your cat having a seizure?"

The cat, offended, convulsed—its rounded spine digging into my side, and spit at the woman, the red Gummy Bear dangling from one of its dagger teeth.

Good kitty.

I walked in my front door and dropped my Super Spy bag and the cat on the floor. The cat shot off for who knows where. Bradley Cole said, "Oh, my God. Davis."

*   *   *

"We have a visitor."

I nodded.

Bradley gets a look on his face when he wants to tell me something but doesn't quite know how. He got it now.

"What?"

"Maybe?" He put his hands on both sides of my head and patted about my ears, trying to tame my mass of red hair. I held up a finger, ran down the hall, looked in the mirror, fainted (no, I didn't), lassoed my hair into a ponytail, dabbed at the blood, then joined him in the foyer.

"Where'd the cat go?" I asked.

"I don't even care." He took me by the elbow, led me through, then introduced me to Griffin Chase.

What had been a pleasantly boring summer for me officially ended on this swamp hot Sunday in late July, the same day I woke up with frosting in my hair, took ten lobster calls, and discovered Holder Darby left home in a hurry without her cat. While I'd been busy with all that, the Independent Bankers of Alabama had been pouring into the Bellissimo, five hundred strong, including spouses, sponsors, and vendors. The vendor sponsoring the conference was Paragon Protection, a company that provided security products and services, and the bankers were here courtesy of them. Not only was Paragon paying for the bankers to be here, they held a top spot on our Valued Business Partner list. We've done business with them since forever. In fact, they built and installed the Bellissimo vault. This week, in conjunction with the conference, Paragon Protection was scheduled to inspect and conduct any needed repairs to the Bellissimo vault—a chore my husband had been working on for weeks. Paragon built the vault in 1995, installed it in 1996, and came back once a year to make sure everything was A-OK. It was a no-brainer to conduct the annual inspection in conjunction with the conference. For obvious reasons, vault operations needed to be kept hush-hush, and this year's inspection could be conducted discreetly, flying under the radar and cover of the convention. Timing is everything.

The process began with a physical inventory this morning, conducted by Griffin Chase, of Hammond Stevenson Morris & Chase, the Bellissimo's outside accounting firm that audits all things gaming. And it was Griffin Chase, managing partner at the firm, who broke the bad inventory news. Missing from the vault:

four million dollars in platinum coins. Present in the vault: four million dollars in fake platinum coins.

"Who has access to your vault, Brad? Do you know who could have done this?"

I did. I knew exactly who could have done this.

"You're sitting on more counterfeit coins than I've ever seen or heard of in one place. And excellent replicas," he said, "amazingly realistic in quality, color, weight, and design. Do you have any idea where they came from?"

I certainly did. I knew exactly where they came from.

"Do you know who might be responsible?"

Yes, I did. You bet I did. I knew exactly who was responsible.

"Do you want me to contact the Treasury Department?"

"No," my husband said. "We'll handle it."

We locked the door behind him, then took shaky steps to the only seating in our foyer, an Igloo cooler the size of a steamer trunk.

"We're not moving home in two weeks, are we, Bradley?"

We met almost three years ago when I first moved to Biloxi. Two years later, on our wedding day, he accepted the casino manager position at the Bellissimo and we moved here. That was nine months ago.

He pulled me in. I buried there. "Probably not."

"Maybe we'll be one of those happy childless couples."

I could feel his chin on my head. "We're going to have ten babies."

Let's not go overboard.

"What's up with the cat, Davis?"

I looked at my hands. Scratched all to hell. No telling where the cat was.

"The cat story is a long one."

I felt him nod. "Maybe later."

(Later.) "Bradley?"

"Yes?"

"I don't really know what platinum *is*."

"Yes, you do." He reached for my left hand. "Your wedding band is platinum. It's a precious metal. The missing platinum was minted into commemorative Bellissimo coins. Like gold or silver coins, but these are made of platinum."

"Why would the Bellissimo have so much platinum?"

"Just an asset, Davis," he said, "part of our portfolio. The vault has gold and silver too."

"For a rainy day?" I asked.

"For a rainy day."

He traced a deep scratch across the back of my hand.

"Four million dollars is how many coins?" I asked. "Bigger than a breadbox?"

Bradley stretched his legs until his shoes ran into a cast iron tub large enough to swim laps in. "Platinum is like pork bellies, traded on the stock market. And the value fluctuates. An ounce of platinum is worth anywhere from fifteen hundred to two thousand dollars, depending on the market." His shoes tapped the iron tub. "Any way you look at it, four million dollars is two thousand coins or better."

"Like dimes?" I asked. Because two thousand dimes seemed stealable. I remembered a story in the news years ago, when a trucker hijacked her own eighteen-wheeler full of dimes. She went to Vegas and hit the Strip with a Dooney & Bourke bucket bag full of dimes. She parked herself between two ten-cent slot machines and went to town. When she ran out of dimes, she went back to the dime stash in her hotel room and loaded up her Dooney & Bourke again. Busted before the day was out. No one has that many dimes.

"Much larger than dimes," Bradley said. "They're measured on the Troy scale, Davis, and they're the size of silver dollars, but heavier."

How does he know all this? How do I not know all this? Who is Troy?

"So the platinum didn't walk out of the vault." I have a beautiful collection of purses—Louis Vuitton, Gucci, and a Chanel— and not a one of them could hold two thousand coins.

"No," he said. "It didn't."

Mr. & Mrs. Bradley Cole, sitting on an Igloo cooler in the foyer of their home, quietly considered the ramifications of a vault breach. And in that contemplative moment I realized this heist, regardless of where it started or how it ended, wasn't so much the missing platinum or even the value of the missing platinum—let's face it, four million bucks in the broad spectrum of casino economies wasn't all that much money—as it was that the platinum was discovered missing on Bradley's watch.

"Have you told Mr. Sanders?"

"I just got off the phone with him."

"Who did this, Bradley?" I held my breath while waiting on his answer.

"Me." He threw his hands in the air. "Richard and I are the only ones with vault access," he said, "and he's not here."

Wrong answer.

"Start at the beginning," I said. "When's the last time you knew the platinum was in the vault?"

"I'm not sure I ever knew it was there. I've been in the vault exactly twice. A walkthrough when I took this job and an inventory six months ago. Both times with Richard. We opened the bins, we looked, they were full of platinum. It didn't occur to either of us to authenticate it. We were there to count it."

"So the platinum could have been fake six months ago."

"Davis, the platinum *had* to be fake six months ago. I haven't been in the vault, I haven't accompanied anyone into the vault, and I haven't authorized anyone for vault entry."

Our eyes locked. I thought about what our futures held if we didn't find the platinum. (Unemployment.) (Indictments.) (Incarceration.)

The front doors burst open and Fantasy filled them with huge shopping bags in both hands. Baylor was behind her holding a carpeted cat playground. "Where's the cat?" she asked. "What happened to your face?"

* * *

We settled around our coffee table, an actual headstone on iron legs. It said, *Hypolite Bizoton De La Motte—1893 – 1959—HE MET WITH DEATH.*

Baylor, the muscly member of our team, who looks, lives, and loves like the lead singer in a boy band, went all over looking for the cat. No cat. "Did you scare the cat?"

"No! Why would I do that?"

"It isn't hiding from you because you were nice to it, Davis."

"Maybe it's hiding from you, Baylor."

"You need to get another cat," he said. "You can't have just one."

"That's ridiculous." Out of the corner of my eye, I could see Bradley's jaw working, clenching, unclenching. "I don't even want one cat."

"It has to have a friend to play with or it will drive you crazy."

"I tell you what," I said. "You take the cat and get it a friend to play with."

"I can't," he said. "No pets in my building."

"They let you in," Fantasy said.

Bradley shot up from his seat, a black velvet Baroque throne thing trimmed in flaky gold, and said, "Not one more word about the cat."

The subject had been Holder Darby. Specifically, Holder Darby's sudden disappearance. We'd gotten sidetracked talking cat. Earlier, while Bradley and I had been waiting for Fantasy and Baylor to (cat shop) arrive, I'd nosed into Holder's personnel file finding nothing out of the ordinary and only one item of interest; she was from a teeny Alabama town, Horn Hill. I called her in-case-of-emergency contact, her sister, Helen Baldwin, who lived one town over in Gulfport.

"Miss Baldwin, I'm with Animal Control in Biloxi, and we're trying to locate your sister, Holder."

"Yeah?" Helen might be Holder's brother. His/her voice was

deep, thick with testosterone. "Me too," Lady Man said. "I've been calling her since Friday. I think she's really busy at work and her cell phone's dead."

Lady Man, she isn't busy at work and *she* might be dead.

"Why is Animal Control looking for her?" Lady Man asked.

"We have her cat."

"She doesn't have a cat."

"Excuse me?"

"No cat. Holder doesn't have a cat. She's never had a cat."

"Are you *sure*?" Did I bring Tasmanian Cat to my home for no good reason? "Big yellow cat with a smashed-in face? I think its Holder's cat."

"Look," Lady Man said. "Holder doesn't have a cat. Period. I've talked to her every other day of my life and have had lunch with her every Tuesday since we were in our twenties. Holder doesn't have a cat. No cat."

All the cat talk had derailed us. Bradley was anxious to stop talking about the cat and start talking about the vault. Specifically, someone replacing real platinum coins with fake platinum coins. We'd gotten sidetracked on that one too. Baylor had a quarter collection, one from each of the fifty states.

"It's one of those things I want to throw away and can't," Baylor said. "I mean it's like four hundred dollars in quarters."

"It is not, Baylor." Fantasy broke the bad news. "It's like twelve dollars in quarters."

Baylor, who's big and burly and in his mid-twenties, has dark curly hair, smooth olive skin, black bedroom eyes and a little dimple in his chin becoming more pronounced with each of his birthdays, makes a pouty face when women turn him down or when he learns the quarter collection he's been dragging around since high school isn't all that valuable. Women rarely turn him down, so we don't see the pouty face too often, he wasn't very practiced at it, and he looked all of sixteen when he made it.

Fantasy patted his knee.

"It'll be okay, sweetie."

Bradley, at the moment, did not care. He may never have a moment when he cared about Sweetie's quarters.

"Enough, please."

We all cleared our throats and sat up straighter.

Bradley walked a slow circle around our crack team. "The conference starts tomorrow. The vault has been compromised. Holder Darby is gone, Richard is gone, and Jeremy is gone. It's just us, and it's up to us to at least keep the doors open." We nodded. Yes yes yes. "I need you three to focus. Starting now."

I could focus until I had a migraine and still not know where Holder Darby had run off to, but we knew where Richard Sanders, who owns the Bellissimo, and my immediate supervisor No Hair, who others call Jeremy Covey, were. They had been on assignment all summer at the site of our new sister casino, the Jolie. Which left us in charge of the Bellissimo. Which was along the lines of the fox guarding the henhouse.

"We have two people to find," Bradley (the fox) said. "Holder Darby and the person who made off with four million dollars in platinum from the vault."

"Bradley."

He stopped behind my chair, a purple pleather recliner. I tipped my head back and looked up. He's just over six feet, with dusty blonde hair he keeps short, metallic green eyes, perfect teeth, a dip in the middle of his chest I can't leave alone, built like a Major League pitcher, and he rocks his lawyer clothes. I guess they're casino manager clothes now, today a white oxford shirt, yellow tie with tiny Carolina blue emblems, and dark gray gabardine pinstripe pants. His sleeves were rolled up, his tie tossed over his left shoulder. "We know exactly who took the platinum."

"Oh, shit, not this again." Fantasy rolled her whole head. "There goes my vacation."

"I am not going back to that woman's house," Baylor said. "That nutjob beat me with an umbrella."

Bradley's grip tightened on my chair.

"When and why were you at her house, Baylor?"

I shot Baylor a do-not-get-me-in-trouble-with-my-husband look.

"My bad." Baylor surrendered. "I've never been beaten with an umbrella."

"Davis?"

"Bradley I don't know what he's talking about."

My husband, who just turned thirty-six, has been in the gaming industry his entire professional life, but from a legal perspective, which is very different from where he is now, in the trenches, the stakes higher, and the pressure tenfold. It was beginning to show in the corners of his eyes, and he hadn't slept well since we married, which isn't about being married to me, but a combination of the job and where we live. His job is a pressure cooker, and even that isn't so much about the day-to-day running of an empire; it's more about his ridiculously large salary. A big-money job comes with a big responsibility to earn out your big paycheck. While making the big bucks, he was still on the Bellissimo learning curve, a ride, I'm afraid, that never ends. It's a laugh a minute around here, with each hair-raising adventure leaving us nowhere near prepared for the next. It's CasinoLand. You never know what will happen.

Bradley, after giving us a round of the suspicious eyeball, thankfully, let it go. He had bigger things to worry about than cats, collectible quarters, and umbrellas. He reclaimed his spot on his black velvet throne and began barking orders. Get in Holder's office, go back to her house, find her. Keep up with the convention, don't drop that million-dollar-revenue ball, and before this day is out, turn all our energies to tracking the platinum. He was at the end of the long list of impossible tasks when the cat scared us all to death by jumping onto his lap. It pawed around for a minute, made two circles, then settled. Bradley held his hands up while the cat did its dance.

"That is one ugly cat you got there, Davis. Its nose is smashed."

"Fantasy." Baylor was offended. "It's a Persian cat. It's supposed to look that way."

"That is not my cat."

Not My Cat was rubbing all over my husband.

"You're stuck with that cat, Davis," Baylor said. "He likes it here."

"That's impossible, Baylor. No one likes it here."

THREE

It was the collapse of the oil industry in the mid '80s that did Biloxi in. Things weren't great before, but they tumbled fast and hard after. What little oil money that had been sneaking Biloxi's way from neighboring Louisiana, and one oily step farther, Texas, mostly by way of shipbuilding and refining, dried up and left Biloxi in a devastating lurch. By 1992, when dockside gambling was approved for the distressed coast of Mississippi, the city was deep in financial ruin, the infrastructure deplorable, the whole place on the verge of implosion. That it was a coastal community was no help, Biloxi being where the Gulf of Mexico took its nap—the beach manmade and neglected, the water brown and polluted, and not even a ripple in the water, much less a wave. With double-digit unemployment and poverty on every corner, there was a mass exodus for greener pastures. Biloxi hadn't repaired a road or built a new school in forty years. A new home hadn't been built in forty-one.

So when Salvatore Casimiro—second generation Italian immigrant with one wife, three mistresses, half of Capitol Hill in his back pocket, four rotten kids, and the seven largest and most profitable properties on the Las Vegas Strip—decided to spread his wings and build a gambling destination in the South, mostly because he needed somewhere to park his daughter Bianca and her new husband Richard, his casino Golden Boy who he'd somehow roped into marrying his narcissistic, amoral, and possibly manic daughter, he knew he'd be building residences too. The first for his son-in-law. There was absolutely nowhere to live in or around

Biloxi. The closest thing to civilization, and for all he knew, indoor plumbing, was ninety miles west in New Orleans.

He built a penthouse mansion on the whole top floor of his Gulf Coast project, the Bellissimo Resort and Casino, the tallest building (to this day) in the state of Mississippi, and, at the time, the largest hotel-casino outside of Vegas proper. He hoped to ship his only daughter to Biloxi and keep her in Biloxi. For as long as they all shall live.

Just below her sprawling manor, he split the floor into two mini mansions. The first for the casino's future general manager, because it would surely take a war chest salary plus a strong residential incentive to find a manager worth his salt who'd be willing to move to Biloxi, and the second, twelve-thousand square feet of celebrity accommodations—four bedroom suites, a dining room for twenty, a personal gym, two pools, sweeping terrace gardens—in hopes of luring A-list entertainers to South, Nowhere. Jay Leno and the like. And that's where my new husband and I live now, in the other mini mansion, the casino manager's residence, down the hall from Jay's place. Directly beneath narcissistic, amoral, and possibly manic Bianca Casimiro Sanders.

We hated it.

The Bellissimo's Casino Manager Residence was decorated by its first residents at the tail end of the three-year resort construction in 1996, and no one had touched it since. I call it the Big Easy Flea Market. The interior was designed by the Bellissimo's first casino manager, Ty Thibodeaux, or rather by his wife Magnolia, a Cajun Louisiana crawfish-loving beignet-addicted nutcase. Every stick of furniture came over with the original French settlers and somehow Magnolia had managed to round it all up and drag it here. The walls were laden throughout with slabs of rusty flaking ornamental iron, pieced together gates and fences she'd probably swiped in the dark of night from crypts and mausoleums. They were welded together and everywhere, creating fake indoor Bourbon Street balconies all through the residence, and on every fake balcony, somewhere, was Jesus Christ on the cross. Big, little, dangling, mounted, bronze, silver, wood, three glow-in-the-dark, all with crowns of thorns and nails in the bloody feet. They were all over the place. And they were all looking up, to the ceilings we didn't have.

The tops of the rooms were gilded crown molding, even in the five bathrooms, so ornate and sprawling they bumped into equally overdone carved ceiling medallions, there to enhance the many chandeliers. The casino manager's residence had seventeen tacky chandeliers, one jazz themed and made entirely of tarnished brass trombones and saxophones, all dripping in brightly colored crystals, mini voodoo skulls, or Mardi Gras memorabilia.

The color scheme of our new home was purple, pink, blue, green, yellow, black, red, gold, and Kraft Macaroni and Cheese orange. There were blooming magnolias everywhere—oils of magnolias on the walls, magnolias on each of the six thousand kitchen backsplash tiles, several magnolia-themed sofas, magnolia bath towels and beddings, wool rugs covered in creeping magnolia designs, and a huge silk magnolia tree in the foyer.

We could make a fortune charging admission and giving tours.

The best part? It's haunted. The whole place. I swear to you, there are ghosts and ghouls and goblins in every corner of the casino manager's residence. Every single day is Halloween. Neither I nor Bradley could get a decent night's sleep. I could barely eat in the middle of all this Creole mess. And I wouldn't even *think* of conceiving a child in this Spook-Spook Bayou Yard Sale.

One person who absolutely loved it? My grandmother.

One thing that wouldn't stop breaking since the day we moved in? The seventy-two cubic foot red refrigerator. In what universe do two people need a refrigerator that large? There's no doubt in my mind Magnolia Thibodeaux kept whole animal carcasses in it and used them for jambalaya sacrifice voodoo ceremonies. Most likely in my bedroom.

Now that I lived at the Bellissimo, there was no "I'm going to run to the store." Because of my Super Secret Spy status, I had to completely disguise myself to walk out the front door. More often than not, I went Unabomber, hoodie and dark glasses. Every five or six days, I made my escape using service elevators and stairwells. I hiked miles to my car, uphill several ways, in the vendor-only lot behind receiving. I drove to the Winn Dixie on Pass Road and bought a buggy full of comfort food. I retraced my steps, this time schlepping groceries on a luggage cart up to the twenty-ninth floor Who Dat Haunted Mansion, then put them away, only to reach for the milk the next morning and it be room temperature, the refrigerator broken again.

There wasn't a department within the Bellissimo that could help. Not engineering, not maintenance, not the heat and air guys. No one at the Bellissimo really knew if the new casino manager's wife lived here or not. They'd never seen her; they'd never set foot in the new casino manager's home. Because the new casino manager's wife worked undercover. To let an employee in the front door (a misty beveled glass tarnished copper number wide enough to drive a car through) would be to blow my cover. So I had to call Sears, like everyone else.

"You say you live where, lady?"

"At the Bellissimo. The twenty-ninth floor."

"You're pulling my leg."

"I am not."

"Okay, here it is, and the computer says we sent someone to fix it two weeks ago."

"It's broken again."

"There's actually fourteen pages of repairs here, lady."

A sad fact I was well aware of.

"Maybe it's time for you to think about a new refrigerator."

Wouldn't that be nice? We couldn't get the old refrigerator *out* to put a new one *in*.

A month into our marriage and new living quarters, after six visits with six different Sears repairmen and no luck, I dragged Bradley into it. I hid in the voodoo pantry, so deep, dark, and cavernous, I'm positive this is where Magnolia kept the dead bodies, while he met with the Sears appliance service manager and a man from the Bellissimo engineering department named Ding Ding. (I wish I were kidding.) (Surely to one of the Jesuses it was just a nickname.)

"Mr. Cole, I don't know how they ever got this refrigerator in here, but I can assure you, we can't get it out without a crane and tearing down a wall or two. If this refrigerator comes out whole, it'll have to go down the side of the building. The freight elevators can't even hold the *weight*."

"Then you're going to have to repair it."

"I'm telling you, Mr. Cole, we're at our wits' end with this monster." I heard him tap on the blood red doors. (The refrigerator has four doors. Four. All red.) "For one, it's a dinosaur. I was in first grade when this thing was built. It's a Jenn-Air custom, we can't find anyone who knows a thing about it, and there's not parts for it or a manual on it, and we've done just about everything we can possibly do."

"And you can't get it out?"

"You see that?" Ding Ding pointed to the top of the refrigerator, where it disappeared into the ceiling. "The problem is none of the wiring or plumbing is behind the refrigerator. Or even below it. It's all up top. The only way to get it out is to come down through the ceiling."

"Go right ahead."

"Well, we can't. We're right below Mrs. Sanders's closet. I've already tried that route. I filled out the paperwork and my boss shot back that he didn't care what kind of repairs were needed below the Sanders's residence, the wife would *never* go for it, and we needed to figure something else out."

Bianca Sanders couldn't care less if we had a refrigerator or not. I could have told Ding Ding that.

"Now, if you could move this saint somebody," Ding Ding said.

Yes. In my kitchen, across from a massive gold-inlaid island was a five-foot-tall garden angel on a two-foot cement cube base, with a wing span of four feet, made of moldy cast resin, and, bonus, it was a fountain. It cried black tears that pooled into its own hands.

When we'd been married two weeks, I spent my first night alone here. On my way to refill my glass of wine, I bumped into the angel. Barely bumped, like grazing the sofa or catching the corner of the bed. Boom. I went down—spread eagle on the floor, passed out, and somehow on the way down, I cracked my head open. That angel knocked me flat on the ground. Probably with its moldy breath. I came to later with a bloody line across my forehead and blood in the middle of both of my palms.

Like Jesus.

"'Cause there's plumbing behind this statue, see?" Ding Ding told him. "And we can get a new refrigerator here."

There were four thousand places to put a new refrigerator in the Fat Tuesday Fort. Every time we were fed up and ready to order one and plug it up in our bedroom, or beside the television, or in one of the many powder rooms, we tried one more time to repair the big red devil, the whole time hoping against hope we'd get to move back to our condo where we had a perfectly wonderful and working refrigerator, leaving this place as we found it. (Haunted.)

"I think we have quite enough refrigerator as it is," Bradley said, "and I don't care if we have to rebuild every motor in it, I need this refrigerator working. Understand?"

"You got it, Mr. Cole."

It had been a full eight months since that day and the refrigerator wasn't fixed yet. It was an ongoing problem, like the ridiculous décor of my home was a problem, the ghosts, good grief, the ghosts were a problem, but my biggest problem lately was Magnolia Thibodeaux.

Several weeks ago, I ran around shaking the fake magnolia trees looking for the real one. I came in from work one day and the whole place was blooming. When in bloom, magnolias produce an unmistakable cloying sticky sweetness, with a wisp of pepper and citrusy undertones, like lemon or grapefruit. There's no missing it and I smelled it. It happened again a few days later. About the same time, I began noticing things missing—a voodoo doll here, a Jesus there—and there wasn't a doubt in my mind Magnolia Thibodeaux had been sneaking in here. Because she probably still has a key and she's one of two people, her husband being the other, who know the twenty-ninth floor setup well enough to sneak past the surveillance cameras on their way in and out. She was so slippery, the cameras couldn't catch her and neither could I. In the past month, I knew for a fact she'd been here no less than five times. I was on the verge of booby traps.

I'd called her. She didn't answer, so I left a nice message. "Mrs. Thibodeaux, I know you've been here and I'd appreciate it if you'd call me the next time you need in. I'll be happy to help you with anything. I mean it, Mrs. Thibodeaux, anything you need or want out of the residence."

I called again the next week. "Magnolia. I know you've been here again. Please give me a call."

I called the next week too. "Look, lady. I'm not going to put up with this."

It happened again about ten days ago. I smelled her all over my house. "Magnolia, I'm telling you, I'm going to catch you running in and out of here like you still live here and you're going to be sorry. It's called breaking and entering."

Calling her wasn't doing any good, so I gathered up a load of her Bourbon Street baubles and had Baylor deliver it to her. He took Jesuses, ceramic alligator busts, Mardi Gras beads, eyes of newts, everything that wasn't nailed down. Maybe what she wanted was in there. It also cleared out one percent of her jambalaya junk. I sent six-foot-tall two-hundred-pound Baylor with a box stuffed full and a dire warning: If what you're looking for isn't in here, too bad. Break into my home again and I'm calling the police. Magnolia beat Baylor up with an umbrella and told him to stay off her property. Then lobbed Jesuses at him. The worst was, I couldn't get anyone to believe me. My immediate supervisor, No Hair, widely addressed as Jeremy Covey, didn't believe me.

"She is not sneaking into your house, Davis."

"Yes, No Hair, she is."

"Why would she do that?"

"She's looking for something."

"And you know this how?"

"Because I can smell her."

Nor did my husband believe me.

"Davis, I swear I don't smell a thing."

"How can you *not* smell it? It's her. I smell *her*."

"Do you want me to have cameras installed?" Bradley asked. "I will. Say the word."

No. No cameras inside. We're newlyweds, for goodness sake.

I stepped out of my inner circle. "Erika? Do you smell flowers in here? Magnolias?"

Nose in the air, sniff sniff. "I smell Mr. Clean and Lemon Pledge."

Erika Cleaning Woman is scared to death of this place. She runs in once a week with a leaf blower, blasts off the top layer of étouffée dust, then runs out screaming. She refuses to be here alone, so now we have Erika Cleaning Woman and Erika Cleaning Woman's Sister, Tonette. Tonette asked me if I'd considered having the residence exorcised. She knew a priest.

And this is where we live.

Apparently, with a cat.

I've slept with animals before (I was married to the same ape twice before Bradley, a long story I don't want to tell), but never with a four-legged furry animal. Bradley and I fell into bed on Sunday night and the damn cat hopped up and settled in between us like it was supposed to be there. I tried shooing it off and it bowed up and hissed at me with glow-in-the-dark eyes, sending me scrambling up the headboard. Bradley reached for the cat and calmed it down until it purred, then it settled at his feet after trying its best to shred my duvet cover into ribbons with its needle claws. We turned to each other in the dark. In addition to the distant gurgling noise from the kitchen, I could hear the cat, who I think might be asthmatic, trying to breathe through its smashed nose.

"Now do you believe me, Bradley?"

"I always believe you, Davis." He traced a line down my nose with his finger, something I'd been watching him do to the cat. "I totally believe in you, Davis."

"About Magnolia."

He rolled onto his back. The cat rolled onto its back.

"Davis, honey, if the platinum were here, we'd have found it by now."

"Bradley, honey, that's why she keeps breaking in. She's the one who stole the platinum, she stashed it here, and she keeps coming back to get it, a load at a time."

"I find that so hard to believe."

"I find it hard to believe we have a cat in the bed."

FOUR

On a normal workday, Bradley hit his desk while it was still dark out, five or so. I usually slept in till seven. Sometimes noon. Monday morning, promising to be anything but normal, found me up and out of the bed at the ungodly hour of six, Bradley long gone, the shower almost dry, and I could barely smell his sandalwood soap. I wondered if he'd slept at all.

On the long list of things I love about being married to him, it starts every day with coffee. He sets up the coffee pot for me before he leaves, so when I stumble to it, all I have to do is push the "brew" button. I stumbled to it, but stopped short, because there was a dead fish in the kitchen. I slapped my hand over my nose and mouth. Beside the coffee pot was a bowl of gray fish mush. With yellow flecks. Cat food.

I'd forgotten all about the cat.

I picked up the bowl with a dishtowel, lest I accidentally make contact with its contents, and from behind me the cat had a fit, screeching and wailing, mad because I'd touched its food. I dropped the bowl to the floor. "Here, cat! Here!"

This was no way to start my day.

Not even five minutes from sleep, I turned back to the coffee pot and the cat was in my face. I let out a yelp. The cat moves at the speed of light. It arched up and tried to slap me with a right hook, followed by an uppercut, claws extended. I danced out of its way, but it continued to howl.

"What, cat? What?"

The food smelled hideous, overpowering the smell of the

coffee, and the cat wouldn't shut up, drowning out my favorite morning sound, that of the coffee brewing.

"What do you *want*, cat?"

It raced back and forth across the island, alternating between crying and lunging at me. I picked up the nasty food and put it back where I'd found it. The cat sat down on my kitchen counter (where's the Clorox?), looked down its smashed nose at the food without touching it, hopped off the island, found its former spot on the rug, and was asleep in three seconds. The coffee was almost ready; the cat's eyes were closed. I inched a hand in the direction of the nasty cat food to move it away from my coffee pot, and the cat, who could see through its closed eyelids, reared up and threatened me.

"Are you kidding me, cat?"

Just to make sure, I inched my hand toward the bowl again, and the cat showed me its teeth. Had it come to this? Feeding a cat on the kitchen countertop? I'd find Holder Darby today. To. Day. It might not be her cat, but she'd know whose it was or could at least resume custody of it.

"You don't mind if I get myself a cup of coffee, do you, cat? Is that okay with you?"

It swished its tail.

Bradley left a note at the coffee pot. *Wife. I'll be in, around, or about the vault most of the day. First, another inventory with the accountants. Baylor will be with me. I'll be in the vault again this afternoon for an inspection with Paragon. I need you to check in on the conference this morning, make sure all is well, look into the Holder Darby business, and don't forget dinner tonight.*

I'd like to forget dinner tonight.

* * *

The call came at seven seventeen. I was snapping on my watch.

"Are you the new Holder?"

No. "How can I help you?"

"This is Megan with Special Events. I work the front desk at the conferences. I just checked everyone in for the welcome breakfast, and there might be something going on here."

"Such as?"

"I think someone's missing."

Someone *is* missing. Holder Darby. She should be taking this call. "Why do you think someone is missing?"

"Because people are standing around waiting on one guy who's not here."

"These people standing around," I asked, "have they asked you about this missing person?"

"No," she said. "It's just weird."

"Weird?"

"Weird. I've been doing this for five years, and this is weird."

According to the conference schedule, it was Monday morning roll call at the conference, including a full-body scan (think airport screening booth) to gain admission to the welcome breakfast (Overdraft Omelet Station and Fiscal Responsibility Fruit Bar) deep in the top-secret banker chambers.

And according to Megan, there was one lone badge left on the registration table. I could hardly see how it was weird or my problem.

"I'm sure whoever it is stayed up all night gambling." I slipped into my jacket. "He's probably sleeping it off."

"I don't know." She hit four octaves on the three words. "I can hear them. They're very upset this man isn't here."

(And I'm supposed to get upset too?) (Is this what Holder Darby did all day?) "Has anyone called him?"

"They say he's not answering."

"Has anyone knocked on his door?" I stepped into my shoes.

"They say he's not answering."

"Who is *they*?"

"I don't know their names. It's the conference techs."

"Techs? What kind of techs?"

"Slot techs."

"Our slot techs? Let me talk to one of them."

"They're slot techs," Megan said, "but not ours. These slot techs are with Paragon Protection."

Slot technicians installed and kept slot machines in working order. We have enough slot techs for a baseball team. Paragon Protection, not in the casino business, shouldn't have even one. Why would Paragon Protection bring its own slot techs?

"How many techs are there?"

"Three," Megan said. "And they're mean."

"Why do three mean techs need one guest?" Maybe this is weird.

"I really don't know," the girl said. "But I thought someone should."

"I'm on my way," I said. "I'll check on the guest."

She gave me the missing man's room number, a big fat suite, then asked what she was supposed to do with his badge. I told her (I don't care) to lock it up. Behind the scenes of the banking industry, much like behind the scenes of the casino industry, is shrouded in secrecy, including, it would seem, a convention. The bankers didn't want would-be bank robbers sneaking in, drawing maps, jotting notes, and walking off with their playbook, so they brought in a boatload of their own security (along with their own slot technicians) and issued badges, all set up and approved by Holder Darby. Who flew the coop.

The conference center, an escalator ride up from the east corner of the casino, starts with a large reception area, and by large I mean football field, and through the conference doors there are three dining rooms, a concert hall-slash-auditorium, an events hall, and breakout meeting rooms to accommodate up to a thousand conference attendees. This week's conference, the one Holder Darby dumped on me, required an identification badge to get anywhere past the reception area.

The badges contained microchips. Fourteen different photo IDs, an interview with your third grade teacher, and a brain scan were required to get a badge, and if you lost it, too bad. No mixing and mingling with the other bankers during keynote banquet lunches, no playing in the conference tournament in the evenings, no Dionne Warwick Friday night.

My job, as I understood it (I've had this convention job twenty minutes), was to make several appearances a day in the reception area, ask if everyone enjoyed the Collateral Chicken Cordon Bleu, and get upset about inoperable microphones and light bulbs. In other words, once the conference began, Holder's (my) job was one of hospitality. My plan for today was to be hospitable for ten minutes, then locate Holder Darby and four million dollars in platinum coins. I had no idea where Holder Darby might be, but I knew where to start looking for the four million. That part would be easy.

My morning list just got one chore longer, because apparently I'm expected to wake up conference guests and kick them to the weird conference. I will admit to being mildly curious as to why Paragon Protection had its own slot techs, but that's it, mild curiosity. I'm sure there's a reasonable explanation, and as soon as I find Holder Darby, I'll get one. Then all I have to do is find four million in platinum.

One last glance in the mirror to make sure I barely recognized myself, and, success, a total stranger stared back. At this point in my Super Secret Spy career, I'm a master of disguise. I use a product called ColorMash, a temporary hair color spray that (comes in sixteen brilliantly dimensional shades) smells good, washes out easily, and briefly turns my hair a different color. Today my caramel red hair was vibrant chocolate and my caramel brown eyes, via colored contacts, were china blue. I put myself through this rigmarole because if I spy around looking like myself, I wouldn't stay super or secret very long.

Today, I dressed in what I thought the rat-fink deserter/missing-in-action Holder Darby might wear to meet and greet conference guests, a power suit: navy blue pants and blazer, no-nonsense white silk shirt, all Diane Von Furstenberg, and on my feet, Kate Spade Yvonne patent pumps. Also new. And several inches of new, because I'm not all that tall and eye contact is a large part of hospitality. I looked like a movie star FBI agent. (Real FBI agents wear no makeup, cargo pants, sports bras, Reebok SWAT boots, and bulletproof vests. Movie FBI agents wear Diane Von Furstenberg power suits.) And I might as well have stayed in my pajamas for this, my first assignment on the first day of what would be a week of dressing up as an FBI movie star and replacing Collateral Chicken Cordon Bleu light bulbs, playing the role of Olivia Abbott, Temporary Special Events Coordinator, because the guest in room twenty-six fifty was, as Megan suspected, missing. In fact, he was gone. There was no guest in room twenty-six fifty.

Weird.

I eyed the closed bathroom door.

It was way too early for this.

I tiptoed over and tapped. "Housekeeping. Is anyone in there?"

From time to time, I think about getting a job at the mall. Or at Sonic, America's Drive-In. Or taking up golf. I love the clothes.

No way was I going into the bathroom alone. I reached in my spy bag and pulled out my gun, gloves, and phone. I tucked the gun in the waistband of my Olivia Abbott pants, pulled on the gloves, and poked on my phone.

"Hey, are you here yet?"

"I'm in the dungeon," Fantasy said.

Our offices are three large rooms located in the underbelly of (Mother Earth) the main building. As the crow flies, we're a tenth of a mile directly beneath Style, a women's clothing store on the mezzanine, in 3B. B is for Basement.

"Grab a print kit and come to room twenty-six fifty."

"What's up?"

"The guest is gone."

"How do you know?"

"Because he's not here."

"On my way."

I'm not going in that bathroom alone.

It looked like he'd stepped out for a paper. Twelve hours ago.

The bed had been turned down, but not slept in. The dresser had a man pile: car keys, loose change, a small folding knife, wallet, and his room key. The closet held a week's worth of conference clothes and a rolling suitcase large enough for four weeks' worth of conference clothes. The television was on. His leather slip-on shoes were beside the door.

The small dining table was set for one with a barely touched meal, highly congealed, the chair pushed back from the table as if he'd just risen. A full glass of pink wine sat to the right of his dinner plate. An acrylic white wine chiller held the rest of the bottle, the ice long melted, everything room temp. His knife and fork were resting neatly on his dinner plate. Something or someone had interrupted this man's dinner three bites in.

Fantasy knocked. Knuckle, knuckle, pause, knuckle, knuckle, bang—our secret knock. I have a passkey that overrides the programming on every electronic door lock in the building. I have one of the two all-access passkeys, Security has the other one locked in a vault, and I guard mine like it's a banker badge.

Fantasy doesn't have a passkey and doesn't want one. For one, she can get through any door, anytime, anywhere. It's her Superpower. For another, she says she has enough to keep up with and doesn't want anything else.

Fantasy, who is six feet tall, my best friend, my wingman and wheelman, looks like Tyra Banks with blue eyes. And she has three boys, two dogs, and one husband who lose all their stuff all the time. They count on her to keep up with everything. Her boys are constantly calling to ask where their this and that are, and she always knows. "You cut that shirt up to make a slingshot last week. It's gone." And, "Your hamster has not been ratnapped. You took his cage to the laundry room Tuesday because you said he needed a time out." And, "No one is wearing your shoes. No one wants to be in the same room with your shoes. You left them in the treehouse." I guess keeping up with a passkey would push her over the edge. So she learned how to get around without one.

"Hey." Her t-shirt said Bring It On. She took in the scene.

"Yow. Where'd he go?"

"Your guess is as good as mine."

"Have you looked in the bathroom?"

"I was waiting on you."

"Davis," she said. "You big chicken."

"If he's in there, Fantasy," I don't know why I was whispering, "he's dead. Like Elvis."

She pulled her gun from where she keeps it at the small of her back, marched over, turned the knob, then announced herself. "Coming in! Cover it up!" She kicked the door wide open.

This is why I called her. Honestly, she's not afraid of anything. Not one single thing. Not spiders, the flying monkeys in *The Wizard of Oz*, or men who may be naked and dead on the bathroom floor.

She poked her head in, then right back out. She stepped away, then swept out an arm. "Take a look."

"Is he in there?" I don't know why I had my gun drawn. If he was in there he was dead, and it's not like I could kill him again. "Just tell me, Fantasy."

"You've got to see this for yourself."

The bathroom vanity was covered in stacks of cold hard cash. And hot off the press cash too. It was new car smell but better, because this was new money.

"How much, do you think?"

"I don't know." I ran a finger down a five-inch stack of one-hundred dollar bills. "Several hundred thousand, at least."

"Good Lord, Davis, look. There's money in the bathtub."

We stood over the bathtub in admiration. "There's a million dollars here," I said.

"Why would someone walk off and leave this money?"

"They wouldn't."

"Look at this." She fanned out a stack. "It's uncirculated."

Where did this money come from?

We threw the deadbolt on the guest room door and got to work. It was just us; neither Bradley nor Baylor answered their phones, so they were still in the vault. I snooped in the man's wallet while Fantasy rolled his suitcase into the bathroom to pack. The wallet was a brown leather trifold. In it, a neat stack of hundreds so freshly printed I didn't even try to peel them apart, but having worked around money for as long as I have, I eyeballed it at two thousand dollars. And nothing else. No driver's license, no ID, no picture of the wife, no Capital One card. I dusted and got partial prints from the wallet, the dinner knife, and the room keycard, and a set of perfect prints from the wine glass.

"Hey, Davis." Fantasy stood in the bathroom doorway. She used the back of one gloved hand to push her hair from her face and in the other gloved hand, she held thirty thousand or so dollars.

"Yeah?"

"This might be funny money."

Casino Employee Lesson Number One: Counterfeit Money.

Fantasy and I probably know more about fake currency than the five hundred bankers here for the conference put together. You could wake either of us from a dead sleep, pass us phonies, we'd identify them by touch, sight, or print quality, then go right back to sleep. Technological advances have made counterfeiting so easy, and casinos are such an easy target for counterfeiters that, at this point, we're experts. We could leave here and get jobs at the Treasury in a snap. We're that good.

Fantasy passed me a banded stack of hundreds. I peeled off my gloves and fingered through the money. It felt right, weight and mass. It looked right, embedded red and blue fibers, embossed images. The printing was excellent with clear and unbroken borders, the saw-tooth points on the Federal Reserve and Treasury Seals distinct and sharp, and the portrait was lifelike, standing out from the background. The problem was in the serial numbers. Specifically the stars. Every bill in the stack was a star bill.

"What about the rest?" I asked.

"The whole tub."

Every note in circulation has a unique serial number. It

consists of three letters and eight digits. The first and last letters denote the series, and can be any letter but O or Z. O too closely resembles the number zero and Z is reserved for test runs. The second letter identifies the Federal Reserve Bank issuing the bill, and it's always A through L. The numbers run the range between 00000001 and 99999999, and every thousand dollars or so, you run across currency with a star.

If a defective note, damaged or misprinted, is found after the serial numbers have been applied, it has to be replaced so the final count will be accurate. It's replaced from a stash of bills printed before the production run in which the last letter of the serial number is a star, and the rest of the serial numbers don't trace back to anything or anyone. Star bills' serial numbers are completely random. There's no way to track a star bill back to production, and therefore, when trying to identify counterfeit currency by serial number, star bills get a pass. The bills would have to have other tells, and these didn't. It was a genius method of counterfeiting, one I'd never heard of. We had a bathtub full of perfect money, every bit of it with green hollow stars.

It was funny money. Very good funny money, the best I'd ever seen. At the same time it was useless unless spent one bill at a time. You could never deposit this money in a financial institution, take it to a currency trader, or even buy in for $500 at a blackjack table and not wind up in prison. Whoever passed this money off would never be caught. Whoever tried to spend it would be. And fast.

"Fantasy, this is a trap."

"What?"

"It's a setup." I shook a few thousand dollars. "The man who left this money here either fell into a trap or he was setting one."

She rocked back on her heels. "You're right. This money is a one-way ticket to federal prison."

Weird.

* * *

The fake money wouldn't fit in the missing man's suitcase. We arranged it several ways.

"He got it in here," Fantasy said. "Surely, we can get it out."

"I'll sit on the suitcase, you zip."

Ten minutes later, me falling off the suitcase twice, I stuffed eighty thousand or so in my bra. Fantasy, after winning the fight with the suitcase, rocked back on her heels. "What's going on? Missing people? Fake platinum? Fake cash?"

"Those are questions for Magnolia."

Fantasy shook her head. "You're giving that woman way more credit than she deserves. She can't put a sandwich together, much less a con. In a million years Magnolia Thibodeaux couldn't fill a bathtub with counterfeit money, rob a vault, and pull off a double kidnapping."

FIVE

When Bradley and I had been married for forty-eight hours and the smoke cleared enough for us to look around and see exactly where we were, I flew into a panic.

"We have to go home, Bradley. This whole New Orleans thing is freaking me out."

"We have to take it a day at a time, Davis." He stared at an elaborate oil painting above the bed of an expressionless alligator with huge marble eyes. Beside the alligator were the words Peace, Love, and Gumbo. "It is a little," he blinked, "much."

He took off for his new job downstairs and I took off for the Bayou Bureau of Printing and Engraving down the hall.

Wrapped in a blanket, armed with a cup of black coffee (my half and half had curdled in the big red refrigerator overnight), I set out to explore the casino manager's residence, huge place, way more than we needed or wanted, to make my peace with it. We might be here a few weeks.

My tour started at the front door with the ridiculous magnolia tree in the cast iron tub. The wide green leaves reached all the way to the copper dome ceiling. I was on my way to the next room, the circular tearoom decorated like a King Cake, when I spotted a door to the right of the magnolia tree in the foyer. A hidden door. It was seamlessly wallpapered against the rest of the foyer, totally inconspicuous in the background of the busy black and gold fleur-de-lis wall. A door I hadn't noticed, having been in and out of the residence a dozen times already, a door that led to a place I wish I'd never gone, a door that once opened couldn't be closed.

Feeling along the seams, I nudged and it protested. It was a swinging door, no knob, hidden hinges, much wider than a regular door and at least ten feet tall. I used my hip to knock it in and when I did, the noise it made was nothing short of a train crash, bouncing off the foyer walls and copper ceiling, scaring me to death. I sloshed scorching hot coffee all over my hand. While I was dancing away the sting, the door swung back and hit me in the head, and there went the rest of my coffee, burning down the front of my bathrobe. (Looking back, I think it was a telekinetic message: Do not enter.) The only thing I'd managed to see was a pitch black open space, and the smell that escaped whatever was behind the door was musty—moth ball, attic, tomb musty, as if fresh air wouldn't dare go there. I bravely reached in with my scalded hand and didn't immediately locate a light switch. Not wanting to set off a bomb or meet up with a gumbo-loving alligator, I marched back to the kitchen, snarled at the refrigerator, and dug around until I found a flashlight. I thought about getting my gun. I pushed through again, same railroad scream from the door, located a light switch on the wrong wall, and flipped it. It didn't help much, but after a minute my eyes adjusted and I found myself in a dimly lit hallway looking at a second door, this one locked. The hallway was wide and empty—no Catholic homages, saxophone chandeliers, or magnolias. Everything was thick, dark wood: paneled walls, ceiling, floor.

The second door had a Kwikset five-pin deadbolt, just like every other deadbolt installed when the Bellissimo was built, with a standard five-pin cylinder. I left again, and this time I did get my gun, and my Quik-Piks, back through the door, down the dark hall, and popped right through the lock. Gun first, I found myself in another dark airless hall looking at yet another locked door, a door that occupied the next two hours of my day.

The lock on the second door was a high-security Medeco, the same lock used to secure drugs, guns, and ATMs. I tried everything short of a chain saw and calling Fantasy, who could bust through anything, to get in. Finally, I did what all good thieves do when faced with a lock challenge (honestly, they don't bother, they happily fire up a blow torch rather than stand there for a week trying to hack a Medeco, but I didn't have a blow torch option), I watched a YouTube video. Word to the wise: Don't believe everything you see on YouTube. I did not get past the Medeco with a #9 nail and a bent paperclip. I wasted a good thirty minutes locating a paperclip in the NOLA Nuthouse. The nail was easier. I tossed ridiculous crawfish pictures and pulled forty nails straight out of the walls until I found the one I needed. Still in my bathrobe. All morning long. YouTube showed me where and how to jab a step protrusion in the lock's interior with the nail, then ping just below it with the paperclip, which should have rendered it toothless, at which point my Quik-Piks would have worked. None of that happened, so I shot the lock off the door. Bang. Then I stepped into a money factory.

I batted my way back to the foyer, closed the door with a screech, fell against it, and slid down the fleur-de-lis wall to the floor where I sat staring at my fuzzy slippers for I don't know how long. I worked on my speech to Bradley about how we couldn't spend one more night in this place. I didn't care if we checked into a regular guest room below us and lived there until we could go home to our beautiful condo. I honestly didn't care if we moved into my black Volkswagen Bug, his new office, or a yurt. I just knew we couldn't live *here*. The people who lived here before us were criminals, and if we stayed here, we'd be accessories. To their crimes. For the most part, I don't care what people do behind closed doors, but my new husband and I had our toothbrushes behind these closed doors. To stay in this place for ten more minutes might mean spending the rest of our lives in separate federal prisons.

We'd only been there two nights, so it didn't take long to pack. I was zipping the last bag when I heard the distant trill of my phone. I followed the noise to the kitchen and saw I'd missed several calls from my new husband while I was exploring our honeymoon hideaway's hidden agenda. Bradley texted: *I've tried to call ten times. Are you lost in that big place? Check your email.*

To: davisway@Bellissimo.com
From: bradleycole@Bellissimo.com

How's my bride? I'm between meet-and-greets with accounting and marketing, and thought I should mention something's up with the refrigerator. Can you call a repairman? For some reason, our new home has always been off-limits to all Bellissimo staff, an odd rule instituted by Thibodeaux. Why, I don't know. Alligators? Privacy? Not a bad policy for us to continue and probably our best effort at keeping your job secure. So call a repairman from the phone book, not anyone with the Bellissimo. Maybe Sears? Just took a conference call from Tunica, Davis, and Sanders wants to step up the Jolie opening by six months, but only if we agree to stay on the property 24/7. I don't see where we have a choice. We can handle anything for six months, right? My last meeting is at nine tonight and if I can still form words after, we'll talk about redecorating. Maybe you'll have time to sightsee through the rest of the residence, find a part of it we'll be more comfortable setting up camp in. It's only six months. Thank you, Mrs. Cole.

*   *   *

"We can't."

"Davis."

"We can't stay here."

"Why not?"

Our first married argument. Two days in.

We were in the kitchen, the big red refrigerator providing annoying background music to our first marital fight. Pandora would call it Drainpipe Hits.

Bradley, after a ten-hour day at his new job, looked beat. He leaned against the kitchen island as he tugged his tie loose and unbuttoned the collar of his shirt. I studied the wine rack above the sink, chose a bottle, blew off the dust, then checked the label for skulls and crossbones. It was a brand served all over the Bellissimo, it was sealed and corked; hopefully we'd live. I opened it and poured. We pulled chairs away from the breakfast table and sat down.

"I don't like it here either," he said.

"It's not that I don't like it."

His eyebrows shot up.

"Which is not to say I do."

He looked relieved. I poured more wine.

"Richard's request is reasonable, Davis. Not only do I agree with him that if he's going to be off-site I should be on, but it will be easier for me to learn the ropes of my new job if I'm here." He tapped the table. "And six months isn't forever."

Then he did this thing he does. He barely tilted his head back so that he led with his chin, and smiled at me with his eyes. It was adorable and I fell for it every single solitary time.

My head hit the table. He patted it. Good girl.

"Come on, Davis. We can handle it."

I looked up. "No. We can't."

"Why?"

"I can't tell you." I used the same tone of voice I'd use to announce the imminent end of the world.

He used the same tone of voice he'd use if he knew the end of the world was imminent. "Why not?"

"Because then you'll know."

Our eyes met and I realized he already knew. His head dropped an inch and shook slowly. We sat in relative silence (gurgle gurgle) until the bravest of us was willing to discuss it further. "Let's go," he said. He stood. He held out his hand.

When we passed the refrigerator something deep inside it exploded. We stopped dead in our tracks, and after, when our lung and heart functions resumed, hand in hand we took a slow walk out of the kitchen, through the King Cake room, into the foyer, past the stupid magnolia tree and down the long dark hall to Crescent City Currency.

* * *

"What happened here?"

"It was a small gun accident."

"Uh-huh."

It had taken four shots to blow through the Medeco. My ears were still ringing. Or maybe that was the refrigerator.

"Who told you, Bradley, and how long have you known?"

"One day," he said. "I've known for one day."

"When were you going to tell me?"

"I wasn't."

Stunned. "What purpose could it possibly serve to keep it a secret from *me*?" Especially considering I snoop for a living.

"The same reason you didn't want to tell me. I don't want you responsible for this information, Davis. And I certainly had no idea you'd stumble back here," he said. "Even if you did, I didn't think you'd get in."

It did take all morning.

We stepped in, our footsteps echoing around the twenty-by-twenty room. All concrete: floor, walls, ceiling. There was barely room to walk around the two huge pieces of equipment. We stopped between them. Big equipment. Machines. As in production factory. One looked like a copier on steroids, and the other was unrecognizable.

"Where are we?" I asked.

"We're in a vault."

We'd been married two days. We still had wedding cake. I'd spent most of the two days (honeymooning) processing the fact that Bradley Cole was the Bellissimo's new casino manager. He was my husband and he was my boss in one fell swoop. To say my head was spinning is to say there's a big round hot thing in the sky during the day.

And now this.

* * *

We sat on a metal desk against the back wall and stared. I counted four exposed electrical outlets, and not for lamps. These outlets were for plugging in Best Buy stores. So whatever these machines did, they did it big. The few bulbs that worked in the overhead florescent light fixtures barely worked; they flickered. The air was old and thick, and everything was covered in a fine layer of oily black dust.

"This will be our only conversation about this room and about vault operations, Davis. So whatever questions you have, ask them now."

I had a million, but no words came. He began answering what I couldn't ask.

"Of the three vaults at the Bellissimo, two, including this one, are obsolete."

Quiet. Mouse quiet.

"We have one vault in operation behind the main cage."

One plus one only equals two.

"The third vault is in the casino. When the Bellissimo was built, there was also a slot machine vault. It went out of operation ten years ago."

About when the slot machines were converted from coin pay (the big, dirty, noisy slot tokens everyone loved) to cash-out tickets. Vault no longer needed. I wondered what happened to it.

"That vault is now the wine cellar in Bones."

Bones, the steak house in the casino. I'd seen the wine cellar. I'd been in the wine cellar. I never knew it was originally a vault. I never knew any of this.

When I finally found my voice, it cracked. "What are these machines?"

"A printer and a press," he said. "Salvatore Casimiro printed his own money."

Well, there you go. My worst fears confirmed.

A country mile later, I asked, "For his personal use? Or business?"

"I don't know," Bradley said. "I don't know what he did with the money and I don't want to know."

Neither did I.

"Blanks were shipped in for the coins," Bradley said. "They're called planchets. The printer," he pointed to the machine on our left, "is a fifty-thousand-dollar optimized DPI Heidelberg. And there's a stash of cotton paper in the cabinets." He pointed again.

"This is so United States Treasury."

"I know."

"Why?" I asked. "Why? Why do this? Why take this kind of risk? Why break this many laws?"

"I don't know why," Bradley said, "but I do know it was all shipped to Vegas. He didn't print money and send it downstairs to the Bellissimo casino."

A good thing. A very good thing.

"Where did the machines come from?" I asked.

"They bought the printer, and the coin press was custom built. Casimiro hired Thibodeaux, and Thibodeaux knew someone. They worked with a family-owned milling company out of Baton Rouge and had the machine built."

"So it was a joint operation between Casimiro and Thibodeaux."

"I don't know the details, Davis, and I'm sure I don't want to."

The less we knew, the better. We already had a moral and legal obligation to do something about it by knowing at all, but several factors came into play. For one, four thousand people, including us, would lose their jobs for the old sins of a few. For another, it was history. No one was minting or printing money in here now. And lastly, both Salvatore Casimiro and Ty Thibodeaux were out of commission. Casimiro had spent the past year getting out of the casino game, and when he wasn't busy doing that he was in the hospital, and from what I'd heard, Thibodeaux had gotten his Bellissimo gold watch, then went straight to his sick bed, where he remained. Both men were in their late eighties, sick, and what good would it do?

My last question, and the one weighing heaviest on my heart.

"Bradley, did Mr. Sanders sanction this?"

"Richard didn't know anything about any of this until Thibodeaux retired six months ago and not a minute before."

Three of us knew.

"Let me get this straight," I whispered. "Cash was printed in this room."

"Yes."

"And coins were minted right here."

"Yes."

"But the refrigerator doesn't work."

"Weird."

We went back to being married and the vaults, vault operations, counterfeiting, The Money Room, Salvatore Casimiro, and Ty Thibodeaux were all subjects Bradley and I hadn't discussed one time since that night. The Thibodeauxs we discussed, but not in this context. And here we were, nine months later, and it was the only subject in town. Holder Darby walked away from a good job, which I'm now suspecting might not have had a thing to do with Hello Kitty. Next, the vault was inventoried, only to discover millions in platinum gone, replaced with fakes, and now, a guest had disappeared and left us with a bathtub full of counterfeit money. Counterfeit money I suspected came from a secret vault room down the hall. Of our home.

Time for me to have a little chat with Magnolia Thibodeaux.

SIX

"What are we going to do with this?" Fantasy and I were waiting on elevators with a suitcase full of counterfeit money. It's exactly one-half of our work day, waiting on elevators.

"I'll take it upstairs to the Bayou Barn. Grab Baylor, if you can find him, and we'll meet at my place and try to track down Mr. Funny Money." I adjusted the stiff stacks of bills in my bra to itch a little less.

"I'm wondering if I should book a room here tonight." Fantasy couldn't stop staring at the suitcase. "It looks like it's going to be a long one."

"You can stay with us."

"No way in hell I'm staying at your place, Davis. I don't have time for all that bad juju."

Everyone hated where we lived. Everyone. Except my grandmother.

While Fantasy took a public elevator to the mezzanine level on her way to our 3B offices to (book herself a room in the hotel) locate Baylor, I took a staff elevator to the lobby, rolled the money around two corners, then caught the private elevator to the Ya Ya Haunted House. Actually, it's a semi-private elevator. When Jay Leno's place is occupied, those guests have access to it too. It didn't happen often that I was in the elevator with anyone else, but of course it happened today. I was dressed as Olivia Abbott, Special Events Woman, so it wasn't a security problem running into anyone, just an annoyance. I was against the mirrored back wall, my hand on the extended suitcase handle, when someone stuck an arm out, caught the doors as they were closing, and rushed in.

I was about to ask to see his passkey for this elevator when he, a tall dark man, looked up from his phone, got an eyeful of me, then slammed himself against the elevator wall, doing his very best to climb it. The whites of his eyes were so very white.

The doors opened on twenty-nine and the guy bolted out and ran for his life, turning the corner to Jay Leno's place. Which meant he must be on Dionne Warwick's front team. Someone always arrived days before the superstars, or, in this case, former superstar, to inventory the honey mustard pretzels and grape Nehi soda we'd agreed to stock Jay's place with. The more former the star, the more detailed the contract demands. We had a has-been '70s rock star recently who wouldn't agree to perform unless all the linens in Jay's place were blue. Towels, bedding, fluffy pillows, in slate blue. The band, all card-carrying members of the AARP, the drummer on a mobility scooter, had one hit a million years ago, "Blue Yonder." The week before, Taylor Swift had asked for nothing but enough space and time to meet her fans. And she said please.

It was only when I dug in my pocket for my front door key, one of those iron skeleton numbers, and why wouldn't it be, that I looked down and saw all kinds of money sticking out of my bra and the butt of my Glock poking out of the waistband of my von Furstenberg FBI pants. That's why the poor Dionne Warwick guy was sweating bullets. He thought I was going to shoot him. I thought he was one of those people who hated elevators.

I opened the front door and the zipper exploded on the suitcase. Money everywhere. At ten o'clock in the morning.

The Igloo cooler large enough to stuff a dead body in, which is our makeshift refrigerator, sits just inside our front door under the shade of the twelve-foot-tall fake magnolia tree in a hundred-gallon cast iron tub, so we don't have to lug ice all the way to the kitchen. It made a perfect shelf for a million or better counterfeit dollars. So we wouldn't trip all over it. I lobbed lobbed lobbed the money. The suitcase was shot. And by shot, I don't mean I shot it, I mean it was history. I was stacking the money when I got a whiff of something. Or someone.

She'd been here *again*. She might still be here. She is *so* in the middle of this mess, whatever this mess is. I am *so* sick of this woman.

"Magnolia? Where are you?" My heels clacked around the foyer. "Magnolia?" I could smell her everywhere and I heard a rustling. It sounded like it was above me, but the origins of noise in Muffaletta Manor were hard to pin down; the refrigerator drowns and distorts them. I got out of my new home, locking her in her old one. Not one to leave anything alone, Magnolia had four huge ficus trees around a black iron patio set in the *hall*. I dragged the iron bench across the hall carpet and blocked the front door. "Gotcha." I dusted my hands. Pulling my phone from my pocket, I dialed Bradley's office.

Of the masses who work at the Bellissimo, I can safely say only three outside my immediate work circle know who I am and what I do. Maybe four. Okay, at this point, maybe a dozen. One who certainly did was my husband's personal assistant, Calinda Wilson. Calinda came with Bradley from the Grand Casino, down Beach Boulevard a few miles, where he was the former lead attorney and she was his former personal and legal assistant. She knew me and my job way before Bradley took the casino manager's position here. She's been well aware of our relationship too, having caught us on Bradley's desk. More than once.

I texted her: *Calinda, I need Bradley upstairs right now.*

He's covered up, she texted back. *Four calls and five people waiting.*

It's urgent. 911.

Is it about the refrigerator?

No.

I'll let him know.

Calinda is in her late forties, knows what Bradley needs before he does, and is armed with a degree in paralegal studies from Georgetown University and a banana milkshake. Calinda drinks banana milkshakes all day every day, trying to stay an ounce above bone thin. She's bone thin, because she has no taste buds. She can't taste a thing, so she cares very little about eating. Every once in a while, she says, she can taste a hint of banana, thus the banana milkshakes instead of chocolate, or my favorite, strawberry, but otherwise, nothing. Wouldn't she be fun at parties? Tossing back jalapeno poppers like they were popcorn?

I waited on Bradley's call behind and between two of Magnolia's ficus trees, with an eye and a loaded gun on my front door and occasionally, the elevator. My phone buzzed.

"Wife." He sounded out of breath. "I've been out of the vault two minutes and I only have one minute to talk."

"Bradley. Magnolia is in our haunted house. I've got her cornered. Get up here."

He ate up half of his one minute with total silence.

"And I have more than a million dollars in counterfeit cash I just took from a guest room."

Nothing.

"Bradley, Magnolia's in our house."

Nothing.

"Bradley! Two and two! Fake coins! Fake money! She's behind every bit of this."

I could hear him breathing.

"Davis, we'll get to the bottom of this, and I promise you, it won't be Magnolia. That being said, I'll be there in a minute. Stay put."

I screamed when the elevator doors opened, my phone flew through the air, I accidently shot the ceiling three times—bang, bang, bang, accident, accident, accident. Baylor and Fantasy flew out of the elevator and drew on (me) the shooting trees, and all this happened on the exact click of the clock as Dionne Warwick's front man was rounding the corner. He let out an otherworldly crazy shriek when he saw me crawling out of the bushes with a smoking gun at the same time Fantasy and Baylor turned on him. They trained their sights between his eyes, and that was when the ridiculous entryway chandelier, a Smart Car-sized lead glass drippy thing garnished with bobbing jeweled magnolias and lucky recipient of the three rounds I'd accidently fired, decided to come tearing out of the ceiling.

Dionne Warwick's guy passed out.

Just then the elevator doors, unprovoked, closed, scaring the living daylights out of us. It's nothing short of a miracle we didn't shoot each other.

There was panting (me and Fantasy) and foul (foul) language from Baylor, the kind of language I reserve for vehicular surprises, like when someone tries to run me off the road, smoke and dust rising from the chandelier rubble in the floor, and it was Fantasy who said, "Holster! Everyone! Holster your guns!" It was a good idea, but before we could click on our safeties and maybe get Dionne Warwick's guy off the floor, the elevator doors opened, again, for no good reason—none of us were pushing elevator buttons—and it was but by the grace of God we did not execute my husband.

*   *   *

Bradley crunched through the chandelier.

I opened my mouth to explain and he stopped me with a hand. "We'll talk later."

Baylor and Bradley went in first to catch Magnolia. Fantasy and I waited in the chandelier rubble, keeping an eye on Dionne Warwick's guy.

"Some people just can't handle the least little bit of excitement."

I fanned him with a branch I'd snapped off a ficus tree.

Fantasy said, "He's cute. Corporate cute. I like his socks." His socks were mint green, with little black birds on them. She kneeled down and checked him again. "Strong pulse. He'll be okay. He smells good." She looked up at me. "What in the *world* is going on here? Holder Darby, the vault, Mr. Funny Money, this guy laid out on the floor. It's summer, you know? We're supposed to be taking a breather."

"The only thing I know is that Magnolia Thibodeaux is behind every bit of it. That's all I know."

"Davis," Fantasy said. "You have to stop with that."

"She's going down."

But maybe not today. Bradley and Baylor claimed she wasn't there. They also claimed to have inspected under every bed, in every closet, and even the refrigerator. They were back in five minutes, which isn't enough time to find an elephant in the French Quarter Freak Show, much less Magnolia, who'd lived here almost twenty years and knew where to hide.

"I'm telling you, Bradley, she's in there."

"And I'm telling you, Davis, she's not."

Past the twelve-foot-tall silk magnolia tree and the Igloo fridge smothered in counterfeit cash, then through the King Cake tearoom, is the great room of the Jambalaya Junkyard. Think high-school-gymnasium-slash-Hooters. This is where the Thibodeauxs, big LSU fans, watched football with two hundred of their closest friends. The room had a total of sixteen sofas and thirty-two club chairs, all arranged around big screen televisions in the four corners of the room. And by big screens, I mean you could park RVs in here and call it a drive-in theater. The fake Bourbon Street balconies closest to the entertainment pits were football themed. Jesus and Tigers, Tigers and Jesus. Bradley and I claimed one of the corners as our own, the one closest to the kitchen, and stayed as far away from the rest of the stadium as we could.

Bradley and Baylor lugged Dionne Warwick's guy to one of the many, many magnolia sofas, and Baylor accidentally banged the poor guy's head as they lowered him onto it.

"Oh. My bad, dude."

I said, "I don't think he can hear you."

Fantasy slipped a pillow that said *Geaux Tigers* under his head. "How do we know this guy is on Dionne Warwick's front team?"

"I rode up with him earlier," I said. "He's got to be on Dionne Warwick's front team or he wouldn't have a key to Jay's place."

She shrugged. I shrugged. There are tens of thousands of people in this building at sunrise on Easter morning. We can't know, or keep up with, every single one of them.

Baylor fell into a green velvet loveseat that sprouted six-inch gold rope tassels from every seam and started singing, "Here, kitty kitty."

I'd forgotten all about the cat.

Fantasy and I sat across from Baylor in side by side matching purple pleather recliners. Bradley, who generally keeps a cooler head than the rest of us, stepped into the kitchen and returned with a drippy kitchen towel. Fantasy took it from him and put it across Mr. Dionne Warwick's forehead. Next, Bradley Cole poured three generous shots of breakfast bourbon from a crystal decanter and passed each of us one. We made quick work of it.

He paced. Back and forth. "Who is this man?"

Three huge shrugs.

"What happened to the chandelier?"

Baylor and Fantasy pointed at me. (Thanks a lot.)

"It was an accident, Bradley."

"Of that," he said, "I have no doubt."

We sat quietly as Bradley paced. After five minutes of wearing the magnolias off the rug, he said, "Stay with him," to Fantasy and Baylor. "You." He pointed. "Come with me."

The man on the magnolia sofa could have been in a medically-induced coma wearing noise-canceling headphones and Bradley would still want to step out of his hospital room rather than discuss anything in front of him. I followed my husband to the kitchen, where the big red monster made enough cover noise to give us privacy.

"What is going on, Davis? First the wedding, which was a disaster, and now this. We have to, at the bare minimum, keep the doors open. So far," he looked at his watch, "two hours into this work week, and we're not doing so well."

"Did you see all that money?" I nodded in the direction of the foyer. "Number one, it came from a guest room. Number two, it's counterfeit. And number three, the guest is gone. Poof, gone. As in Holder Darby gone."

"I saw the money. I tripped over the money. And the first thing I need you to do is get the money off the property. I don't want it anywhere near the conference game."

A conference perk: Conferences get private slot tournaments in the events hall of the conference center. Last year, we hosted a cupcake conference, and their slot machines were all cupcakes. Fortunes and Frosting. So cute. (Not real cupcakes. You can't get a cupcake inside a slot machine. The slot machine graphics were cupcakes. When the players hit the right combination of cupcake and frosting, they won. The jackpot was three birthday sprinkle cupcakes in a row. The candles lit and the player won $25,000.)

"Obviously," I said, "we want the counterfeit money out of here. But why specifically away from the bankers conference?"

"So there'll be no confusion."

Which confused me.

"So the counterfeit money won't end up in the conference game," he explained.

"The conference game? *In* the game? How could it end up in the game?"

"The bankers have a cash game, Davis."

"What?" I'd never seen a cash game. "Cash *in* the game?"

"Yes," Bradley said, "they're in the money business. They have a cash game."

"Bradley, how is that not a security nightmare?"

"It's Paragon's problem," he said. "It's their money, and their job to safeguard it. They brought their own security specifically for the game."

"And they brought their own counterfeit money for it too."

He shook his head. "No. No they didn't."

"The conference people were waiting for the counterfeit money, Bradley."

"You said they were waiting on the guest. No one said they were waiting on the money."

Something made me think of prison food, which would be our steady diet for the rest of our lives if we allowed a game to be played or paid out in counterfeit money. The Bellissimo would close, and we'd all be in prison.

"There has to be a reasonable explanation," he said, "because Paragon would no more deal in counterfeiting than we would."

"Fake coins. Fake money." I tipped my head in the direction of the counterfeit production plant hidden deep in our home. "The only other reasonable explanation is Magnolia Thibodeaux."

He threw his hands in the air.

"Okay," I said, "if you want me to get to the bottom of this, and, as you say, keep the doors open, get me into the conference and I'll take it from there."

"You are in. You're Holder Darby."

"I need farther in," I said, "past the reception desk. All the way in."

"There's no way to get you in without setting off alarms. Last week, we could have worked it out. Now that the conference has started, I don't think it's a good idea. We will not put this conference under a microscope."

"I need to see the game."

"You're not going to."

"Okay, I *want* to see the game."

"You're not going to."

That quieted things down for a minute.

"It's odd to me, Bradley, that we're not allowed access to our own facilities."

"Of course we are," he said. "But not the way you're approaching it, locked and loaded." He looked me in the eye. All the way to the back of my head. "Davis?" He was so tall. Top of my world tall. "Stay away from the conference game. And Magnolia Thibodeaux has nothing to do with anything. Don't waste time. Understand?"

I did not understand.

"Find the missing guest and you'll have your answers." He kissed my forehead. "I have to get back to work."

*　*　*

We sat as still as church mice in Bradley's wake until Fantasy reached for the bourbon and poured us a round of brunch. At some point, Dionne Warwick's guy, without us noticing, assumed a sitting position on the magnolia sofa. "Who *are* you people?" He looked around. "Where *am* I?"

SEVEN

This place was creepy enough without a jumpy cat hiding in it. A cat who, again, I'd forgotten. It was a simple noise that petrified and produced it.

A mundane task, pulling a bottle of water from my Igloo refrigerator, scared the cat, who'd been hiding somewhere in the magnolia tree above the cooler, out of its skin. All I did was reach in and pull out a bottle of water for Dionne Warwick's guy, causing ice to collapse around the space, and not in a gentle way, which sent the cat tearing out of the magnolia tree, landing square on my head, which had hardly healed from the cat's last dance on it, then scraping its way down my back with its claws.

When it happened, I didn't know if Magnolia Thibodeaux was slashing me with a butcher knife, if I was being sucked into a mulching machine, or if a bomb had gone off and I was full of shrapnel. I wound up spread eagle on the floor, panting. I could taste metal, and all I could see were stacks of fake money.

Footsteps pounded behind me. I heard gun safeties click. Fantasy, after some sailor language, helped me to a sitting position. Baylor, after some kitty kitty baby talk, cradled the cat, petting long strokes down its back.

The cat's eyes were closed, its thick tail whipping back and forth, and I asked if I had any hair left in the back of my head.

"Your jacket's not going to make it," Fantasy inspected, "but your hair is fine."

"You can't scare cats, Davis. Haven't you ever heard 'scaredy cat'?"

"Thank you, Baylor." Fantasy helped me up. "Your cat tips are invaluable."

I sat on the Igloo refrigerator, still trying to catch my breath, holding up a finger: Give me a minute. Fantasy opened the bottle of water, which had rolled across the floor, and passed it to me. I took a long pull. I found my voice.

"Baylor, find something to pack up this money in, hide it somewhere out of the building, and get the cat settled down. When you're finished, get us lunch. Something decent. Do you hear me, Baylor? Edible. Fit for human consumption. Not Taco Bell. Fantasy, take care of Dionne Warwick's guy." My temples felt like someone was hammering both sides of my head. "I'll check on the conference, then nose around Holder Darby's office. We'll meet downstairs in an hour and look for the man who brought the money."

And Holder Darby.

And four million in platinum.

*   *   *

When I got it together enough to move on with my life, granted, from here on out with post-traumatic cat syndrome, I changed into a different suit. One that hadn't been in a catfight. I hid behind Chanel sunglasses the size of kiddie pools, then stepped out the front door of Beignet Bungalow and around the crew clearing away the chandelier remains. Multicolor wires dangled from a big black hole in the ceiling. For the next eighteen minutes, I traveled from the Gumbo Garage Sale to the Alabama bankers. Three elevator changes, through the lobby, and all the way through the casino.

As the escalator rose to the convention level, the gambling din faded. When I stepped onto the gold floral carpet, it was as if the casino below me didn't exist. I walked the length of the room, past Impressionist oils in gilded frames, twenty or more seating areas scattered to my right and left, where gold pendant lights dangled over round settee sofas with recessed buttons forming diamond shapes in the gold upholstery, all the way to the reception desk, gilded too, where a girl was bent over her phone, double tapping Instagram pictures of hedgehogs. I cleared my throat. She finally looked up.

"I'm the new Holder."

She smiled. Braces. She had to be thirty, with a mouth full of hardware. "Right. I'm Megan."

"Olivia."

"Nice to meet you, Olivia."

Her voice and diction matched that of the girl who'd called me this morning.

"How's it going?"

"Oh, it's going," she said. "They're all locked up back there." She tipped her head to the double doors behind her.

I took a step past her desk. "I'll go check everything out."

"Wait." She pushed her phone aside. "You can't go back there." This again.

"Isn't it my job to make sure everything's okay?"

"Yes," she said, "but we can't wander in and out. There are men right through those doors and if you don't have a badge, you can't get past them."

"Let me borrow your badge."

"I don't have one," Megan said. "We're supposed to leave them alone."

"Are all conferences this way?" I asked.

"Never, but this is the first time we've had bankers here."

So weird.

"Did you find that man?" she asked.

"That's why I'm here," I said. "Where are the techs who were looking for him?"

"Oh, they're gone," she said. "As soon as they set up the game, they took off."

What? "When?"

"Oh," she said, "an hour ago?"

An hour ago, the counterfeit money we confiscated was all

over my foyer. Which meant the techs weren't waiting on it. Specifically. But that didn't change the fact they'd been waiting on the man. The counterfeit money, the man, and this convention are connected. Somehow. (I think Somehow is named after a tree. And that's not Maple.)

"Thank you, Megan," I said. "Call me if you need me."

"Will do."

She went right back to the hedgehogs and I went right back to wondering what was going on behind the locked doors of the bankers conference.

To do list: Get a banker's pass.

* * *

My second stop was the Executive Floor, a level above the Bellissimo Spa and Salon on the other side of the property. Sixteen minutes, two elevator changes, four long halls, in heels, to the Special Events office. If the Bellissimo is nothing else, it's big.

Another girl at another reception desk, but this one a regular office and no braces.

"I'm Olivia Abbott," I said. "I'm the temporary Holder until we get a new Holder."

The girl scratched her head.

"Have you heard from her, by any chance?"

The girl shook her head.

"Can you give me a list of everyone at the conference?"

She scratched her neck.

"Today?"

The girl had yet to speak.

"Do you know if she had a cat?"

She tapped her nose thoughtfully.

"Do you mind?" I pointed at Holder's closed door.

She shrugged a have-at-it.

Holder's office was dark and dusty. On my way to her desk, I scanned the room for personal pictures—no cats—then sat down in her chair and powered up the computer. Of course, it was password protected. Personal Computer Hacking 101: Start the computer in safe mode, log in as administrator, change the password. Fifteen seconds tops.

The Independent Bankers of Alabama folder was on her desktop, wedged between the Goodman-Ramirez wedding and the Simpson-Wheeler wedding, and it too was password protected.

There's an easy way and a hard way to open password protected files. Easy: Copy it in a different format that doesn't recognize the security feature (try converting it to an eBook or a spreadsheet) and boom, you're in. Hard: Download and install file-hacking software, like NSIS or LMI (Let Me In), send the locked information to it, then let the software try to guess the password, sometimes over a period of weeks. When I got in the easy way (two minutes), I sent the whole file to myself by email.

Just to be nosey, I took a quick peek at the task manager history on Holder's computer to see what she'd been up to the day she walked off, no different than peeking in the medicine cabinet, and me snooping around her computer was a little after the fact, since I'd already rifled through her panty drawer and I had her cat. Her computer activity just kept on coming. Holder Darby had been all over the Bellissimo system. Why would a wedding coordinator be snooping around cyber Bellissimo—payables, receivables, front desk, human resources—at a level reserved for me? I clicked open the web browser, and found it just as curious. Holder spent a lot of internet time at her bank, moving around large quantities of money. She also rented a car last week. Why? She had a perfectly fine Audi S8 in her garage. All told, it was odd enough computer activity that I'd need to hijack her hard drive. I could copy her files and folders pretty quickly, but I needed her entire operating system.

Take a note: When cyber stealing someone's computer, steal the whole enchilada. You can't simply copy the files. You need the drivers and directories too, due to hardware and software differences between the data you're stealing and your own system.

You can send the files to yourself ten times, but if you don't swipe the whole system, you won't be able to access ninety percent of them. Either steal the whole kit and caboodle or don't bother. You're welcome.

From the web browser, I downloaded CloneMonster. I copied Holder's complete hard drive to a .zip file and sent it to myself. Then I wiped her computer as clean as my mother's kitchen, good luck finding anything on this sucker ever again.

"Has Holder been back at all?" I asked the reception girl. "Have you spoken to her? Do you know how I might be able to reach her?"

The girl shook her head. Didn't say a word, just shook her head.

To-do list: Call this office. I bet this girl picks up the phone, holds it to her ear, and that's it.

* * *

My final destination of the morning, our offices on 3B. I swiped myself in. "Baylor, where's Fantasy?"

"MICHIGAN!" I could see his arms and legs paddling off both ends of the sofa. "I CAN'T SWIM!"

Baylor, who could swim all day long, has a special sleeping talent, in that he can sleep anywhere, anytime, on anything. Floorboard, bathtub, park bench. If he can stretch out, he can sleep. He falls asleep in an instant, and wakes just as quickly, talking about Twinkies or, last week, a girl named Candy Corn, or today, aquatics.

"Wake up, Baylor." I sat on the coffee table, leaned over, and patted his rosy cheeks. "Wake up."

"DIVE, MERMAID PIZZA!"

"Hey!" I snapped my fingers. "Get a grip."

He shook himself awake.

"Make us some coffee, Baylor."

"I don't drink coffee." His head was cocked to one side and he had a knuckle going on one of his ears, trying to get the water out.

"Then make me coffee."

Of the three rooms that make up our offices, room one is a den of sorts, I call it the bullpen, where Fantasy and I watch "The Price is Right" and Baylor takes cat naps. To the left of the bullpen we have a dressing room, where we camouflage ourselves to wander around the resort and in the casino without being recognized or remembered. And the third room is control central, full of computers, where I regularly go on cyber scavenger hunts when I'm not hijacking hard drives, shooting chandeliers, or being attacked by cats.

I woke up three computers. Baylor placed a cup in front of me. I peered in. Something was floating in it. Cornbread, maybe.

"Baylor, coffee isn't supposed to be this color or eaten with a spoon."

We looked at each other. This went on for a minute or four. He blinked first.

"Dammit."

"Get a large cup, Baylor. The bucket size," I said to his back.

Five minutes later, he was back with my bucket of coffee. "Guess who's in the coffee shop."

I didn't look up.

"Fantasy," he said.

I looked up.

"She's with Diane."

"I doubt that's his name, Baylor."

"That's what *you* called him."

"I called him *Dionne* Warwick's *guy*."

"Who is Dionne Warwick?"

"Baylor." I peeled the lid off my gallon of coffee. "Get me a coffee cup, a clean coffee cup, and 'Do You Know the Way to San Jose?'"

"California?"

Someone save me.

I texted Fantasy: *Hey, do you mind?*

She texted back: *Davis. We scared this man to death. I'm doing damage control. Be there in ten.*

"Sit down, Baylor. Help me." I patted Fantasy's chair. "What did you get us for lunch?" The brown take-out bags on Fantasy's desk smelled like the Fourth of July.

"Ribs."

"Have you ever seen me eat a rib?"

His eyebrows drew together. "Come to think of it, no."

"What do we always want for lunch, Baylor?"

He concentrated really hard. "Not ribs?" He snapped his fingers. "You want strawberries."

It's not like I'm addicted to strawberries. I am addicted to Pop Tarts, because they're easy to eat on the run and they're a good source of seven vitamins and minerals. Strawberry Pop Tarts just happen to be my favorite; it's the flavor the supermarket is never out of. In addition, my favorite quick-lunch Bellissimo salad happens to have strawberries in it. It's a chicken salad—romaine, grilled chicken, strawberry balsamic vinaigrette—and the sliced strawberries are just a bonus. To give it a little pop. But somehow I have a reputation going back to grade school as being strawberry addicted. Which I'm not. But now I was starving. For strawberries.

"Let's get to work, Baylor. You can have the ribs and I'll eat later."

"Done." He peeled the foil away from a slab of ribs as long as my leg. "I should've gotten napkins."

EIGHT

I cracked Holder Darby's conference file while Baylor was out fetching my coffee. I printed a list of attendees while he ate ribs. I printed a list of sponsors and vendors while he took a bubble bath, because he was covered in rib gravy. All that done, and finally, he was ready to work. He sat down beside me smelling like a bar of soap as I was going over the conference schedule, which was unimpressive until the last day, when everything was scheduled on an impossibly tight clock, with the Dionne Warwick concert and the slot machine tournament running neck and neck. Why schedule both events at the same time?

I passed Baylor the list of attendees and a fresh legal pad.

"Start entering these names, Baylor. Dig in their guest portfolios, and write down what room number they're in and where they work. We're trying to find the missing counterfeit money supplier, so we need to know if he's a banker or not. Over here," I tapped, "write down the ones who work at banks and over here— " I lost him. Baylor has the attention span of a gnat and can only do one thing at a time. "Just start looking up these people."

"What are you going to do?" he asked.

"I'm going to see what might be going on with this cash game."

It was just after lunch (Direct Debit Double Cut Pork Chops) and according to the schedule, the bankers were taking their first crack at the tournament game. Of all the questions bouncing around my brain—Where is Fantasy? Why doesn't my refrigerator work? How will I ever catch Magnolia Thibodeaux?—the question at the front of the line was about the slot machines at the bankers conference. Specifically, what's in them? I reached for the house phone and dialed Casino Operations. Let's see what they don't know about this game.

While the phone rang, I asked Baylor, "Did you take care of the counterfeit money?"

"Check."

"Did you get it out of the building?"

"Yes." At the same time, a man answered the phone in my other ear. "Casino Ops."

"Hi," I said. "This is Calinda Wilson from Mr. Cole's office. I need to speak to the techs who set up the convention game."

"Hold on." Soon enough, another male voice said, "David Sandoval."

"David, hi. Are you one of the techs who installed the slot machines for the convention this week?" Dead silence. "Hello?"

"Yeah, I'm thinking." When he finished thinking he said, "We didn't install those."

"Is this Casino Operations?"

"You bet."

"The department that installs slot machines?"

"That's us."

"If you didn't install them, who did?"

"I don't have any idea. But I'm looking at our schedule. Our last installation was a bank of Wicked Winnings in section fourteen, and our next installation is four new Downton Abbeys in section twenty-nine next week."

"How in the world does Downton Abbey translate into a slot machine?"

"What?"

"Never mind."

"I know the conference game is up and running," he said, "because we threw the switch on it an hour ago, but that was just pushing a button. We didn't set them up. We haven't installed a conference machine since the ladybug people were here."

The Entomology Conference two weeks ago. I knew about it,

because some nut in receiving opened a crate marked "CAELIFERA THIS SIDE UP" and let ten thousand crickets loose. Those crickets were still all over the place. I said thanks and hung up.

No one in this building knew a thing about the bankers game.

I turned to Baylor, who looked like he was taking the SAT, chewing on a pencil eraser, pouring over the legal pad plugging in names.

"Baylor, what did you mean when you said you said you took care of the counterfeit money?"

"What I said. I took care of it."

"How?"

"What do you mean?"

"How did you take care of it?"

"By taking care of it, Davis."

This is why people pull their hair out. "Let's start over, Baylor. Where is the counterfeit money?"

"I put it in your car."

Of course he did.

"Why in hell would you put it in my car?"

"Because I drove your car to get you lunch."

"But you didn't get me lunch. And why did you drive my car?"

"Because Fantasy has a flat tire. Two flat tires."

"Two?"

He held up two fingers.

"Why didn't you drive your truck?" I asked.

"Because it's out of gas." He rolled his eyes, duh. "What is your point?"

He was getting irritated with *me*.

"I don't want to drive around with counterfeit money is my point!"

"Where do you need to go?"

"Forget it," I said. "Let's get back to work."

The problem wasn't Baylor; the problem was summer. We'd sat around since Memorial Day watching Sandra Bullock movies, and now, all of a sudden, we needed to be firing on sixteen cylinders, and Baylor was always the last to load. On the other hand, he's funny, he's cute, he's strong, and he's a dead-eye. Most days it's like Fantasy and I have joint custody of Baylor more than anything else, but when things got tight, as they've been known to do, he comes through like a champ.

Thirty minutes later and I still hadn't connected the slot machine dots.

"The bankers slot machines are up and running, but we didn't install them." I was thinking out loud. Looking at Baylor, but thinking out loud. "The game is full of money, but not counterfeit money, because the counterfeit money is in my car. So why were the conference people waiting on the man who brought all the counterfeit money, and what's in the game?"

"I don't know." He racked his rib-addled brain. "Am I supposed to know?"

"And if the counterfeit money wasn't for the game, what was it for?"

"To pay someone off with counterfeit money?"

His words slid through me. Then settled.

*　*　*

The slot machine questions wouldn't be answered until I could find a way into Exhibit Hall B and take a look at them, and I thought I'd better (wait until the conference people were asleep tonight) not bust in on them the first day. I put the slot machines aside for the time being; they weren't going anywhere. I turned my attention to the man who brought the counterfeit money to the Bellissimo. Who was he, and where is he? After that, I'd track down four million in platinum. And Holder Darby. All in a day's work.

I reached for my phone and dialed the County Coroner's office on 23rd Avenue.

"Hi. I'm calling from the Bellissimo. I need to know if you have any information on the body you picked up here. The family has arrived and wants to know something."

"Who is this?"

"I'm calling from Mr. Cole's office. Do you have any information about our dead guest?" I could hear keyboard tapping.

"Lady," the man said, "we didn't pick up a body at the Bellissimo. We haven't had a fresh one at all since the middle of the night Friday, and it was from Memorial. The last cadaver we got from you was the toothache man."

This is a big place, a million guests pass through these doors every year, and we're going to lose a few. (Think actuary statistics.) Two months ago a man from Gautier (pronounced *go shave*), right down the road, a Bellissimo regular, died of a toothache. He was playing a $2 Bonus Frenzy with an infected tooth. The tooth went septic and hit his bloodstream, boom, out of that slot chair. It scared the hell out of us, sent us screaming to our dentists.

"What about Holder Darby?" I asked. "Do you have a Holder Darby?"

"Lady," the man at the coroner's office said, "I don't know what kind of roll you're taking, but you can't just call here and get an inventory. Check the obituary section of the paper if you need to know who's passed."

"Is that a yes or a no on Holder Darby?"

"Who did you say this is? What's your name?"

"Ooops," I said. "Wrong number."

Just in time for me to get a hit on missing money man's fingerprint I'd loaded into the National Fingerprint Database. I might not have found him in his guest room, or laid out on a slab at the coroner's, but I did locate him in the system. If you've ever been on the wrong side of the law, in the military, in law enforcement, or visited a Disney park, I can find you.

Christopher Hall. The man in room 2650, who'd left dinner on the table and counterfeit money in the bathtub, was an inmate at the United States Penitentiary in Pollock, Louisiana. He was convicted on January 21 five years ago on multiple counts of conspiracy to manufacture, distribute, and deal in counterfeit obligations of the United States in violation of 18 U.S.C § 370, four counts of counterfeiting currency in violation of 29 U.S.C § 470, and fourteen counts of dealing in counterfeit obligations in violation of 20 U.S.C § 255.

I found the master counterfeiter.

Why would Christopher Hall be in high-security federal prison for counterfeiting? He should have been (convicted—it's, duh, illegal to print your own money) in medium security for ten to twenty, not federal for life. A few clicks later, I had my answer. He had a bonus manslaughter charge tacked onto all the counterfeiting counts. His partner, a man named Grover Walsh, died during the commission of these crimes. Christopher Hall was sentenced to fifteen years in prison on the counterfeiting charges. The bonus conviction of one count of involuntary manslaughter during the commission of a federal crime put him in for life without parole.

Where? Where did all this happen?

Click click.

Harrison County, Mississippi. City of Biloxi.

There wasn't a doubt in my mind these crimes were committed in a place I call home. Grover Walsh was crushed to death under a piece of equipment down the hall from where my husband and I sleep.

I took several slow steadying breaths. I could feel my pulse skipping. Small dots swam in front of my eyes. I felt like I was in a dark tunnel and I was dizzy. I sat there a full ten minutes processing my horrific findings.

Eventually, I turned back to the story. I read police reports, case files, court transcripts, rulings, and every article written about the crime, capture, and conviction. Christopher Hall showed up at the Emergency Room carrying his gravely injured partner, effectively turning himself in. He was taken into custody.

Detectives found $1.8 million in counterfeit currency and another half million in fake platinum coins under the floor in Hall's house. They suspected there was much more where that came from, but repeated searches hadn't produced anything.

"I can assure you there's more money," a United States Secret

Service Criminal Investigator testified, "millions and millions. Plus equipment. It's out there too. We can't find the money and we can't find the production plant."

In all that, under oath, Christopher Hall claimed that he and Grover Walsh acted on their own. Not one mention of the Bellissimo, Salvatore Casimiro, or the Thibodeauxs.

Who sprang this man from prison? And where was he now?

* * *

I'd lost track of time and Baylor had slipped out. I tipped my chair. "Baylor?" I was alone in Control Central. No Baylor, no Fantasy. "BAYLOR!"

"FLOAT ON YOUR TEETH! YOUR TEETH!"

He'd gone down for another nap.

I texted Fantasy: *A little help, please?*

And from her: *Be there in ten.*

Which is exactly what she'd said earlier.

I'd like to have called, popped in, or otherwise pestered my husband with the new findings, but I'd learned long ago to not bother him every three minutes so he could work. When he needed me during the day, he called. When I needed him during the day, I rolled my wedding rings around my finger.

After going through the list of conference names twice, I still didn't find Christopher Hall. I went into the Bellissimo system and found where he'd registered. As Bill Dollar. Cute. Back to Baylor's legal pad, where he had a big blank beside Bill Dollar's name.

So he wasn't registered at the Bellissimo as a banker, a conference sponsor, or even part of the conference. He paid cash when he checked in, which might mean we had counterfeit bills circulating in house, oh yay. But he had to secure the room with a credit card.

Forever and a day later, I tracked the Visa account used to secure Bill Dollar's room to First Federal Bank in Baltimore, Maryland. Which might as well have been the North Pole, because

Baltimore didn't connect him to any of the bankers attending the conference, who were all from Alabama, or Magnolia Thibodeaux, who'd probably set foot above the Mason-Dixon exactly never, or Holder Darby, not yet anyway. Maybe Christopher Hall's connection was with the conference sponsors, Paragon Protection. I rolled my chair to the computer full of Holder's old computer and clicked open the conference file to read their profile.

Paragon Protection manufactured and installed vaults all over the US of A. Their other products included armored trucks and pneumatic transfer systems for financial institutions with drive-through services. They were a veritable superstore for anything and everything to do with securing or moving money. And they had forty representatives here at the conference, which they were sponsoring.

It was on their dime that five hundred bankers were at the Bellissimo, in hopes of selling them equipment and services. The problem I had with it, in addition to it being utterly ridiculous for Holder Darby to have given them the green light on practically banning Bellissimo employees from Bellissimo property, was the fact that I think there might be a connection between the escaped convict Christopher Hall and Paragon, and worse, that my husband would spend the entire week with these Paragon people.

Paragon Protection's home office was located in Oakridge, Illinois, with production and distribution facilities in (click click) Mattawa, Washington; Wickenburg, Arizona; Bottineau, North Dakota, and Galax, Virginia. Their most recent property acquisition was in Horn Hill, Alabama. Which stopped me dead in my tracks.

Now I was getting somewhere.

I tracked Paragon down in accounts payable. Six weeks ago they paid the Bellissimo eighteen thousand for the bankers' custom slot machines. The invoice was for fifty software and graphic installations for a custom game called Mint Condition. (Cute.) I almost clicked out of the agreement—legal jargon, legal beagle, legal eagle—when I reached page four and fell out of my chair.

Paragon Protection put down a one million dollar deposit on

platinum. Platinum on loan from the Bellissimo vault for the Mint Condition game.

What? The bankers' game had cash *and* platinum in it?

I couldn't get my husband on the phone fast enough. Except I couldn't get him on the phone. I called Calinda.

"Calinda. I need Bradley. Right now."

"Is this about the refrigerator?"

"No!"

"Davis, he's in the vault. I can't call him out unless it's life or death. I can have him call you the minute he gets out."

I sat perfectly still until the phone rang, quietly contemplating a job at Subway. I could Eat Fresh. I loved the assembly line of it all. And the peanut butter cookies.

My phone and I jumped.

"Why didn't you tell me there was platinum in the banker game?"

He sighed.

"That's how you found out the platinum in the vault was fake," I said. "The accountants were doing an inventory, but they were also pulling platinum for the Mint Condition game."

He sighed again. "Yes."

"Does Paragon know they have fake platinum in the slot machines?"

He inhaled like it was the last breath he'd ever take.

"No."

"What are we going to do, Bradley?"

"We're going to find the platinum, Davis."

And by we, he meant me.

"Can we talk about this after dinner?" he asked.

Dinner. I forgot about dinner. Would this day ever end?

On my way out, I gave Baylor a nudge. "Hey, wake up and go home."

"TRUCK SNORKELS IN THE TREE."

On my way to meet Bradley for dinner, it occurred to me Paragon Protection might have the Bellissimo's platinum. They had access—the annual inspection. And they had it hidden in plain sight. Inside their Mint Condition slot machines.

How in the world did Magnolia Thibodeaux orchestrate all this?

NINE

Richard Sanders, president and CEO of the Bellissimo Resort and Casino since the ribbon cutting, having climbed Mt. Biloxi, and having finally hired a casino manager in whose capable hands he could entrust his billion dollar baby, raised his stakes and spread his wings. He secured controlling interest of the Bellissimo from his ailing and retiring father-in-law, Salvatore Casimiro, then tackled the next item on his list: He branched out.

Mr. Sanders's job has always involved a fair amount of travel, but as long as I've worked for him, he's always left town bent on returning as quickly as humanly possible to (keep an eye on his wife) be at the helm of the S. S. Bellissimo. That is, until he hired a likeminded first mate, my husband. Bradley and I were married on October 22nd, he was sworn in as operating casino manager on October 23rd, and Mr. Sanders left for Tunica on October 24th.

For us, it meant leaving a home we loved, to live here, in the Booyah Bordello, Bradley working a ninety-hour week, with me reporting directly to him. It's been an adjustment.

For Richard and Bianca Sanders, it meant a physical separation, because Bianca Sanders wouldn't even say the word Tunica aloud, much less go there. She barely goes here. It's been frustrating.

Tunica is the number two gambling venue in Mississippi. It's in the northwest corner of the state, as far away from Biloxi as you can get and not cross the state line, and the only things in Tunica are farming, wildlife, and gambling. There's nothing in, around, or under Tunica but coyotes and a strip of three-star casinos in the middle of cornfields.

All that was about to change.

Mr. Sanders had been ready to put his dog in the Tunica fight for years, and broke ground for the city's newest and grandest casino, Jolie, the week I would have otherwise been honeymooning, and the worst of it for me turned out to be he took my immediate supervisor, No Hair, with him. Since then we'd barely seen either of them. Mr. Sanders was three-for-four—three days here, four days there—for nine months. When he is here, he had his desk to clean off, his spoiled rotten wife to appease, and his new casino manager to conference with for eight-hour stretches. As soon as he finished those chores, he was back on his Gulfstream 650 to the Jolie. That plane could probably fly itself to Tunica and back at this point.

"Tell me about the wedding, Davis. I heard you wound up with cake on your face. And what's this about you having a cat?"

"Oh, dear Lord." Bianca Sanders. "A *cat?*"

Mr. Sanders—forty-five years old, blonde hair lighter at his temples, blue eyes behind small, round, tortoiseshell glasses—wanted to hear my version of the Hello Kitty wedding. We arrived for dinner at the Sanders's at seven and before we'd taken a sip of our cocktails, I was already in the hot seat.

"The wedding got out of hand, Mr. Sanders. And before it was over, we were all covered in frosting."

"Honestly, David." Bianca Sanders was disgusted. "Show some decorum."

My name is Davis.

Bianca Sanders is, at (most) times, the bane of my existence. She's almost ten years older than I am, but in spite of our age difference and aside from pesky details like coloring, scruples, and general disposition, we look just alike. Part of my job is to dress up and prance around making public appearances for her, and she's addicted to it. She's forever telling me I'm the face of the Bellissimo, and what she means by that is *do it for me.* She says it all the time— I'm her face—as if it's a compliment. I don't want to be her face, I don't have time to be her face, but after three years of running her each and every public errand, her activities beyond the 30th floor penthouse had dwindled to one: commuting to Million Air, the private airport, to board a Bellissimo jet to anywhere that wasn't here. She could jet set for as long as she pleased, because she had me to cover for her. Bianca didn't hang around long after Project Tunica started. Ten minutes, maybe. The Sanderses had been here together no more than five days of the month for nine months running.

The day he left for Tunica, she took off shopping. She was gone three (glorious) months, only stopping back in to (torture me) drop off her goodies to make cargo room for more, and the whole time no one knew she was gone because I was being her face.

She toured Europe first and we didn't hear a peep from her for six weeks. From there, she hit Tokyo. Then she slowly made her way back to Biloxi via San Francisco, Las Vegas, Austin, Chicago, and NYC, Mr. Sanders in Tunica the whole time. Finally fed up with living out of seventeen Louis Vuitton trunks, she got home and had me on the phone within an hour, threatening death by boredom. My death, if I didn't do something about her boredom.

"And I'm ill, David! Something dastardly is going on with my physical person! I need a team from Johns Hopkins here today. Did you hear me, David? Today!"

Sadly, with Mr. Sanders and No Hair absent, exercises like these (cost a small fortune) were all mine.

A team of life-saving physicians were ripped away mid life-saving procedures and flown here. Guest suites were revamped into five-star medical facilities for the four different specialists. At the end of two weeks—she's a terrible patient; pricking her finger is an all-day affair—it was determined Bianca was in excellent health. The only thing the million-dollar doctors found was she'd gained five pounds since the last time they'd been summoned for a luxury vacation at the Bellissimo because she'd sneezed, and they attributed it to fluctuating hormones, perfectly natural, at her age.

She had a fit like no other fit in the history of fits.

"David."

It's Davis.

Bianca had dark circles under her eyes, her neck red and splotchy, and I could see a thin sheen of moisture across her top lip. "I want them all fired for incompetency. I want lawsuits filed. Talk to your husband. Today. I want their credentials stripped! Their grants revoked! Their licenses rescinded!" She demanded I have her top-notch physicians taken out back and shot while hiding the extra five pounds under ten yards of a black silk muumuu. It was a designer nun's habit. She stomped back and forth in front of me, the black silk billowing around and trailing behind her. "I need a new team of doctors. STAT, David. I am offended at their delivery, their incompetency, and never has anyone been misdiagnosed so erroneously."

Never has anyone fought aging with the energy, investment, and arsenal as you, Bianca.

"Write this down, David."

I'd been taking notes the whole time: *Mrs. Bradley Cole. Mrs. Bradley Cole. Mrs. Bradley Cole.*

"I will *not* make a public appearance until I lose this weight. Not one! Do you hear me, David? It's all you."

It's Davis. And you haven't made a public appearance since the day you met me.

"I need you to lose five pounds, David. To offset the temporary bloating I'm experiencing from so much travel. Immediately." (Does that make any sense at all?) "And just to be *certain.*" Bianca sat down beside me, black silk pillowing, scanning the room to make sure none of her staff was eavesdropping, and moved in for the kill. Her cat-green eyes were bloodshot. "Make an appointment with my gynecologist. You know her. The Brazilian girl."

Yes, I knew her gynecologist, who was Asian. I knew all of Bianca's people because I was her face. Bianca ignored the fact that sending me to the gynecologist for her didn't exactly work. So to keep from wasting my time, not to mention wearing the lovely paper gown, I scheduled her appointments then went to lunch with her gynecologist. "Have a thorough examination, David," Bianca said, "and make certain these idiots aren't suggesting what I think they're suggesting."

Which made even less sense.

The next day, she had me arrange a Johns Hopkins cosmetic intervention party, then dig up high-dollar personal trainers. She flew them in from all over, conducted probing interviews, and hired the one who loved her most, Hans Solo. Hans Something. I call him Hans Solo. And he was a big believer in sculpted muscles. "The body is as the clay. We must *mooooold* it."

I don't know what kind of *mooooolding* Hans had Bianca doing three times a day (she claimed she and Demi Moore do the same workout), but after several months of it, Bianca looked like she was training for the Olympics. Boxing or Freestyle Wrestling. She had newly-acquired abs of steel, First Lady guns, and she'd bulked up her butt to the point of having her implants removed. (That had to be fun.) So that we might see all her muscles, she was wearing two ounces of a satin slip dress, threatening with her every breath to burst at its satin seams, and mile-high stilettoes. All black, as usual. She pressed a tall glass of designer water to her hot cheeks, because not only had Hans pumped her up, he cleaned her up too. She stopped drinking ten martinis a day, quit her happy pills, gave up gluten (I have no idea what gluten is), and had Cartier custom build a diamond jacket for her Fitbit bracelet. Guess what? She hadn't lost the weight.

"David." She fanned herself. "I'm hot. And you need to meet with Hans. You're getting mushy."

I'm about to get a lot mushier, the initial reason for our dinner date with Richard and Bianca Sanders. While I thought it would be better if we took care of a few things first—the crime rate, international terrorism, the economic collapse, climate change— Bradley was ready to start a family. He couldn't do it without me, I usually changed the subject, and yet here we were to inform the Sanderses we intended to move back home to our condo at the Regent, just five little miles away, when Jolie opened in two weeks and Mr. Sanders resumed full-time residence here. The plan, for me to get pregnant five minutes after we moved home, had been in place for months, a date way off in the future, yet here we were. And if all went according to plan, and I spend the rest of my life trying to protect a little guy who looks just like Bradley from armed conflict in the Middle East, infectious disease, and the fact that there will be no drinking water by the time he's ten years old, I couldn't be Bianca's face for who knows how long. Depends on how mushy I get.

That was the agenda when we made this dinner date weeks ago, to break it gently to the Sanderses together, because I needed someone between me and her, so she wouldn't kill me. We stood outside the Sanders's front door at five till seven wondering if, in light of the events of the past few days, we should even bring it up.

"Let's wait," I said.

"To have a baby? Is this about Social Security?"

Social Security is a big fat mess, no doubt about it, but that wasn't what I meant. Specifically.

"Let's wait to talk to them about it."

He was a patient man.

"We have more pressing issues right now, Bradley."

"Let's play it by ear."

"Good idea," I said.

He was just about to knock on the door.

"Are you ready?"

"Yes." No.

A little bit of Bradley went a long way with me, and right now, it was just a finger of his hooked with one of mine. Passing between us in that small touch, a promise, a confirmation, and a hope for the future. Surely, something could be done about the budget deficit between when I got pregnant and gave birth.

The Sanders's new butler (I've never seen this guy in my life) opened the door, Bradley and I shared a look and, in that split second, decided to wait.

To tell them.

"We're not staying for dinner either," Bradley whispered as we walked through the foyer.

"Amen," I whispered back.

A tuxedoed waiter tiptoed around topping off everyone's drinks. Bianca yawned, demanded a thicker slice of lime for her fizzy water, admired her manicure, and crossed her legs the other way every three minutes just to make sure we all caught her ripped hamstrings, while Mr. Sanders and Bradley conducted their version of small talk.

"All's well in Tunica?" (Bradley.)

"It was when I left two hours ago." (Mr. Sanders.) "How about here?"

"We're at sixty percent occupancy, half of that the bankers." (Bradley.)

"As expected." (Mr. Sanders.)

Then revenues, profitability, activity, disbursements, gross pay, gross earnings, gross negligence, such fun cocktail talk, I thought I might lose my mind.

"I have a headache," I announced.

"Well, you've given it to me, David."

We shot off in opposite directions. Me, for the front door. Her, for a hot flash.

TEN

A glass of wine to calm my nerves later, I heard Bradley key himself through the front door, explaining the missing chandelier to Mr. Sanders. Then he told him why we had an Igloo refrigerator in our foyer, and by the time they reached me in Who Dat Hooters, Bradley was telling Mr. Sanders about the babbling brook in the kitchen.

"Sears?"

"Sears," Bradley said.

Mr. Sanders surveyed. "You could have redecorated five times by now." Bradley poured and passed him a short bourbon. He looked at us and said, "You don't want to redecorate. You want out of here." He sipped the whiskey. "I don't blame you."

"Sit, Richard."

Mr. Sanders chose a magnolia sofa. "I haven't been here in forever." He stared at a voodoo doll on the wall. "One forgets." He stared at the Jesuses. "How are you managing, Davis?"

"I'm fine," I lied.

"You absolutely hate it, don't you?"

Yes, but I absolutely liked Mr. Sanders.

"Let's talk," he said, "so I can get back to Bianca."

*　*　*

Earlier today, while I was in 3B (supervising Baylor's naps) gathering unwelcome information, Bradley had been busy in, around, or on top of vault business. A second physical inventory conducted by the auditors with Hammond Stevenson Morris & Chase came up clean, everything else accounted for. Even so, Bradley had the vault contents relocated.

Bellissimo armed guards dressed as waiters pushed covered food trays loaded with tens of millions in cash, casino chips, stock certificates, deeds, gold, silver, and a treasure trove of Bianca Sanders's jewelry she'd gotten bored with straight through the casino, into public elevators, then to three connecting Deluxe Double guest rooms on the 8th floor. The guest rooms around, across, above, and below were cleared, the guests moved. (Upgrade!)

The loot was piled on the beds; the guards piled on the sofas, where they ordered room service and still-in-theaters movies.

The only thing left in the vault was a rotating series of human gorillas with tattoos and Ruger AC-556 assault rifles. Bellissimo bank deposits were rerouted to the human gorillas, who lobbed it into laundry carts. At shift change, two gorillas covered the loot with pool towels and rolled the carts to a receiving bay, where they handed it off to armored trucks that delivered it to the bank.

Bradley filled in Mr. Sanders.

"How many more days do we have assets and revenue in guest rooms, laundry bins, and on receiving docks?" Mr. Sanders asked.

"If the vault inspection goes well and no repairs are needed," Bradley said, "one. If Paragon finds they need to do any work in the vault, it might mean up to four days. At most five. I plan to leave the vault contents where they are until the inspection and updates are completed."

We were wide open, fair game, an easy target for the next one, four, possibly five days. And we knew it. We hoped, for the next one, four, possibly five days, no one else discovered it.

"When will we know?" Mr. Sanders asked.

I sat quietly. Chugging wine.

"I'll meet with Paragon first thing tomorrow," my husband said, "and we can expect repairs. They've come prepared. They brought a tech team, and they say they'll have us back in the vault quickly."

Note to self: Paragon brought their own tech team for vault repairs and slot machines. To do list: Find out if it's the same crew.

"Who knows the vault is empty?" Mr. Sanders asked.

"In addition to the three of us," Bradley said, "only our guards and Paragon."

* * *

In the pecking order of things, moving money around a casino gets the top spot. So for the next half hour, we pored over the details. Routes, timelines, personnel, procedures. When Mr. Sanders began looking antsy and glancing at his watch, I steered the conversation my way. The vault was Bradley's job—to safeguard the contents and oversee the expected refurbishing, a job he'd be doing around the clock for the rest of the week. My mission was to find what was missing. People and platinum.

I asked Mr. Sanders to tell me everything he knew about the escaped convict Christopher Hall. After his shock at even hearing Hall's name again in this lifetime, he told me all he knew. Which was no more or less than what I'd learned earlier. I asked if the fake platinum found in the vault could have been an old sin committed by Christopher Hall and Ty Thibodeaux.

"So you're suggesting that sometime before his retirement, Ty Thibodeaux and Christopher Hall stole four million dollars in platinum from the vault and replaced it with counterfeit?"

"Yes."

"I don't see it, Davis," Mr. Sanders said. "Ty Thibodeaux would have never stolen from Casimiro."

Stealing from Salvatore Casimiro would be a death sentence.

"Thibodeaux was a good casino manager." Mr. Sanders loosened his tie. "I'll give him that. Which is not to say I didn't suspect my father-in-law had him running illegal errands behind my back, but none of it on my books," Mr. Sanders said. "Nothing criminal crossed my desk, and I had enough on my desk without asking for more."

"Did you know Christopher Hall, Mr. Sanders?"

"I never heard his name until the day he was arrested," he said, "and even then I had no idea who he was. I didn't know we had a counterfeiting operation in-house until Thibodeaux retired." He tugged at his collar. "I socialized with the Thibodeauxs as little as possible, and I was only a guest here a handful of times through the years. It wasn't until they moved out and I did a walk-through that I found the equipment. Which is when I realized that not only had my father-in-law sanctioned it, he'd installed and operated it, literally under my nose." He stared at a Jesus dangling from a balcony. "It's one of several precarious predicaments he had me in that I wasn't aware of until after the fact. For what all could have happened to me since the day I met Salvatore Casimiro, I'm lucky I'm not in prison."

Well, I thought, you are stuck with Bianca.

He told us why, upon discovering the printing and coining equipment, he didn't dispose of it. It couldn't be physically removed from the residence without sounding copious alarms. Which made sense. You can't really roll a coin minting machine the size of a minibus out the front door without raising a few eyebrows. "Not only that," he said, "I'm not sure I want the equipment out of the building."

Right. Keep the secrets close. He, we, a lot of people could be indicted. The equipment down the hall could close the Bellissimo doors for good. Four thousand employees on the street. Innocent people would go to prison. Bradley and I had known about it for nine months, Mr. Sanders a little longer, and none of us had made a move. We were culpable, all three of us. We were liable and we were in a tight tough spot.

Mr. Sanders went on to tell us he'd hit the same moral, legal, and personal wall we'd hit. The sins of Casimiro's and Thibodeaux's past would jeopardize too many presents and futures to pursue it. "What am I going to do? Send my only child's grandfather, my wife's father, an old man who doesn't know what day of the week it is, to prison?"

We sat quietly, except for the gluck gluck from the kitchen.

"Bianca's father is almost ninety," Mr. Sanders said. "He has dementia. He's out of the casino business altogether. Even if I went to him and demanded an explanation or retribution, it wouldn't happen. I could ask where the missing platinum is a hundred times and never get an answer. From what I understand, Ty Thibodeaux isn't in much better shape. We're at a dead end."

When I hit a dead end, I put it in four-wheel drive and keep going.

"What about Magnolia Thibodeaux?" I asked. "Let's say you're right, Mr. Sanders, and Ty Thibodeaux had nothing to do with stealing platinum from the vault. But what about her?"

My suggestion was met with extreme skepticism.

"Have you met her, Davis?" Mr. Sanders asked. "Granted, I didn't know her that well, but I do remember she had great difficulty navigating," he fumbled for words, "simple tasks. To breach our vault would be a gargantuan undertaking that I don't believe she's capable of."

Am I the only one? Seriously?

"I'm not saying she masterminded a vault heist, Mr. Sanders. But I believe she knows about the platinum and she thinks it's here." I used both hands to present Jambalaya Junction in all its glory. "In this residence."

"What makes you think that, Davis?"

"Because she won't stay out of here. She keeps breaking in. She either doesn't know where it is and she's looking for it, or she knows where it is and she's hauling it out a little at a time."

And with that, I lost them. I couldn't get anyone on my Magnolia bandwagon—some say witch hunt—and when this is said and done, when I've nailed her, I'll remind these men of this moment when they looked at me as if I'd lost my very last marble.

Richard Sanders shook his head at our grave marker coffee table.

"Magnolia could not have known about a counterfeiting operation that even I didn't know about."

"She had to have known Christopher Hall was running in and out of her home. How could she not?"

Mr. Sanders shook his head.

"Bianca doesn't pay a bit of attention to anything that happens in our home unless it's directly related to her."

Which needed no explanation.

"Do we know how this man got here from prison?" Mr. Sanders asked. "Or why he had a million counterfeit dollars in one of our guest rooms?"

"I have a theory," I said. "But at this point, that's it. A guess."

They were listening.

"I think the money was a payout."

"To whom?" Bradley asked.

"Someone he wanted to take down."

"What makes you think *that*?" Mr. Sanders asked.

"The money we gathered from his guest room was a trap. A deliberate trap."

"What kind of trap?" Mr. Sanders asked.

"A go-straight-to-jail trap," I said.

Gluck, gluck.

"Who would Christopher Hall want to go straight to jail?" Bradley asked.

"Magnolia." They looked at me as if they'd heard me wrong. Again. "We may have stumbled into the middle of a fight between Magnolia Thibodeaux and Christopher Hall that has nothing to do with us."

My husband and Richard Sanders weren't buying it.

"If you don't like that theory, you won't like this one either," I said. "Because if it's not them, it's Paragon."

"Absolutely not." (Mr. Sanders.)

"No." (My Husband.)

"Listen," I said. "Several months ago Paragon Protection bought property in Horn Hill, Alabama."

"Horn Hill?" Bradley tried to place it in reference to my Alabama hometown of Pine Apple.

"Horn Hill is in Covington County," I said, "a hundred and fifty miles northeast of Mobile, on the other side of the Conecuh National Forest. Six people live there, and there's nothing there in Horn Hill but a long-gone sock factory, dilapidated warehouses, and one gas station."

Bradley and Mr. Sanders waited patiently.

"Holder Darby is from Horn Hill."

Bradley broke the long stretch of stunned silence when he asked, "When did you learn this?"

"An hour ago."

Mr. Sanders asked, "Is it possible *all* these people are involved in a sting revolving around this convention?"

"Who would be the ringleader?" Bradley asked. "It couldn't possibly be Conner Hughes. He doesn't have a semblance of a life beyond Paragon Protection."

"And it's not Magnolia Thibodeaux," Mr. Sanders said, "she simply isn't capable."

I was shaping the right words to tell them I'd find who was behind it, but in the meantime, we'd better get our guard up for what was getting ready to go down, when from the foyer we heard a decidedly atrocious noise. It was a ticking retching rhythm that grew louder until it crescendoed into a choking gag, and for once, it wasn't the refrigerator. Someone or something was being strangled near the front door. Someone was *dying* in the foyer.

I was the only one with a gun. I clicked the safety off my Glock, the homicidal noise growing louder as I made my way toward it, clearing the King Cake room, finger on the trigger, Bradley and Mr. Sanders on my heels.

It was coming from the fake magnolia tree.

"What the hell?" (Mr. Sanders.)

"Furball." (Bradley.)

ELEVEN

Dark and early Tuesday morning I woke to see my husband standing ten feet from me, backlit by the closet, buttoning his sleeve cuffs. I'm married to this man. A shock and a thrill every morning of my life.

He whipped his tie around and, before I could yawn, had it in a Windsor knot. He adjusted his collar around the tie. His shirts are so starched they can stand up by themselves, and the collars are pressed to a razor sharp edge.

"Isn't that uncomfortable?" I asked once.

"No, Davis, I'm used to it." He tugged a lock of my hair. "Are bras? Your shoes?"

"Yes, hell yes, and I'm not used to it."

He caught me watching him and sat beside me. "Good morning."

I rolled his way.

The cat followed him out of the closet and landed between us.

"Jeremy's already looking for you this morning, Davis." I pulled a pillow over my head. Bradley lifted it. "Anything you want to talk about?"

"No." I smiled. "I'll call him."

I'd been avoiding No Hair's calls for days. Not that I didn't miss him. I just didn't want to talk to him. But I'd have to suck it up and do just that, because right after I woke up and remembered I was married to Bradley, I also woke up and realized everything else wasn't a midsummer night's dream. Missing people. Counterfeit money. No refrigerator. Fake platinum. A cat.

We went over Bradley's schedule, which took all of two minutes. He'd be the captain of this industry for the next twelve to fourteen hours. "And," he gave me a game-show host smile, "you'll like this, I'm going to drop in on the convention."

Now I'm up. "Can I go?"

"No. You'll shoot someone."

"Surely you don't mean that." I never shoot people who don't need to be shot.

I twisted my hair into a knot, a morning motion I perfected when I was seven years old, and Bradley, in a morning motion he perfected when he was thirty-five, passed me a pen from his shirt pocket. I put it where it belonged, in the middle of my knot of hair, and ta-dah, no more bedhead. I stood. He stood. The cat stood.

"If you make any headway today," he said, "platinum or otherwise, let me know. And call Jeremy."

"You need a gun with you today." I fixed his jacket, where it always caught his shirt collar. "I'll send Baylor when he gets in."

"I'll be fine. I'll have Bellissimo guards with me everywhere I go. Keep Baylor."

"You need your own gun every minute you're with Paragon Protection until we get to the bottom of this. If you don't want Baylor, then I'll go with you."

"Nice try." He kissed the top of my head. "I don't need a babysitter."

I followed him. The cat followed me. "I'm talking about a babysitter with an assault rifle, Bradley."

"Which is even worse."

"Seriously, Bradley, it's not a good idea for you to go into the vault alone with anyone from Paragon Protection until we get to the bottom of this." Whatever this might be. "If you have to, please let one of us go with you."

"Davis," he stood in the open door. "The vault is empty."

Right.

The cat cried when he left.

* * *

Showered and dressed before I left the bedroom, I called Fantasy on my way to the coffee pot, cat on my heels. The coffee was ready, my favorite cup waiting.

"Hey," she said. "What?"

"Are you up?"

"No. Why?"

"We're going to the conference. Meet me at the office in an hour."

"Got it."

Then I called Baylor.

"Oh, my God, Davis, no. The sun isn't even up."

"Get in here, Baylor. I need a favor. And bring breakfast."

* * *

My ex-ex husband Eddie Crawford is a pig, the rottenest human in the state of Mississippi, a raging idiot, and he's on the weed whacker crew at Jolie.

Yes. I married him twice. I get really tired of explaining it.

I also divorced him (several times), left Pine Apple, got a job, fell in love, and I'm happily married. Which is to say I moved on. Eddie Crawford, on the other hand, had only done one of those things. He left Pine Apple. And there wasn't a doubt in my mind that situation would be corrected quickly. Bad Penny Eddie. He currently *had* a job, but he didn't *get* a job.

He was handed one on a silver platter by Richard Sanders, and this to reward him for being in the exact right place at the exact right time and not totally screwing up. It was, the cosmic timing of it all, a very weak moment for Mr. Sanders, and a flat-out miracle for Eddie.

In my wildest dreams, I never thought my ex-ex-husband, Eddie the Snake-in-the-Grass Crawford, would, or even could, actually work. Much less work for the same corporation as I do. And even in my wildest dreams when hell froze, pigs flew, I won the lottery, and Eddie actually *did* work, and it just so happened to be under the same corporate umbrella I stood under, I'd still have never believed *his* job, snuffing out dandelions in Tunica, Mississippi, four hundred miles away, would interfere with *my* job.

Yet, here I am.

They hid Eddie, who has an IQ of twelve, on the new Jolie golf course, Even Money, and told him to stay out of everyone's way. For months, the reports (I didn't want) were uneventful—when he did show up for work, he slept the day away in the backseat of his car, a 1962 baby-food-green Cadillac Eldorado convertible with big bull horns mounted to the front grill and a sawed-off shotgun in the passenger seat.

Have you ever?

As the story goes, he was asked to take care of a pest problem on the fourth hole. Instead of thinning the brush along the fairway, like he was told to, he built a hunting blind. For two weeks he showed up for work at four in the morning with a Hefty bag full of cheese popcorn, sprinkled it along the fairway, then shot animals large and small. Not what they meant. The golf people were scared to death of him, No Hair hadn't managed to catch him, and he'd been spotted with gopher skins duct-taped by their heads to the soft top of his convertible Cadillac. Eddie Crawford was driving around Tunica with gopher skins flapping around on top of his stupid baby-food-green car. The car with the bull horns. And the sawed-off shotgun.

No Hair wanted me to do something about it before PETA did. I'd been avoiding No Hair's calls because the last one had been so rough.

"If you'll wait it out," I advised, "he'll surely shoot himself. Problem solved." It got quiet. "No Hair?"

"Davis, listen." (He said this all the time, as if most of the time I didn't listen.) "If you'll do me a favor, I'll do you one back."

"I'm listening."

"You say Magnolia Thibodeaux is running in and out of your place."

"She is!"

"If you'll talk to Eddie, I'll talk to Magnolia."

"And say what to him, No Hair? 'Stop shooting gophers and duct-taping them to your stupid car?' He doesn't listen to me. And besides, I'd *rather* talk to Magnolia than Eddie, and that's saying something, because I think she needs to be in a straitjacket."

"Every time you call her and leave a message chewing her out, she calls me and leaves a message chewing me out. I'm willing to call her back. See what she wants. Help you get to the bottom of this. I'll scratch your back, Davis, and you scratch mine."

That was almost two weeks ago. No Hair had left me ten messages and sent countless mean texts and howler emails, and I knew there'd be hell to pay when I dialed.

"Hey, No Hair!"

"Don't you hey me, young lady."

"I'm sorry I haven't returned your calls. I've been busy."

"You most certainly have not been busy. I know you're busy now, but don't lie to me about not returning fourteen phone calls."

The cat's voice was as close to microphone feedback as it got. Just as abrasive, and just as painful.

"What the hell?"

"Oh dear Lord, No Hair, it's Holder Darby's cat. Who, as it turns out, isn't Holder Darby's cat."

"Whose cat is it?"

"I wish I knew." I swear, the cat knew when I was talking about it. It hissed at me.

"Is it a Tom cat?"

"No collar, No Hair. I don't know its name."

"Is the cat a girl or boy, Davis?"

"Honestly, No Hair, how would I know that?"

Five more minutes of cat, five minutes of Holder Darby, five minutes of Christopher Hall, two minutes of Baylor, and two minutes of Fantasy.

"Why is Fantasy in the hotel?"

"For one," I said, "everything around us has blown up. We're busy. And for two, her tires are slashed. And for three, Reggie and the boys are on their summer trip to Saints camp."

Fantasy's husband Reggie is a freelance sports writer, covers all things New Orleans Saints, and takes the Erb boys, K1, K2, and K3—I never get the right K name, so I go by size and call them K1, K2, and K3, and even at that, I still mix them up—on a two-week summer trip every year to see the Saints at training camp. These are the best two weeks of Fantasy's year. She calls it her vacation from family life.

We spent the entire two weeks last summer in a Bellissimo high-roller cabana at the high-roller pool. We stretched out on lounge chairs with built-in cool water misters (napping and drinking frozen fruity cocktails) until the sun went down watching for bad guys. For two whole weeks. (No bad guys.) (Lots of pool boys, no bad guys.)

"Who slashed her tires?" No Hair asked.

"I don't have a clue."

"Where was she parked?"

"Behind me."

"Were your tires slashed?"

"Not that I know of."

No Hair wanted to talk about focus, specifically me focusing, for the next little bit. We both felt an obligation to locate Holder Darby, agreeing her disappearance didn't bode well, and No Hair said he'd use his former MBI (Mississippi Bureau of Investigation) clout to call the warden in Pollock, Louisiana, and see how Christopher Hall's release and/or escape had gone down. He'd get back with me. We wouldn't find the platinum missing from the vault until we found Christopher Hall, who surely was behind the manufacture of the counterfeit platinum.

"And the counterfeit money, No Hair. Don't forget we found a million fake bucks in his room."

"What's your take on that?"

"I think it's a payoff to someone he doesn't think very highly of." I explained how good, and how bad, the counterfeit money was. "It's the best I've ever seen, and at the same time, it's a flaming red flag ticking time bomb."

"Do you have any idea who it was intended for?"

"My best guess this morning is Paragon Protection."

"Guess again," No Hair said.

"What?"

"First of all, Conner Hughes would spot it. You're good at it, and so is he."

"Okay, then it's Magnolia."

"Don't you start that, Davis."

I started. Somehow, someway, Magnolia Thibodeaux was in this up to her voodoo earrings. No Hair strongly disagreed. Things were heating up between us when out of nowhere the refrigerator backfired. It happens every few days. Like someone walking in the front door, sneaking up behind you, and shooting a rocket launcher. It has scared us to death in the middle of the night, interrupted very private moments, and even got us up close and personal with Ray Romano when he was staying next door at Jay Leno's place. He beat on our door wearing a red bathrobe and blue Chaco flips, thinking the building had been bombed.

Well, the cat had never heard it.

Airborne, it shot over my head, out the kitchen door, and straight through to Who Dat Hooters. The noise it made was that of a wide open bullet train trying to stop on a dime. I took tentative steps after the cat, wondering how I'd explain its sudden death to Bradley.

"My God, Davis. Are you alive?"

"Sorta," I said. "But I'm not so sure about the cat. Hold on."

Touring Who Dat Hooters, I found the petrified cat hanging from the bars of a fake balcony. Disturbed Jesuses on both sides of it were dancing. The cat had clawed its way up and was hanging on by a thread and two paws. It was panting and its tongue was hanging out the side of its mouth. This cat could get itself in more predicaments. I stood under it doing the "here, kitty kitty" until it was obvious the cat didn't intend to drop that far. I dragged a lime green crushed velvet Queen Anne chair under the balcony, climbed onto it, and held up my arms until the cat loosened its grip on the bars and fell screaming onto my head, used it as a launch pad, then shot off like a missile.

"You're welcome." I rubbed my head.

"Are you there?" I picked up my cell phone, conversation, and coffee cup.

"Davis, you need to move."

"Boy, don't I know it. But before I move, I need to sneak into the conference."

"Why?"

"To nose around."

"You can get to the meeting rooms from the service hall behind the main kitchen," he said, "but bring a pillow."

"Why?"

"You'll fall asleep. Conferences are boring, Davis."

"I want to see their slot machines. I need in the exhibit hall."

"There's only one door in and out of the exhibit hall. No sneaking in. You know that. And why do you want to see their slot machines?" he asked. "There are thousands of slot machines in the casino. Go look at them and stay away from the bankers' game. Don't you have enough to take care of? It sounds to me like you have a full-time job taking care of your cat."

"Not my cat, No Hair, and stop changing the subject. Did you know the bankers have a cash game?"

"That's what I hear," No Hair said.

"What if Paragon Protection teamed up with Christopher Hall, and the slot machines are full of counterfeit cash?"

"No. In a million years, no. And you need to make up your mind, Davis. Which is it? Who are you after? Magnolia or Paragon?"

"Both."

"Neither," he said. "Find Holder Darby. Find Christopher Hall.

Find the platinum. Leave the conference alone, including the game, leave Paragon alone, and leave Magnolia alone."

"It's all connected, No Hair."

"None of it's connected, Davis."

"I'm going to see that game."

"You'll never get in the room. Your best bet is to watch live feed of the surveillance video. Wait a minute," he said. "It's an exhibit hall on the conference floor. You'd better check. There might not be enough surveillance in there to do you any good."

He was right. Not a high-risk area, the conference facilities. I'd already scanned surveillance video trying to catch a glimpse of the techs who'd set the game up yesterday and came up empty. There might be twenty cameras total in the entire conference area, unlike a blackjack table, with three dedicated camera for every five feet of game. (Don't ever scratch anything when you're playing blackjack.) "I'll check, No Hair. If there's not enough surveillance to do me any good, I'll get in."

"You're not getting in, Davis. You don't have a badge. You can't just show up."

"I'm going."

"How?" No Hair asked.

"I'll come up with something."

"You could have come up with something a week ago. If you try to pull a fast one right now and show up on the conference doorstep, you'll do nothing but cause trouble. Your goal should be to stay out of trouble."

(Pfffffft.)

"Now, Davis. About Eddie."

Bang, bang, bang, my head against the wall.

"I'm happy to take care of it for you," No Hair said, "but I'm just giving you a heads up. If I handle it, word will get to Richard. And Brad. Where one little phone call from you might do the trick without either of them the wiser."

In response, I asked, "Do you think it's okay for Bradley to go into the vault with the Paragon people?"

"Yes. The vault was emptied yesterday, Davis. He'll be fine. And stay away from the conference."

I called Calinda.

"Mr. Cole's office."

"Hey, Calinda, it's me."

"Good morning, Davis."

"Good morning. Calinda, do you know when Bradley will be at the bankers conference?"

"Let's see," she said. "Two o'clock."

"Thanks."

Don't want to get caught.

* * *

Somehow I made it downstairs to 3B before Baylor, who lives two minutes away and can be ready to go anywhere in five, and Fantasy, who was taking a vacation from her family in a guest room upstairs. I flipped on lights and computers, then checked on my missing people. First, I listened in on Holder Darby's sister's phone, which I'd bugged. Lady Man took a fourteen-minute call last night from a burner phone. Bingo.

"Miss Baldwin? This is Animal Control. I'm calling about your sister's cat."

"That cat is not my sister's, lady. Someone dumped that cat on her and she doesn't want it. It has anger issues. Put it up for adoption."

Gotcha, Holder. You're on the run. And you might be right about the cat.

Holder Darby might be in danger, or some kind of trouble, but she'd contacted her sister, so she wasn't dead and stuffed in a dumpster and probably wasn't being held at gunpoint. Terrorists don't let you make fourteen-minute phone calls about cats.

Five minutes later, I was two for two pinging my missing people, because Christopher Hall may have run out of his guest room leaving (millions in funny money) his wallet, but someone used his credit card, the one issued by a Baltimore bank. The same credit card Bill Dollar had used to check into the Bellissimo. The credit card had been swiped last night at Langolis on Pauger Street in New Orleans. Dinner. A big dinner. More than five hundred dollars of dinner. So I had loose evidence of Holder Darby's and Christopher Hall's mutual safety and welfare. Granted, they weren't exact locations or explanations, but they were steps in the right direction. And the best news of all? Who lives in New Orleans? That's right. Magnolia Thibodeaux.

(I knew it.)

Baylor dragged in with a gallon of Mountain Dew and breakfast burritos from Taco Bell. Before he could offer me an enchilada pancake, I said, "Get that out of here, Baylor. It smells like the cat's food."

He brushed by Fantasy on her way in the door. She clapped a hand over her nose and mouth. "Baylor! How do you *swallow* that stuff?"

"You two are so damn picky." He went into the hall with his Taco Bell.

I gave Fantasy a look.

"How was your spa day?"

"Davis, it's my vacation." That was quickly followed by, "Are we working all day?"

"Why?" I asked. "Is today your pool day?"

"Maybe."

"Have you seen your car?"

Her brows drew together. "No. Why?"

"You need two new tires."

"I'm not going anywhere anytime soon." She smiled.

"You're going to a bankers conference."

From the hallway, mouth full of nacho waffles, "Cool."

"Not you, Baylor. You're going to Tunica."

TWELVE

The Bellissimo banquet uniform was ugly and uncomfortable, cut straight from cardboard. We were in our dressing room. Dressing.

"We need cash," I said. "How much do you have on you?"

"Not much. Ten bucks, maybe." Fantasy adjusted the knot of her banquet tie. "We'll stop by the casino for a minute and you can get all you want."

"That's not true." But it was a good idea.

"You know it's true." Fantasy tied her black apron. "You're lucky. You have the gift that keeps on giving." There was no denying I had a special knack for the slot machines. "I don't care what you're playing, you win."

I found a twenty in my purse; I stuffed it in my apron pocket. On our way to the main kitchen behind the Plenty Buffet, we made a casino detour and stopped at the first slot machine we came to, Pink Diamonds. On my third spin, I lined up three blue diamonds and won $200. Fantasy threw her hands in the air. We zipped to a cashout machine, traded the payout ticket for two crisp hundreds, then hightailed it to the main kitchen, because employees aren't allowed to gamble at the Bellissimo in the first place, especially in uniform.

"There they are." I spotted the crew preparing the bank lunch. I passed Fantasy one of the hundreds. "Find one who looks hungover."

"They all look hungover."

"And they all look stupid in these hats."

"No," Fantasy said, "that's just you."

My red hair, all of my red hair, was stuffed in the black banquet beret, so it looked like I had a squirrel nesting in mine. Everyone else's sat flat on their heads. I tried to smash it down.

We found two waitresses filling tea glasses and offered them cash for their lunch shifts. They took the money and ran.

Ten minutes later, Fantasy and I were in a kitchen service elevator on our way to the convention dining room one floor up, a cart with four metal shelves of lunch, Savings Ratio Salmon Caesar Salads, wrapped in cellophane between us. We looked at each other across the Savings salmon.

"Tell me what we're doing," she said.

"We're going to see the conference slot machines."

"Why?"

I studied a salad. "I don't know yet."

"Funny feeling?" she asked.

I nodded.

"Me too." The service doors opened and we wrestled the food cart through the doors. Fantasy said, "But my funny feeling might be these salads. They smell nasty."

✳   ✳   ✳

We claimed the two tables closest to an emergency exit at the back of the banquet hall, slung Savings salads at bankers, sloshed water in their glasses, and Fantasy told her table we were out of pepper, all of the Bellissimo and not a flake of black pepper in it.

"How are we going to get away from these people?" Fantasy asked. "I've got one lady who's lost three napkins. How hard is it to keep up with a napkin?"

We waited until no one was looking, then slipped out. By slipped out, I mean we left our lunch tables to fend for themselves, tiptoed out of the dining room back to the food cart, rolled it to a mop room, climbed on top of it, popped an air vent, hoisted up, then crawled down an air duct to the events hall.

(Four miles. Four feet wide, two feet tall, and freezing.)

"This is filthy," Fantasy said. "Why doesn't anyone clean these things?"

Creeping along on elbows and knees is slow travel, but we finally reached Event Hall B. We peeked through a vent to see a twenty foot drop. We kept creeping along until we got to the game.

"Holy moly," Fantasy said. "Can we get one of these in my car?"

"We can't even get ourselves in the room, Fantasy. How are we going to get one of these in your car? And news flash, it might not be real money."

"It sure looks real."

Yes, it did. One look at Mint Condition, the conference tournament slot machine, and it was easy to see why they didn't want anyone in the room.

Seating areas were stretched along both walls, and the long room held three full bars, plus the slot machines through the middle. There were five circles of machines, ten to a circle, so fifty in all, and from above they looked like arcade games slash slot machines. They had properties of both. There were armed Paragon Protection security guards in the four corners of the room and two at the entry doors.

Fantasy sneezed twice, and we froze in place.

"Security guards are worthless," she whispered.

"Would you feel better if they heard you sneeze and shot us?"

"Probably not." Sneeze. "Why is there so much damn dust up here?"

We crawled to an air vent almost directly above a gaming kiosk to get a better look.

Mint Condition had a bonus round, my favorite kind of slot machine. On a standard slot machine, the player knows they've lost before the last reel stops spinning, but with a bonus round, the last reel can land on the bonus symbol and they're right back in the game. The play screen of Mint Condition was your basic three-reel slot, but the third reel had a surprise. It looked like a gold combination lock, like a vault lock. If it landed on the payline, the bonus round ensued. The bonus round was played above the machine—think big wheel on Wheel of Fortune slots. Instead of a wheel, Mint Condition had a clear cabinet full of money. Row after row of money.

The player used a joystick to guide a metal grabber to stacks of cash, and by cash, I mean moola, green stuff, major bucks. Line up the metal claw just right and close it just so, then pull away a stack of money. That dropped. Right into the player's lap.

I've never seen a cash game. Ever.

"That is a lot of money," said Fantasy.

"That is a fantastic game," said me.

We bumped elbows for better views.

"The bottom row looks like one-dollar bills," I whispered.

"Yeah, but it's an inch thick," Fantasy said. "It's probably a hundred dollars, and that's not a bad bonus."

There was a time element. I knew this because of the digital countdown clock beside the joystick. The goal was obviously to win enough time to maneuver the money grabber to the second row and grab a stack of five-dollar bills before the joystick timed out. Or the third row, with a fat stack of ten-dollar bills. The fourth row, guess what, twenty-dollar bills.

Above the rows of money, and obviously the grand prize, was a big fat stack of hundred-dollar bills, and perched on top of the inch of cash was a round Lucite roll. Full of something.

Coins. Big coins. Coins the size of silver dollars. But they weren't silver dollars.

"What in the world?" Fantasy whispered.

"It's platinum. Platinum coins."

"No!"

Yes.

"The hundred-dollar bills add up to ten thousand. Easy," Fantasy said. "And no telling what those coins are worth. What do you think?"

"I don't know," I whispered, "another ten thousand? Fifteen?"

"So, make it to the top and a twenty-five thousand dollar payday drops in your lap? I want to be a banker."

We'd come full circle. Platinum coins missing from our vault; platinum coins in the conference slot machines. I didn't know if the coins in the game were fake or real. I hadn't gotten that far yet. I had, however, gotten this far: It couldn't possibly be a coincidence that the very thing we were missing was the grand prize of this game. I asked the burning question: "How in the hell does Magnolia Thibodeaux even *know* about this conference?"

Fantasy's head dropped. She let it hang there for a dramatic moment, then she cut her eyes at me. "What? Davis! Have you lost your mind? Magnolia doesn't have a *thing* to do with this conference! There's no way we're going to find the platinum, Holder Darby, or the money guy, if you don't stop blaming *everything* on that old woman, who has nothing to do with anything."

"Whose side are you on, Fantasy?"

It's hard to make good points when you're whispering in an air duct dangling above slot machines. She geared up to sneeze again, a big one this time, and I think I broke her nose a little, slapping my hand over it. Then there was some poking, a few loud-whisper threats, and some rude name calling. The security guards didn't move a muscle, and the aftermath of her sneeze was totally averted when we heard a scuttle. Just a little scratch. Somewhere near our legs. Our wide eyes met, and we proceeded to get the hell out of the air ducts. Fantasy wasted no time backing up, but I grabbed for her, getting a handful of hair. "Wait a second."

"Owww, dammit!"

I turned my phone upside down and eased it between two slats in the vent to snap a picture of the machines, specifically the platinum coins in the machines, while she grumbled her way back to me. She got there just in time for us to watch the doors to Event Hall B open—and my husband walk through.

We froze.

"I thought you said we had until two."

"I thought we did. Be quiet."

I barely had a grip on my slick phone with my thumb and index finger. Most of it was dangling below the vent. Fantasy held her breath and I did my best to hold my phone as Bradley and a man in a suit walked to the middle of the room.

"Who is that?"

"It's Bradley!" I can scream and whisper at the same time.

"The other man, Davis. Who is the other man?"

"He must be the Paragon Protection man, Conner Hughes, and I'm going to drop this phone."

"Do not drop that phone."

"Help me catch it. It's slipping."

"I can't help you catch the phone, you goof. You're taking up all the arm space. Do not drop your phone."

I pinched harder, which did nothing but propel it out of my fingers. It dropped straight down and landed on the carpet with a muffled thud, ten feet from my husband and five feet from Conner Hughes. Fantasy and I stopped breathing.

"What was that?"

Conner Hughes's head snapped and he turned in the direction of the noise. A few of the security guards woke up. Hughes spotted my phone on the floor, then looked up. At us. Frozen in place. He marched directly under the vent we were above.

My heart was beating out of my chest already, when Conner Hughes bent down and picked up *my phone*.

"Where could this have come from?" He stood, turned my phone over a few times, then tilted his head back and looked hard. For us.

"Let me see."

Bradley took it from him—he knew exactly where it came from. How many people have phone cases with *I* (Heart) *Pine Apple*? He dropped it in his pocket, steered Conner Hughes the other way, then swung his head back and gave us a hellacious dirty look. I hadn't taken a breath yet and I hadn't moved a muscle.

Conner Hughes turned back too, craning and straining to see

in the vent, while Bradley did everything he could to direct his attention elsewhere.

It's not like we could get out of there. Or even blink.

"Has anyone been in this room, Brad? Your people? Gamblers from the casino?"

"No, Conner." I could hear Fantasy's heart beating and I'm sure she could hear mine. "Absolutely not."

Bradley led Conner Hughes in the direction of the door, but not before he threw one parting nasty look at us. I don't know how long we stayed that way before Fantasy began crawling backwards again. "Let's get the hell out of here."

"Not me," I whispered. "I'm staying here for the rest of my life."

"No, you're not. Come on, Davis."

It was a good decision to stay, paralyzed with fear of divorce and pending unemployment, because three men dressed in solid black picked that moment to file into Event Hall B. I reached for Fantasy, got another handful from the top of her head, and it became clear to me that Bradley might not be able to kill me for crawling through the air ducts and spying on the bankers, because Fantasy was going to beat him to it if I didn't stop yanking her hair.

"What. The. Hell?"

"Hush."

They looked like Navy Seals. All three wore black cargo pants, long-sleeve black t-shirts, and black ball caps, and all three were all the way around big, burly, and mean. One spoke up. "We got this, boys. Take a break."

The Paragon security guards left their posts and filed out the door.

The man who dismissed the guards toured the floor in a loopy figure eight, weaving in and out and bending to look in the general vicinity of the play area on every Mint Condition machines. He stopped in front of one. "This one." He bounced a fist off the top of the game cabinet. He took four more steps. "This one." He did it again. "This one."

"What the hell are they doing?" Fantasy asked.

"I don't know."

The men in black stood at the three chosen machines, opened the cabinets, sat in the chairs, and went to work. From our vantage point, we couldn't see exactly what they were doing, but I had a good idea.

"What is going on?"

"They're switching out the data chips in three of the Mint Condition slot machines."

"Why?"

"They're rigging the game. Give me your phone."

"So you can throw it at them?"

* * *

With no room to turn around, we crawled backwards the whole way to the mop room, at least five miles, where we dropped onto the food cart and, in the process, knocked it over, which sounded like the building imploding. We scrambled up, knocked as much of the dirt off each other as we could, then stepped into the service hall as if all was well, if all was well means filthy, breathless, and in big trouble with our boss. Double trouble for me, because I'm married to the man. A waiter carrying a tray of waxy cheesecake spotted us and was so busy staring, he almost ran into a wall.

"Is there another way out of here?"

Fantasy's head darted around. The three doors in front of us led to the dining room, where the bankers were having dessert and someone at a microphone was keynote addressing them. To our right was the main kitchen, but it was the long way. On our left was nothing but solid wall.

"Doesn't look like it," I said. "We'll have to go through the dining room."

We slipped in quietly, hugging the back wall, until I spotted a very familiar face. One I'd grown up with. Cooter Platt. I stopped cold to make sure it was him, and Fantasy ran into me. What in the world was Cooter Platt doing here? A man seated at one of the banquet tables asked Fantasy if he could have more coffee.

"No," she said. "You've had enough."

Clearing the dining room, we made our getaway. We ran past Megan with the braces, down the wide conference corridor, thump thump, bounced down the moving escalator skipping steps until we reached the casino, sprinted through it, then took the lobby staircase two steps at a time to the mezzanine level, where we dashed around Scoops, the ice cream shop, scanned ourselves into the Super Spy elevator, raced down the dark hall, and only after we'd coded ourselves into our 3B offices did we stop for air.

My phone was on the table in front of us, the screen busted into an intricate spider web—thank you, rotten Apple—and under it, a note: *Dammit, Davis.*

I passed the note to Fantasy. She read it and said, "Ouch," then she sent her banquet beret sailing across the room. After ten minutes of total silence, we dragged our sorry feet into Control Central, where I reached in a bottom file drawer and got a new phone from the stash.

I bit the cellophane off the box, then hacked Verizon—if they ever track me down, I'm dead meat, because I hack them all the time—deactivated the busted one, and activated the new one, saving myself an afternoon at the phone store.

"Let me see your phone, Fantasy."

"Why?"

She had a brand new phone, and not because she destroyed them on a regular basis like me. Her phone was the size of an unabridged dictionary, did everything but sweep the porch, and she was protective of it. With me anyway. Understandable, given my phone history.

"I want to see the pictures of the men in black."

"I'll send them to you."

Rolling my chair to a computer with the energy of a flea, a flea who had the flu, a flea who had the flu and her flea husband was fed up with her, I logged in to see emails flying in.

"How many pictures did you take?"

She looked up from her phone. "I didn't. I shot video." She shook her phone. "Sixty frames a second," she said, "so I think I'm sending about five thousand pictures."

"Well, stop." The emails fell all over each other as my inbox tried to keep up. "Click through there and find the best shots you can of the three men and send those."

She used her thumb and forefinger to push and pull the screen, poking this, prodding that, then sent three high resolution photographs straight to the printer. I rolled back and caught them.

"How'd you get such good pictures?"

She shook her dictionary phone and smiled.

"How'd you get the air vent lines out?"

"Picasa," she said. "Editing software."

I scanned them into the Bellissimo system to see who these guys were. Not surprisingly, they were Paragon Protection's tech crew. Our surveillance caught them riding the escalator to the conference level several times Sunday, the day they checked in, then again on Monday morning, loitering around the conference reception area.

"They're the ones who were waiting on Christopher Hall," I said.

"They started all of this," she said.

"Magnolia Thibodeaux started all of this."

"Pitiful," Fantasy said. "You're pitiful."

We were up to Monday afternoon when surveillance caught them in the casino, but not together. They were scattered along the main aisle. Watching the contents of the Bellissimo vault being rolled through by waiters. More shots of them, later Monday afternoon, with a very familiar face. My husband's. As he accompanied them into the cash room.

The three-man Paragon tech crew who installed and rigged the Mint Condition machines was the same three-man Paragon tech crew who inspected the Bellissimo vault.

"Keep watching, Fantasy." I logged onto another computer. "If you see them interacting with anyone, freeze the shot. Tell me what they ate for breakfast and follow them to the men's room. We need to know every step they've taken since they walked in the door."

I didn't have names or fingerprints. Just photos. Scanning them into any national database with nothing but their square jaws, wide foreheads, and crooked noses would take forever and a day.

"What else can your Picaso do, Fantasy?"

"Picasa," she didn't look up from the monitor. "These men spend more than half their time with Conner Hughes, the Paragon Protection man, and Picasa can do anything."

"Go back to your phone," I said.

"And what?"

"Something, anything. Find me one of these guys with a distinguishing characteristic, some kind of identifying marker. I need a scar, a missing tooth, a third eyeball."

She pulled her phone to her nose and began poking. "Uh-oh." She flipped her phone around. "I got tats."

"Yeah?"

"Prison tats."

I rolled my chair closer to her. "How'd you do that?"

"X-ray."

"You can see through their clothes?"

"Not straight through, but enough." She tilted her phone. "See the tattoos on this guy's hands and neck? They're covered with something, makeup. Picasa can filter out makeup."

That's terrifying.

Where was I?

Prison tats.

I scanned their tattooed mugs into the National Criminal Database. Ten minutes later, I got a hit on one. I asked for his known associates and found the other two. All convicted criminals. Between the three men, they had eight convictions. All burglary or burglary related. All banks. The longest stretch had been a nickel, the other two had done three years each. Model prisoners, all three.

"Damn." Fantasy read over my shoulder as I scrolled through

the three men's records. "No robbery. Just burglary. What's up with that?"

I tore my eyes from the monitor. "They didn't go in when the banks were open, Fantasy. They broke in when the banks were closed. It's burglary because their crimes didn't involve victims." When a bank is robbed, masked gunmen endanger others by blasting in with Uzis at high noon on payday, and everyone has to hit the floor. When a bank is burglarized, it's the dead of night, or Sunday morning, and the perpetrators aren't charged with endangering human lives. Just burglary.

"We need to find them on the property," I said. "I'll check surveillance in the hotel. You check the casino."

Two sets of hands clicked across keyboards.

"Found them." Fantasy won.

I rolled my chair to her screen and watched as the three convicted vault thieves entered the count room on their way to the Bellissimo vault. With my husband.

THIRTEEN

Contrary to all *Ocean* movies and general public perception, casinos keep the money in the bank like everyone else. Most casinos gather it and pass it off to armored trucks at odd and varying hours, then the trucks take it to the bank where it's deposited. This isn't exactly how we do it, but in general, that's how it's done. Which is not to say casinos don't have vaults. We all do. But there isn't anywhere near as much currency in a casino vault as people imagine. It's also a myth that casinos keep enough money on hand to cover every bet on the floor. That would be tens of millions of dollars, if you factor in the possibility of thousands of slot machines hitting synchronized jackpots (never gonna happen) (although it would be fun) (for the players) (not so fun for the casino), so no. It's not true.

One closely held secret is where casino vaults are located. I'll tell you where ours is, but don't get any bright ideas. And if you do, bring your scuba gear, because the only way to get to it is by water. The vault is under the casino, which means it's submerged, because the Bellissimo casino is built on barges. Our casino is built on three huge semi-submersible barges. They're two hundred feet wide and two hundred feet long, ten feet deep, and they're anchored by steel pipe piles that run one hundred and twenty feet into the Mississippi Sound. (A Mississippi law, amended after Hurricane Katrina, but alive and well when the Bellissimo was built—Mississippi casinos had to be on water.) (Dockside gambling.)

The only operating vault at the Bellissimo today came with one of the barges. It's a concrete cavity built by Paragon Protection and dropped below the floor into one of the barges. So to get to it, you'll have to swim. Then get through the perimeter cage (think shark tank), at which point you'll be electrocuted, along with all marine life in the Gulf, and even then, you're not in the vault. You still have to penetrate twenty-four-inch thick precast concrete walls all the way around, with sensors that alert half of Mississippi if a tadpole gets too close.

A better bet for today's burglar would be the count room. Behind the main cage in the casino is a room where cash is constantly on the move, being counted, banded, then sent out the front door to the main cage or downstairs to the vault. Money goes to the main cage in bags or in a till; it goes to the vault in a box built to withstand an atomic blast. After the box is (full) sealed, it takes a heavily documented and witnessed ride to the vault, directly below the count room, and stays there all of three minutes before it tunnels through a below-ground conduit system built by Paragon Protection directly to the bank. If you think you can catch the money on the way to the bank, think again, because you can't dig ten feet under city streets without (hitting a gas line) someone noticing.

Attention all thieves: It would be easier to break into the Antwerp Diamond Center (Gem District, Antwerp, Belgium) than the Bellissimo vault, and chances are you'll only be arrested and convicted if you go for the diamonds. Set your sights on the Bellissimo vault and you won't get off so easily. You'll be pushing up daisies.

There's another way, the land way, and humans can get to the vault that way, certainly, but only after going through the count room. The two doors into the count room are trapdoors and the system is called mantrap. (Which I think is sexist.) When you enter the first door, you're alone inside four steel walls and the door in front of you, which gets you into the count room, won't unlock until the door behind you is locked. If you get that far (which you won't) and are deemed unauthorized, you won't get any farther, because you'll be mantrapped. If you attempt count room entry and you aren't authorized, you sit there, mantrapped, until half of the badges in Mississippi are in place and ready to untrap you, at which point you get cuffed and hauled off. Mississippi has a zero tolerance policy for casino thieves.

Access is granted to the count room for Mr. Sanders and Bradley, a very few department heads, and the dedicated security detail. The count and vault clerks, who are the worker bees, the middle men, the money shufflers, are also granted entry, and they all go through screening to get in and out like they work at the White House. Shoes, keys, and jewelry in a bucket. No personal items, including cell phones, in or out. Then the employees are x-rayed, weighed, and wanded all over. This happens every time they clock in and every time they clock out.

Once cleared for entry, the count and vault clerks pull up currency and tokens from the vault at the beginning of their shifts, verify its accuracy, then distribute it to cash clerks, who pass it out to the cashiers, who allocate it out in the casino. During their work day, the count clerks accept deposits from the same cashiers, who've received it from the casino floor, then pass it to the vault clerks, who send it to the vault. Back and forth, the same money, with the excess, of which there is a ton, shooting through concrete tubes to the bank.

At the end of a count and vault clerk shift, they're required to reconcile all these transactions. They get to go home when everything balances to the penny, and for all this effort, working in a box with two-way mirrors, cameras, and guns trained on them, they make just above minimum wage. One of the lowest paid jobs in the casino. Go figure.

Two interesting things. The best count room heist ever was when a minimum wage vault clerk dropped sealed vault bags stuffed with cash in the garbage can under her desk all day, threw up in it, then happily carried out her own trash and they never saw her again. (Not here. It happened in Atlantic City.) (Disgusting.)

Second interesting thing? The count room is where we found Baylor two years ago. We needed an additional warm body in a hurry and to save the time of vetting someone, No Hair nabbed Baylor from security detail in the count room, where he guarded the vault entrance.

So on this day, the last Tuesday in July, a day I believed my husband to be in mortal danger, I called Baylor.

"I need in the vault."

"What?"

"Baylor. Listen up. I need to get into the vault. Tell me how to get into the vault."

"You can't," he said. "No one can get into the vault."

"Bradley's in the vault, Baylor, with criminals."

"What?"

"How can I get to him?" I was hot and I was cold. I couldn't blink. I tried to, I couldn't.

"Call the count room and they'll get him for you."

Fantasy grabbed the phone from me. "She tried that, Baylor. The count room won't put her through. Please tell her there's no way to get in the vault." She listened, batting me off, then said, "We'll see you when you get back."

"Fantasy! *What?*"

"Davis, calm down and sit down." She demonstrated. She sat down, crossed her legs, gently placed my new phone beside her on the sofa and said, "I'll talk to you when you settle down."

I was at her mercy for the information Baylor had given her, so I sat down across from her, my heart in my throat, and started counting. Ten, nine, eight—if I got to one, I'd shoot her.

"You need to get a grip." This is how she talks to her sons. "First of all, the vault is empty. There's nothing to steal. Second, there are armed guards carrying Ruger assault rifles with him, Davis, and Bradley is safe."

She rose, crossed to the refrigerator, reached in, and pulled out two bottles of water. She opened hers and poured it down her throat. I moved mine around on my face.

"I trust you, Davis." She screwed the lid on the empty bottle. "You know I do. But you need to settle down. Yes, there's something going on. Yes, we need to figure out what it is. And we will. But right now, you're crossing the line between business and personal. You need to get your head on straight."

"You're right. I've crossed the line. It's very personal. It's my husband. I'm going, Fantasy. Right now. Are you in or out?"

Conflict worked its way across her face. "When this is done, Davis, don't say I didn't warn you."

"What did Baylor say?"

"He said you could get in the count room if they think you're Bianca."

* * *

I sprayed myself Honey Kiss Bianca Blonde and dressed (Helmut Lang—cropped black sleeveless turtleneck over skinny black mini mini skirt, bare legs, and Zenith back-zip leather six-inch sandals), in record time. Then I beat on the door of the count room, demanding to see my diamonds.

A count clerk looked through the security window. "Mrs. Sanders?"

Two minutes later, I was mantrapped. I can get away with looking like Bianca Sanders seven days a week, but I didn't win rounds two or three, retina scans and fingerprint matches. The minute I was mantrapped, the vault automatically locked down. With Bradley, Conner Hughes, and the three men in black in it. As I would learn later, the gorillas with assault rifles did their jobs and held the five men, including my husband, at gunpoint until the all's clear signal came from above.

Bradley was told that a woman trying to pass herself off as Bianca Sanders had tried to breach the count room. They didn't take the gun off my husband until I was safely tucked in the back of a squad car and all said and done, cash room security is impressive.

Fantasy, dressed like a high roller in a Jean Paul Gaultier strapless gypsy dress, waited for me just outside the count room door in VIP Player Services, where if she angled just right, she had a sliver of a view of the cash room door. She dragged out an application for an outrageously large casino marker for twenty minutes and when she couldn't stretch it out one more minute and I still hadn't come out the door, she pinged my phone and found me on my way to the city jail on Porter Avenue. She snagged Austin Burgess, the head of the Bellissimo legal team, and together they explained the "misunderstanding" when I was midway through intake, just about to be booked.

Fantasy got nose to nose with the booking officer. "Do you really want to arrest Bianca Sanders? You better give it some thought, young man. You better think about your future."

"But they said this *wasn't* Bianca Sanders."

Fantasy spun around. "Bianca?"

I pointed a finger at the booking officer, swirled an air circle aimed at his nose, and said, "Die, police person."

They let me go.

We rode back to the Bellissimo in Austin's Buick Enclave. I sat in the back seat with his dry cleaning, two umbrellas, and a twenty-five pound bag of Old Roy dog food. He drove like my grandmother, gunning it, then backing off, gunning it, then backing off. Lurch forward, slam back.

"Sorry, Mrs. Sanders." Sweat rolled down Austin's pale face. "Ooops. My bad, Mrs. Sanders." This, when he was checking me out in the rearview mirror and veered into oncoming traffic.

Fantasy patted his arm. "Calm down, Austin. This isn't her first trip to jail."

I searched for a seatbelt under the dry cleaning. "Not a word of this to Richard, Austin." When I spoke to him directly, his foot must have slipped and he floorboarded it, almost running us under a casino-hopper mini bus.

"Really, Austin." Fantasy pushed buttons until she had the air full blast, then pointed the vents at Austin's face. "Settle down. It's her own fault she was arrested. She dresses like a prostitute."

Which gave Austin a small choking fit.

"Pull this thing over. I'm driving." She turned to the back seat.

"This is your fault, Bianca."

"This is Baylor's fault." Baylor always leaves out the details. Like retinas and fingerprints.

Back at the Bellissimo, security swarmed. Radios buzzed with the good news that the First Lady had been located. I was escorted to the Executive Offices. When I walked into the casino manager's office, his secretary gave me the uh-oh/good-luck look.

"Sit." The casino manager pointed.

The clock ticked for a full five minutes. This is how it feels on the chopping block, in the plane going down, at cheerleading tryouts. Then I caught him checking out my legs. I didn't consider how short this skirt was when I put it on.

The first thing I "didn't need to know," according to Bradley, was that the three convicted burglars I thought were trying to kill him in the vault were actually *on* the Paragon payroll, as contract consultants and technicians. They did their time and now they made a living showing one of the nation's largest suppliers of banking security how to render their products and services even more secure.

"Conner Hughes trusts those men, Davis. He doesn't take a single step without them."

"And you knew this?"

"I'm talking, Davis. You're listening."

Another thing I "didn't need to know" was the money inside Mint Condition was, as per the agreement Holder Darby made with the Gaming Commission on behalf of the Bellissimo and in conjunction with Paragon Protection for the Independent Bankers of Alabama Conference, genuine. Real money. Federal Reserve issue.

My actions had forced him to stop what he'd been doing, come clean with Conner Hughes about his trigger-happy in-house investigation team, and the results, he presented to me, indicated Paragon Protection was following every rule to the letter in every way, and the only problem, according to Bradley, was *me*.

"We're lucky you weren't thrown in the back of a patrol car

and hauled off to jail," he said, as mad as he's ever been at me, "and no, I won't be home tonight. I'll be at dinner with Conner Hughes cleaning up the mess you made."

Working together, after today's events, he told me, was something we'd need to have a long talk about when he got home tonight. I blinked back tears. Up to that point I sat there and took it, but with that, I got misty.

It didn't seem like a good time to tell him I actually *was* thrown in the back of a patrol car and hauled off to jail, or to tell him the bankers' game was rigged. It was clear that the only way out of this mess for me was Cooter Platt.

* * *

Cooter, tall, willowy thin, with a mop of white curls and bright black eyes, had ears that bloomed out and wrapped around like soup ladles stuck on either side of his head. If ever a case could be made for cosmetic plastic surgery, it was Cooter Platt, who needed an ear job in the worst way. With those mighty ears, though, Cooter could hear the sun come up, he could hear hair growing, he could hear ants clap and cheer when they found a picnic. For his best trick, he could hear money. If you filled your palm with coins, then dropped them on a flat surface behind his back two at a time until they were gone, Cooter could give you a total.

"That's four dollars and sixteen cents, little missy."

And every time, he was right.

We didn't have birthday clowns or giant waterslide parties when I was growing up in Pine Apple, Alabama; we had Cooter. He could turn a sheet of white paper into money, he could change a Dixie cup of red party punch into a silver dollar, he could whip his long spindly fingers around a one-dollar bill for thirty seconds, then hand you a five-dollar frog.

Cooter's grandfather established Pine Apple's one and only bank, Pine Apple Savings and Loan. Cooter had worked there since he could count and, now in his sixties, owned and managed the bank. He was attending the Alabama Independent Bankers Convention at the Bellissimo Resort and Casino. As it turns out, Cooter's real name was Henry. I'd totally missed him on the list of conference attendees. I'm one of three people from Pine Apple who doesn't have a nickname, and no one believes me. Davis is my mother's maiden name. And the name on my birth certificate. There are two cashiers at the Piggly Wiggly, Pine Apple's only grocery store. Their names are Cranberry and Trampoline. I've known them all my life. The names on their birth certificates are Cindy and Susan. Right now, I needed Henry. Known by one and all as Cooter. Call him what you will, he could get me into the conference, and once in, I could call on my special slot machine talents and win a roll of platinum coins. Because the coins were all I had left. If I couldn't catch Paragon lying about something, I was up a creek.

"We have to find Cooter and get his badge."

Fantasy and I were in 3B. She wasn't saying she told me so, but she was keeping me company while I licked my wounds. She's a good friend.

"And then what?"

"Play Mint Condition and win the platinum coins."

"Are you trying to push Bradley all the way over the edge, Davis? How much do you think that man can take? And haven't we had enough excitement for one day?"

"Bradley and Mr. Sanders may trust Paragon with their lives, but I don't trust them at all," I said. "The platinum coins in the game have to be ours." I had Holder Darby's paperwork spread out on the table. "And that's Paragon's endgame. To sneak out of here with our platinum."

She shook her head. That's all, just shook her head.

"This is my last resort, Fantasy." If Paragon didn't steal the platinum from our vault, then everyone's right and I'm as wrong as I've ever been in my life."

Of course, there's still Magnolia. I hadn't given up on her.

For now, though, I thought it best to take a different approach at nabbing Paragon, one that might not end in divorce. The Cooter Platt approach. Track down Cooter, borrow his banker badge, and get into Event Hall B while Bradley is at dinner with Conner Hughes, and get my hands on some platinum. It would be real, ours, and I'd be off the hook.

This was my only shot at redemption.

How hard could it be?

* * *

"Are you sure, Davis? Are you sure you want to do this?"

I wasn't sure of anything this week. "It can't hurt," I said. "I know Cooter. Cooter knows me. If this doesn't pan out, at least I'll know I turned over every rock."

"If this doesn't pan out, Davis, the people from Paragon are going to be throwing rocks at your head." She patted my leg. "You're sure?"

"Yes." No.

"You're making me miss my family," she said.

I washed the blonde out of my hair while Fantasy scanned Cooter's face into our facial recognition software. It took her way less time to find him entering room 1940 than it did for me to get back to red hair. I found her studying Cooter's picture.

"What is wrong with his ears? Is it a birth defect thing?"

"No, and that's so mean. He just has big ears."

"Dumbo."

"Let's go."

We rode a few elevators, because that's what we do, then knocked on the door of 1940.

"Cooter? Are you in there?"

We waited a decent amount of time (two seconds), then Fantasy jimmied us into Cooter Platt's empty ocean-view room.

"How do you do that?"

"My BP card." She flashed it, then slipped it into her back pocket.

It's her superpower.

"What's this?" Fantasy held up a mason jar full of clear liquid.

I unscrewed the lid, sniffed, then went blind for three minutes. "It's Pine Apple moonshine."

"Put the lid back on it," Fantasy said. "The fumes are making me dizzy."

I nabbed the two glasses on a tray beside an empty ice bucket. "It's good." I knew I could use a sip of something about now. I hate going to jail.

"I'm not drinking out of that glass, Davis. Those things are filthy. Don't you watch 'Dateline'?"

I held up the mason jar. "This will kill anything those glasses can throw at us."

Cooter Platt keyed himself in three hours later. Fantasy and I were passed out in his bed.

* * *

Something was going on with my foot and wouldn't stop. I slung an arm out and lobbed it across Fantasy's head. "Shtopth kicking meeth."

"Whaaaaa?" Somehow, she managed to get up on her drunk elbows. Then screamed.

"Hold on there, little lady!" (Cooter. Who had been shaking my foot.) "This is my hotel room."

I peeled one eye open, to see Fantasy lunging for Cooter, but she wound up spread eagle face down on the floor.

"Cooter?"

Cooter Platt's ears spun my way. "Davis? Davis Way?"

"Coleth."

"What?"

"Cooter." I flopped back on the bed. "I got marrieth."

"You and Eddie again?"

"Nooooooo. Hell, noooo." I pulled a pillow over my face, then slung it right off, because someone had filled it with bricks.

"You girls have been dippin' in the sauce." He held up his almost empty jar of moonshine. "Oh, boy, there's a headache comin' your way, Davis Coleth."

I tried to pronounce my married name again for him. No luck. From the floor, Fantasy said, "Oh my God shomeone hepp me up."

Cooter's room, like all the conference attendees' rooms, was a mini suite. He led us to chairs at a round dining table that seated four, closed the drapes for us, hit the mini bar up for all the bottled water it held, and got Fantasy a cold wet hand towel to drape over her face. Her whole face. She was splayed out in the chair, long legs sprawled, head tipped all the way back, wet towel across her face, ready to be waterboarded.

"What's up with that rotten moonshine, Cooter?"

"It's pure grain alcohol, Davis. You should have learned the Pine Apple Moonshine lesson in high school."

Fantasy peeled back half of her wet towel. "What the hell ish up with your ears?"

"Fantasize!" I tried to kick her. I wound up on the floor. Cooter rushed to help me, but I waved him off and crawled up on my own. "I got thish." I stopped to rest halfway to the chair. Maybe I didn't got thish.

We stayed in Cooter's room until we sobered up. For the next two hours, Fantasy and I both took cat naps mid-sentence several times, inhaled two pots of room service coffee, and shared a triple order of room service fries (to soak up the moonshine), and finally, around six o'clock, we sobered up enough to walk.

We didn't want to walk, ever again, but if someone held a gun to our heads, we could've. A few of the exchanges during those lost hours:

"Why do we do this to ourselves?"

"So your ear deal is about your grandmother marrying her first cousin? She did that? Really?"

"I can't get this licorice out of my throat."

"Your daddy knows exactly how to get in the vault. He's my backup."

"Is there a cricket in here?"

"Davis, your grandmother took Cyril somewhere and got him Botox. Now the poor old thing can't close his eyes all the way and his mouth is just plain ole crooked."

"It was a very private wedding. Just us, Mother, Daddy, Meredith, and a few others."

"I might be hallucinating."

"My legs hurt so bad, I can't see ever shaving them again. Ever." (Cooter.) (Kidding.)

"This is one beautiful place, but I had some red chicken on a salad earlier that tasted like fish."

"My husband is a black man. Black men just don't have the ear hair problems white men do."

"The vault people invited me here. Then my name got picked to play that money game. I won five hundred dollars last night."

"You're going to have to come get me, Bradley, or call me a cab. I can't drive."

"Seventeen." (Fantasy said that for no good reason whatsoever. Several times.)

"I'm not sure I'd want to put firecracker chili on top of those fries on top of that moonshine, little lady."

Never again, and I mean it this time, I will never drink again. Ever. I'm giving up everything: carbs, alcohol, gambling, Pop Tarts, Tuesdays, all forms of laundry, and Molly Ringwald movies. I saw the light and I don't ever want to see it again. I hit rock bottom and it hit me back. I was three hundred sheets to the wind.

FOURTEEN

"Davis."

I was in my own bed, post brain surgery. Or maybe I'd been shot between the eyes. I might have walked into a swinging wrecking ball. Something.

Bradley gently placed an ice cold washcloth on my forehead.

"I'm leaving for work. You'd better sleep awhile."

I peeled one eye open, saw my husband's elbow and a lion. Someone had smashed the lion's nose in. Bradley kissed the top of my head, which did two things: One, it told me he wasn't still angry with me, and two, it broke my brain. I didn't remember anything else until much later. It was daylight, and someone was biting my hair. The bedside clock said it was nine o'clock on Wednesday morning and the cat was trying to pull my hair out of my enormous head with its gigantic teeth.

After twenty minutes of an ice cold shower, I thought I might— might—live. I stumbled back to the bed, reached for the house phone, and speed-dialed housekeeping, valet, and the front desk before my finger found the room service button.

"This is Calinda Wilson, Mr. Cole's assistant. He needs four big blue Powerades and a bottle of Excedrin Super delivered to his residence on twenty-nine. And he wants the Excedrin Super without the lid. Keep the lid." I didn't have the energy to track down any painkillers and even if I did, I sure didn't have the wherewithal to line up arrows. "And bring a large bucket of ice. Leave it at the door and do not ring the doorbell."

The room service person wanted to argue with me.

"Mr. Cole, for your information, does *not* have an ice maker, and even if he had fourteen, he still wants a large bucket of ice. Okay?"

Mr. Cole—who, by the way, does have an ice maker, an ice maker that is exactly one-fourth of the big red monster refrigerator, but it doesn't work, because the ice bin, which is the size of a bathtub, is nothing but a solid slab of cloudy gray ice perfect for hosting individual women's figure skating events—left a note by the coffee pot.

What in the world did you get into last night? You fell off the bed twice (remember?) and talked in your sleep all night. On and on about crickets. Baylor called and left you this message: He's stolen Eddie's car. I suppose, Davis, when you feel up to it, you can explain why Baylor seems so pleased with himself for stealing Eddie's car. I smoothed everything over with Conner Hughes last night, so all is well and I'm not upset. Call me and let me know you're okay. I love you, even drunk you. Super drunk you. Ridiculously drunk you.

I called Baylor before I called Bradley.

"Baylor." I couldn't see out of my left eye, and I couldn't feel anything below my knees. My head weighed four hundred pounds and I could taste Windex. "Where is your truck?"

"My Ford?"

"How many trucks do you have, Baylor?"

"One?"

"That's what I thought. Where is it?"

"In the parking lot."

Like talking to a wall.

"I have a very important question for you, Baylor. Listen up."

"Okay."

"How did you get to Tunica yesterday?"

"I drove your car."

"*What?*"

"Mine didn't have any gas."

The days of banging phones against things were over, because cell phones couldn't handle the abuse. And if I tried banging my head against the wall, it would explode. So I kept going.

"I told you to hide his car, like in a cornfield. Not steal it."

"I mixed that up."

"Did it not occur to you, Baylor, that when he sees his car gone and my car there, he's going to figure out who has his car? And what am I supposed to drive?"

"Do you need to go somewhere?"

"That's not the point."

"What is the point?"

This could have been worse. I didn't know how, but things could always be worse. Just then, it popped into my brain *how* they could be worse. "Where's the counterfeit money, Baylor?"

"Oh, right."

It will be the end of the world as I know it if Eddie Crawford finds a million counterfeit dollars in my car. The very end. Curtains. It's been real. Sayonara.

"I brought it back."

And with his words, I collapsed in a hungover heap. "Where are you, Baylor?"

"In the office," he said. "I'm taking a nap till you and Fantasy get here."

"Go back to Tunica. Do it right this time. Hide Eddie's car, somewhere he can't find it, and bring my car back."

I texted my husband: *Sorry about last night. I'm good. I'll NEVER drink moonshine again.*

He texted back: *I'm covered up. We'll talk later.*

Then the phone rang. "David. Get up here right this minute."

*　*　*

I thought I might freeze to death.

For one, I'd taken an ice shower, dressed quickly, and made my way to Bianca after drying only three of the red hairs on my head. I still felt, four Super Excedrins in, moonshiney, and the noise of the hair dryer proved too much. For another, Bianca had it like a meat locker. And it wasn't just me. Her manservant of the day (she went through butlers like I went through phones) had a wool scarf around his neck and fingerless white gloves on his hands. It wasn't one degree above fifty, and Bianca was flushed, drinking a tall glass of ice water, and half naked. Muscles everywhere.

"David." She pointed to the most uncomfortable chair in the room. Cold white leather with no arms. I could feel her jungle green eyes on my back as I took my assigned seat.

"What is *wrong* with you?" She was lounging on a white leather sofa with her Yorkshire terriers, waiting for someone to feed her grapes and fan her with banana leaves. Her dogs good-morning growled at me and I, under my breath, growled back. "I called you to talk about *me*," Bianca said, "how *I* feel, and somehow you've managed to make this about yourself."

Honestly.

"Say something, David."

"Mrs. Sanders, it's freezing in here." I hugged myself, rubbing my arms, the bottom half of me bouncing, trying to get the blood flowing. "Could I have a blanket?"

"You may have this, David." She tossed something in my lap.

It was multicolored, Valentino, about the size of a wallet. I opened it, then zoomed it in and out, trying to focus.

"Is this a calendar?" I flipped through. Month after month of clustered red hearts and single black Xs, this month noticeably missing a black X. I've been a girl long enough, all my life, to know exactly what I was looking at.

"Take it to the Brazilian doctor," Bianca said. "Find out what's wrong with you."

"What's wrong with *me*?" Which is when a terrible moonshine truth came into play: You can sleep it off, give it an ice shower, throw Super Excedrins at it, and it's still going to take two days to sober up from it. The moonshine spoke up and said, "Mrs. Sanders." The moonshine shook the Valentino calendar. "I can save myself a trip to your doctor. This is called menopause."

We were in Bianca's day room—full ocean view, all mirrors, glass, white fur rugs and white leather furniture, and someone standing on the other side of the door dropped a china cabinet. The noise of the crash bounced off the mirrors, walls, and marble floors, and Bianca, stunned, didn't react to the blast, because she was too busy being shocked by what (the moonshine) I'd said. And so was I. But (the moonshine) I kept going. "I can drop everything, Mrs. Sanders, have Dr. Caden drop everything to get here, and let her look over this," I shook Valentino, "only for her to tell me you're in your forties and life as you know it is about to change."

The room grew still.

I'm not sure I heard myself right.

The headline would read: *It was Mrs. Sanders in the White Day Room with her Bare Hands.*

My head fell as I watched a lonely tear cut a path straight down Bianca's cheek. I squeezed my eyes closed and wanted very much to turn back time. "I am so sorry, Mrs. Sanders." Her large (large) chest rose and fell steadily. "I shouldn't have said that." I didn't know she owned a tear. Had I known, I'd have never guessed I'd be the one to drag it out of her. Waving a white flag, I whispered, "I could be wrong."

Nothing from her.

"It could be, Mrs. Sanders, it looks like…" I wasn't about to say the word again, "…one thing, but it's really another."

I might be onto something.

"Maybe I really should talk to Dr. Caden."

Nothing.

"I will, Mrs. Sanders. I'll call her right now."

Nothing.

"Because," I was fighting for my life, "sometimes it looks like one thing when it's another."

Something was tickling the back of my brain. The front of my brain was full of moonshine and *run for your life, Davis.*

"We need to look at the big picture, Mrs. Sanders."

Nothing.

I collapsed against the cold leather at my back. Passing through my brain were the words *big picture, big picture, big picture.*

The room was so eerily quiet, I swear I heard her open her mouth. I grabbed the sides of the chair, bracing myself. She took a deep breath and met my eyes dead on. She finally spoke, a calm whisper. "I've gained two more pounds."

Choosing my words so very carefully, I said, "Big picture, Mrs. Sanders. Look at the big picture. Muscle weighs more than fat." (Hail Mary Moonshine Hail Mary Moonshine Hail Mary Moonshine.)

"Are you saying that, David, or do you believe it?" No venom from her. Something was so wrong.

"I truly believe, Mrs. Sanders, there's more to this. I think I should have taken all the evidence into account before I jumped to a conclusion."

She was absentmindedly twirling a lazy pattern on one of the dogs' heads with a finger. Gianna, I think. She didn't look up when she said, "You may go now, David, and close the door behind you."

It's Davis. And Davis needs a nap, so she'll be rested when Bianca has decided how to kill her.

* * *

Davis didn't wake up from her nap until eight o'clock that night when a cat with four wet paws jumped on her. Cue Davis screaming.

What really woke me up, though, were the white water rapids. Lugging the cat under my arm, I tracked the raging river to the kitchen, where water was gushing from the bottom of the refrigerator in a flood. I sloshed through, cat in tow, and gathered my phone, my laptop, and a note from my husband. *Dinner with the Mayor and City Council. Get some rest. No more moonshine for you.*

First, I hacked into the maintenance department's operational site and turned off the water main for the 29th floor. Next, I pulled all three magnolia bedspreads off all three magnolia guest beds, and used them as mop rugs in the kitchen, the cat trailing behind me the whole time. Cat and I settled on a magnolia sofa in Who Dat Hooters, ordered room service pizza—pepperoni for me, anchovy for it—and it was then I remembered the thing I'd been trying to forget: The conversation I'd had with Bianca. I checked my phone and email, nothing from her. She must still be putting my end-of-life plan together. Nothing from Mr. Sanders, Bradley, or No Hair on the subject, so she obviously intended to act alone; no witnesses. I figured I'd better hurry and get a little work done before she kills me.

If I found the platinum, I could redeem myself in four million ways, and Bradley's last memory of me wouldn't be humiliating him with my failed attempt to get in the Bellissimo vault. Or the moonshine. Or what I'd done to Bianca. I didn't know which of the three was the worst. I did know this week needed to be over.

Logging into the Bellissimo facial-recognition software, I loaded these pictures: Holder Darby, Christopher Hall, Conner Hughes, and Magnolia Thibodeaux. Because I needed to look at the big picture. One of these people stole the platinum.

"Stop playing with your food, Cat." It was standing in its pizza box, batting at the anchovies, tossing them through the air, then pouncing on them. It finished its pizza first, stared at me while it licked its paws, and not only did I not have a drop of water, I didn't have enough computer screen to hold Holder Darby and Christopher Hall. Not one hit on Conner Hughes or Magnolia Thibodeaux with each other or the other two, but major paydirt on the couple. Holder Darby and Christopher Hall weren't casual acquaintances. Back in the day, according to the photos, they were inseparable. And there was no doubt in my mind they were together now.

"Cat." It was still working its paws. "Let's go downstairs."

For one thing, I had no water, and wanted to hot shower away the last traces of Pine Apple moonshine. For another, I might finally be on the right track and needed more computer; I couldn't always be the keyboard cowgirl I needed to be on a laptop. I packed a quick bag—pajamas, fuzzy slippers, cat—stuffed my hair into a big floppy hat, out the Creole front doors, and caught the elevator.

We made it to 3B without incident. There, in my pajamas, with the cat asleep on the sofa, I placed the first piece of the puzzle. Holder Darby and Christopher Hall. They're together. I didn't know if they'd been abducted, and if so, by whom, or for what reason, but there wasn't a doubt in my mind they were together. I didn't know if they ran, where they would've run to, or why, but all the evidence says they ran together. And I don't know what got into me to talk to Bianca that way, but I know she's going to get me back.

I sat at the computer desk rolling my chair between four screens for the next two hours. Searching every Bellissimo database within my reach—surveillance, accounting, photo archives—I found nothing even halfway connecting Holder and Christopher to Magnolia and/or Conner Hughes. If evidence existed that these people interacted, it was not to be found in the Bellissimo system.

I did learn a few interesting things. Holder Darby, never married, originally from Horn Hill, Alabama, was from a banking family on her mother's side. It was when Holder's career Air Force father was transferred to Keesler Air Force Base in Gulfport that the family moved to Mississippi. Holder was thirteen. She's four years older than Christopher Hall, who had a record before he was convicted of involuntary manslaughter and counterfeiting: two driving under the influence charges.

Magnolia Thibodeaux, back in the day, had a Bellissimo boyfriend. A leathery-skinned pool boy who wore his messy brown hair cut in a mullet. The grainy surveillance video and old pictures caught him and his guitar case running in and out the Big Easy Haunted Flea Market more than her husband Ty had.

Conner Hughes? Next to nothing, which I found in and of itself interesting. No wife or kids, no girlfriend, no golf or tennis. He lived in a modest split-level '70s home in a boring neighborhood. He paid off the house twenty years ago, had no credit card debt, and drove a dull four-door sedan. Conner Hughes might be the most uninteresting man on Earth. The only thing I found remotely resembling a life outside the vault business was a board seat at an organization called Greater Oakridge Animal Shelter and another board seat at Crestview Animal Control.

I was on my way to see what manner of animal Conner Hughes was interested in controlling—termites?—when my phone beeped with a text from my husband: *Davis. I just took a call from someone on Dionne Warwick's team. There's no water next door in the Leno Suite. Do we have water?*

FIFTEEN

The saints came marching in at 7:01 on Thursday morning. My eyes popped open and I bolted up. In the bed: one cat, zero husbands. Neither I nor Bradley had left this building in days, and yet we hadn't had an actual conversation since I can't remember when. The moonshine, I guess, was the last time we were face to face, and that was a blur. I fell back on my pillow, but then there were the saints again. I may be the only person in the world with a doorbell that plays a bagpipe rendition of "When the Saints Go Marching In." And we couldn't find a way to adjust the volume, which was set at ear-splitting. I had a big note over the doorbell (NO!), but everyone could see the flashing fleur-de-lis under my warning and rang it anyway. My feet hit the floor jogging to make the saints stop.

I looked through the leaded glass and copper bars to see the distorted image of the all too familiar Sears repairman uniform. I cracked the door. "Can I help you?" I tugged at my t-shirt, hoping I was wearing something underneath.

"I'm here to replace the defrost timers on the refrigerator."

Of course he was.

I opened the door and hid behind it. "Help yourself."

Sadly, he knew the way. All the Sears guys knew their way around Bayou Bungalow, except for when Sears hires a new repairman, which I hate, because I have to go through the new guy's shock and awe. "Cool! Awesome! There's Jesus! Damn, lady!" On the other hand, one day Sears might hire an appliance repairman who actually knows what he's doing, so there's that.

"I came on Monday," Sears said over his shoulder, "but the lady who was here wouldn't let me in."

"What?" I used the magnolia tree for cover. "A lady was here?"

"Yes, and I told her if I didn't replace the timers in the freezer, that big slab of ice in the ice bin was going to thaw and the drain wouldn't be able to handle it, which would back that ice into the input line and freeze it, then it would thaw and the whole thing would blow. And what happened? Exactly that."

"What'd she look like?" Erika Cleaning Woman would have let Sears in. Erika Cleaning Woman was very well versed in all things Sears, because she was the one who had to clean out the refrigerator when everything turned green and grew fuzz.

"Who?" Sears asked.

"The woman who wouldn't let you in."

"Mean," Sears said. "She looked mean. And she had a mean little friend."

Magnolia. I knew it. I knew she'd been here Monday. Did I not tell everyone she was here and no one believed me? "Hold that thought, Sears." I got in another half mile jogging back to the bedroom to pull on a pair of shorts. I got all the way to the kitchen door when I decided a bra might be in order. As far as being productive today, I was well ahead of my own game. I'd already worked out, and so had the cat, racing back and forth with me.

"So you came Monday?" Sears had kicked the wet bedspreads out of his way and was on the floor with a flashlight. I looked at the coffee pot. I had no coffee because I had no water.

"The lady said come back later."

"What was she doing when you got here?"

He looked up from the floor. "I have no idea," he said, "but she was holding a welding torch."

Of course she was.

I ran to the alligator gumbo bedroom, grabbed my phone, and ran back to the kitchen, stopping along the way at my Igloo refrigerator and grabbing three bottles of water so I could make six cups of coffee, all of which I needed. (Two miles in. Before coffee.) I hopped up on the counter and poked my phone to video. "Sears. If you would. Tell me the whole story again. I'm going to record you. For the insurance people."

Sears fluffed his hair, smoothed his moustache, sucked his teeth, then tipped his head back and sang, "La la la la la!" He looked at me. "Warming up."

"Let me know when you're ready." I'd been filming the whole time.

He cleared his throat, then held up three fingers, starting the silent countdown. When he got to one: "Good morning!" And I still hadn't had a single sip of coffee.

Sears told the whole story again while I recorded his testimony. I prompted him a little. "A welder, you say?"

The cat was on the counter beside me, eating a crunchy fish-shaped breakfast Bradley had left for it, ignoring the interview.

"All I saw was the torch," he angled for my phone, "but I recognized it. Craftsman. One of ours."

"Would you recognize her again if you saw her?"

"Well," Sears said, "maybe if you put a welding helmet on her."

I stopped the video, thanked him, and hopped down to try to make coffee around him. He said if I needed any additional footage to give him a call. Whatever he could do to help.

"Now, let's see what we got here." Sears opened the big red freezer door and an unexpected gush of ice water, gallon upon gallons, poured out. He danced around. "Shit! It's cold! Shit!" He used his wet boots to scoot one of the bedspreads back to the fridge, while I pulled open a drawer and tossed magnolia kitchen towels at the new tidal wave.

While we were mopping up, the cat, who'd been eyeing the open freezer door, propelled itself past us in a big yellow blur, through the air, between me and Sears, and into the freezer. It landed in a cavernous freezer bin somewhere near the middle and let out a yelp. Dammit.

"What the hell?"

"It's the cat," I told Sears. "It's so nosy. Gets stuck everywhere.

You'd better stand back. It has a bad habit of going for your head when it's scared."

I don't know where or how the "meow" business started, because I had yet to hear anything close to "meow" come out of this cat. This cat could be where the Emergency Broadcast System got its siren.

Sears scooted backwards, pushing the dam of wet blankets and dishtowels behind him. The cat was screaming and running circles inside a freezer pull-out bin the size of a grocery buggy. Here I go, rescuing the cat again. "You got yourself in there, Cat. Why can't you get yourself out?" I pulled on magnolia oven mitts so it wouldn't scratch me to death, then reached in for it. The cat let me know it didn't like the oven mitts by having one of its loud and obnoxious cat fits and attacking them. Not one sip of coffee yet this morning, not one sip.

"You want me to help?"

"No, Sears," I sighed over my shoulder. "I got this."

I pulled the freezer bin out an inch and wedged my head in. "Cat. Come on. It's me."

It was plastered against the back wall, letting out tornado warnings and trying to murder the magnolia oven mitts. I couldn't reach it, and that's how deep this damn refrigerator was, so I pulled the drawer out as far as I could, then another inch, and climbed in farther. Now I was half in and half out of the freezer. I could barely hear Sears over the cat. "Are you sure you don't need help?"

"I'm good." What I needed were ear plugs. Between my voice and the cat's car-alarm distress, bouncing around a plastic box, I'd go deaf before I got the cat out. "Just stand back, Sears."

Four seconds later, I heard Sears let out a war cry as a Boeing 747 landed in my kitchen. It shook the whole red refrigerator.

Cat and I froze. We stared at each other. Its eyes were big green marbles, its mouth gaping open. I could see all its dagger teeth and its white sandpaper tongue.

"Sears?" I tried to pull out, but now I was stuck. "Sears? Are you okay?" I could hear the Bellissimo crumpling and Sears crying out for help behind me, and somehow I found the adrenaline to escape the freezer, scraping the hell out of my shoulders and slamming my head into the ice bin above. I slid across the wet floor to rescue Sears, who was under the statue rubble of Saint Somebody. "What *happened*?"

"I have no idea! The damn thing fell over on me!"

He must have backed into Saint Somebody and sent it toppling off the concrete base. Saint Somebody had crashed down, all over Sears. He was covered in Saint Dust. He would have been covered in Saint Dead had Saint Somebody not been caught through the middle by the granite island, cutting itself in half and splitting the island straight through the middle.

I pulled Sears up from the wreckage, my phone began ringing, and we both turned to the cat, who'd decided it wanted out of the freezer, but was now trapped between the bin it flew into and the ice bin above, which I'd knocked loose with my head, and the cat didn't have enough room to squeeze through.

Sears was bent over the half of the granite island still standing, catching his breath, waving through the Saint Somebody dust, repeating, "Oh, boy. Oh, boy. Oh, boy."

"Are you hurt?" I patted Sears down, not finding any weapons or broken bones, the cat, the whole time, singing the fire alarm song, my phone, the whole time, ringing.

"I'm okay," Sears said, "but for God's sake, shut the cat up."

I slid back to the cat. I tried to lift the ice bin, the cat begging me, at top volume, to hurry. Turning to Sears, I asked, "Can you help me lift this thing? Grab one side." The cat had moved on to Air Raid Siren, and no coffee yet. The whole time. No coffee. Not a drop. Not one drop.

Sears shook it off, shuffled over, and together we fought to lift the ice bin.

"Why is it so heavy?" I asked.

Veins popped through the Saint Somebody dust on Sears's face. "I have no idea. It's not even an ice maker, you know," he grunted. "It's an ice machine."

"Is there a diff—?"

And that's when whatever had the ice bin tripped up and stuck gave way, just in time for the cat to shoot out in a blur of yellow fur and the front panel of the ice bin to snap, split, and spill thousands of platinum coins all over me, Sears, down the freezer, onto the floor, and all across the kitchen. None of us—me, Sears, or the cat—could do anything but watch the deluge of coins spill out of the freezer. It was so, so, so *Pirates of the Caribbean*.

Just then my husband, wild-eyed and red-faced, burst into the kitchen, stopped dead cold, and tried to take it all in—me, Sears, Saint Somebody, the cat, who was hanging upside down from the swinging chandelier where it had landed, the kitchen island destroyed, and the platinum, so much platinum, still clinking and settling. Lots and lots of platinum.

Sears found his voice first. "I'd say all this has been the problem with the refrigerator the whole time."

SIXTEEN

"Calls came in from all over the building, Davis."

"It was loud," I said. "So loud. Really loud."

My husband stood, surveyed the destruction a little further, then turned to Sears. "Obviously," he said, "I need you to use a little discretion here."

Sears locked his chalky lips, then threw away the key.

Bradley pulled his phone from his pocket, dialed, and said, "Calinda, I need a cleanup crew on twenty-nine." A pause. "Yes," he said, "the refrigerator, then some." Another pause. "At least twice the number of people it took to clean up the chandelier Monday." A pause. He ended the call, then his eyes fell on the empty coffee carafe. He was momentarily stunned, as if it was the strangest thing going on in the kitchen. He turned to me. "You need coffee."

My head rolled around in affirmation.

He called Calinda again. "Have someone from Beans bring Davis a pot of coffee right away."

I love him.

Bradley, Sears, and I started lobbing frozen platinum coins into the cat's freezer bin. We got the last of them into the bin and the three of us dragged it across the tile floor to a remote corner of Who Dat Hooters, where I tossed a dancing crawfish fleece blanket over millions in platinum, then called Baylor in to see it safely to the temporary vault where Magnolia Thibodeaux would never find it.

"Do you hear me, Baylor? Go to the eighth floor and get yourself two big guys carrying two big Rugers, bring them here, then move the platinum to the temporary vault and nowhere else. Not my car or your truck."

He told me his truck was still out of gas.

Good to know.

Bradley, hands on hips, turned to me. He opened his mouth to speak and I waved him off. He knew I knew he was sorry he hadn't believed me about birdbrain Magnolia running in and out of here and I didn't, I would never, make him say it. Maybe I'd redeemed myself. And if I was several million to the good with Bradley, in spite of the spying and vault business, so be it, because I'd need the leverage when he found out I actually had been hauled off to jail while he was being held at gunpoint in the vault. He kissed me bye, thanked Sears again, and left for his office just as the cleaning crew entered.

Sears, mopping sweat, fell into one of the purple pleather recliners. I collapsed on the purple pleather beside him.

We sat in silence for a good long while. Numbness set in when I realized if we had the platinum, Paragon Protection didn't. If we'd just located all the missing platinum, it wasn't in the Mint Condition slot machines. I'd need a good count on what we'd just rescued to know. If Paragon wasn't stealing platinum from us, I'd have to write this week off to wrong roads, dead ends, jail, a cat, and menopause. Then try to move on with my life.

"Where'd your cat take off to?"

"Not my cat," I told Sears, "and I have no idea."

* * *

Sears capped off the water line to the red refrigerator, the only thing left standing in the kitchen, then water was restored to the twenty-ninth floor. I walked him to the front door. He wrote his cell phone number on the back of an appointment card. "If you ever need anything."

"What's your name?"

"You can call me Sears."

"Do you have a truck full of tools, Sears?"

"Oh, yeah."

"What do they pay you?"

"Fourteen an hour," he said. "No benefits, but I get mileage."

Have I got a deal for you, Sears.

The cat jumped out of the magnolia tree in the foyer and followed me to the alligator gumbo bedroom where I finally had a cup of coffee. Soon enough, I was showered and feeling human. While I was getting dressed, the cat had been busy pulling Bradley's Armani and Brooks Brothers pants off hangers and kneading them in to a fat bed in Bradley's closet.

I didn't have the energy.

I told it to stay out of the way and out of trouble in our bedroom until I got back and it didn't even look up, just swished its fat yellow tail.

The noise of the cleaning crew still at it, removing the vestiges of Saint Somebody, forced me to go all Audrey Hepburn before I stepped out—scarf tied under my chin, square dark sunglasses—so if they told anyone they'd actually seen Mr. Cole's elusive wife, they wouldn't have details beyond she's very sophisticated and has a cat.

When I reached the foyer, my fifth mile of the day, I had to step around a wooden pallet stacked waist high with Saint Somebody leftovers. The man in coveralls securing the pieces, arms and a concrete sandaled foot, looked up at me. "Did you know someone cut out the whole back of this thing with a welding torch?" he asked. "Made it unstable."

"Terrible," I said, then stepped out the front door, something catching my eye down the hall at Jay Leno's place.

A big dark something at the door. I took a few tentative steps, then broke into a run, digging in my spy bag for my gun and my passkey.

Honestly, it was barely nine o'clock in the morning.

Before I reached the door, I stepped out of my brand new $650 Alexander Wang white leather open-toed wedge booties so I wouldn't ruin them, then dropped them into my spy bag. My feet sank into the wet carpet. I swiped the door to Jay's place, pushed it open, and a gush of water rushed out the door, over my feet, and into the hall.

Note to self: Stop flooding the building. Last weekend, the Hello Kitty wedding hall. Yesterday, my kitchen. Today, Jay's place. "Hello?" I took in the scene. The whole scene. "Hello?"

I sloshed through to the master bath, where the waterfall fixture on the Olympic-sized bathtub was wide open, releasing gallons and gallons of water per second, spilling over the rim of the bathtub, across the marble floor, down the hall, and out the front door. I was in water up to my ankles. I wasn't about to swim into the tub, so I shot a towel bar off the wall, bang bang, reached for it when it floated my way, and used it as a hammer to turn off the water, thud thud, then rode three thick guest towels down the hall and out the front door, scoot scoot, which dried my feet. Safely out, I traded my gun for my phone and stepped back into my shoes.

"Hey, it's me."

"Hey!"

Someone was awfully chipper this morning.

"Road trip," I said. "Meet me at my car."

"Where to?" she asked.

"New Orleans."

"Are we going to kick Magnolia's ass?"

"Something like that."

"I like it," Fantasy said. "Have you smoothed things over with Bradley?"

"I think so." To the tune of four million big ones.

"You can tell me all about it on the way."

And you, Fantasy, can tell me all about Dionne Warwick's guy.

* * *

Mile six, to my car. I called Bradley. I thought it best to butter him up first. He caught on right away. "Just tell me."

"When is Dionne Warwick checking in?"

"Oh, no, Davis. No."

"It's not that bad."

"Just tell me. What happened?"

"When is she checking in?"

"Her band gets here today. Four o'clock. What happened?"

"I'm not really sure, but we need a cleanup crew at Jay Leno's place quick. Some wet-vacs, and maybe a little carpet." And that was when I stepped out of the building and saw what was parked in my spot.

* * *

"This is truly disgusting beyond words. We could drive my car, you know."

"You have two flat tires, Fantasy." My appointment with Bianca's gyno was in four hours. Just enough time to get to New Orleans, have a little chat with Magnolia Thibodeaux, and back to Biloxi. "Get in."

I could barely maneuver the nasty boat of a car to the Starbucks drive-through speaker, and only after I'd destroyed all of Starbucks' landscaping did we make it to the coffee, where five Starbucks people were squeezed in the window to get a better look, all of them glazed over.

"How much!" I had to yell over the knocking engine.

One of the Starbucks people waved me on. And that might be the appeal of this humiliating clunker to Eddie the Ass. Free stuff.

Fantasy finally pulled her sweater down from her face so she could drink her coffee. "Why does it smell so bad and what's up with the stupid bull horns?"

"I have no idea."

"You look like a twelve-year-old driving this rattletrap."

I couldn't begin to see above the boat helm of a steering wheel. I needed a booster seat. It had no power steering, and we weren't ten miles from the Bellissimo before my arms, shoulders, and neck were exhausted.

"The glove compartment is full of condoms, Davis. This is disgusting."

"I'm going to kill Baylor," I said. "I'm just going to kill him."

"I'll help."

We rode in relative silence, considering how loud the damn car was, for several miles, until Fantasy figured it out.

"You don't want to go to New Orleans and kick Magnolia's ass, Davis. You want to trap me in this ridiculous car of Eddie's and kick my ass."

"I'm trying to save you."

"I don't need to be saved."

We were on I-10 West, sixty miles of straight road ahead. Now my legs hurt, because both the gas and brake pedals needed extreme coaxing. The Cadillac burned oil at a rapid rate too, leaving a trail of sooty smoke, and the damn thing lurched every sixteen seconds for no good reason. Like just now, sending Fantasy into the dash.

"Shit!"

"Don't try to change the subject, Fantasy."

"Pull over somewhere, Davis, and let's hitchhike. We'll buy a car, rent one, or call a Bellissimo limo to come get us. And I'm not trying to change the subject." She couldn't find a cup holder, because they didn't make cup holders during the Civil War when this car was built. "The subject is I don't need you to save me."

"Then tell me why your Jean Paul Gaultier dress is hanging off the lampshade at Jay Leno's place, and tell me who drank four bottles of champagne, and then tell me why the bathtub water was on. That thing's a lap pool, Fantasy, and you, or Dionne Warwick's guy, or both of you ran out of there naked and forgot to turn off the faucet. When the water was turned back on this morning the whole suite flooded. I don't know where we're going to put Dionne Warwick, and *I* will get blamed for this, because *I'm* the one who turned off the water main last night while *you* were running a bubble bath." I caught my breath. "What is going on with you? What are you *doing*, Fantasy?"

"I didn't run out of there naked, thank you."

"Did you sleep with that man?"

She stared out a filthy window the size of Macy's storefront. "No."

The next ten miles were nothing but bald whitewall tires and hearts turning.

She stared out the filthy window the size of a Macy's storefront.

"Yes."

I let my forehead bounce off the horn cap of the steering wheel.

*   *   *

Twenty silent minutes later, I wrestled the Cadillac to the curb at Ty and Magnolia Thibodaux's house. Google Earth didn't do it justice. It was a three-million-dollar Garden District home on 3rd Street, 7,000 square feet of Crescent City's finest. Eight bedrooms, and no telling how many ghosts. It was pink, with twenty lime green shutters, and six iron railed balconies jutting from six sets of French doors, which Magnolia surely loved.

The Thibodeaux's street was as good a place as any.

"Look, Davis. It's my vacation."

"So?"

The engine wheezed and popped long after I'd turned it off.

"Two weeks of my year, I don't have to be home," she said, "cook dinner, do homework, laundry, or answer to anyone."

"Do you cheat on Reggie every time you don't have homework or laundry?"

"*No!*"

"Have you ever cheated on him before?"

We'd never had this talk. There'd never been a reason to have this talk. I wish we weren't having it now.

"No."

"Are you going to cheat on him again? At work?"

"I work all the time, Davis. If I don't cheat on him at work, when am I supposed to cheat on him?"

Out of the corner of my eye, I caught a flash of something behind one of the lime green shuttered windows.

"Aside from the fact that you're married and have three kids," I said, "do you realize what a security risk it is for you to sleep with a guest? Do you even know this man? Did you bother to check him out at all?"

Her eyes rolled to the battered convertible headliner of Eddie's disgusting car. "Of course I did. He keeps his credit cards in alphabetical order."

"Fascinating. I'm not impressed. Did you bother to run one of the credit cards? See how many women he might be sleeping with?"

"Davis, that's just mean."

Maybe.

"His watch chimes, like a church bell, every hour."

"Oh, that would have me peeling off my clothes too."

She had nothing to say.

"What were you thinking?"

She let her head fall back on the seat, stretched her legs, closed her eyes, then said, "I have no idea. I wasn't thinking. The chandelier fell on him, we had coffee, then drinks, then dinner, then—"

I held up a stop sign. I know what comes after dinner. "Does he have a name?"

She looked at me with dreamy eyes. It was all so high school. Except for the fact she's married with three kids. "Miles."

"Miles," I repeated.

"Miles."

For how his name came out of her mouth, you'd think she slept with Mr. Darcy Pope Francis Johnny Depp.

We were in deep trouble. Big trouble, bad trouble, unbelievable trouble.

We didn't see it coming when Mini Me started beating on the dirty car window. Fantasy and I screamed out a lung each.

* * *

A small woman in a black and white maid's uniform straight from the wardrobe department of *The Help* showed us in, placed a tray of drinks in front of us, then took a position at the door, glaring, curling her lip, and daring us to touch something.

A minute later, a honey cloud of blooming magnolias entered the room well before Magnolia did—she surely bathed in it—and it's exactly what I smell when she's been on one of her French Quarter treasure hunts in the Creole Crazy house.

Fantasy the Adulterer sneezed.

The maid shuffled out of the way when she smelled Magnolia coming.

"That'll be all, Teensy."

Teensy took off.

Hostile posture was assumed by all.

"I know you," Magnolia announced. "You're Jeremy's girl, married to the new casino manager."

"My name is Davis."

"That's a stupid name."

Said the lady who's named after a tree.

"Why are you here?" she asked. "What is it you want?"

I reached in my pocket and pulled out one of the fake platinum coins found in the Bellissimo vault. I flipped it off my thumb and through the air, a trick I learned from Cooter Platt when I was six. The heavy coin twirled and twisted, landing on her powder blue skort, two points for me, you'd have thought I tossed a tarantula in her lap.

She stared at it for the longest. "Is this real?"

"Is that real?" (Mini Me.)

Magnolia sat on a big gold throne in the middle of a big gold room. Mini Me, her personal assistant, bodyguard, liveried servant, who fought all her fights and lied all her lies, stood at the ready to the right and just behind the throne. We called her Mini Me because (she's a foot shorter than Magnolia, but just as wide) the two of them were always together and permanently dressed in old lady tennis clothes, including color coordinated visors. No telling what their helmet hair looked like under them. All I could see on both heads were short, stiff, putty-colored curls fighting for freedom. They were both shaped like pears: small on the top, huge on the bottom. Mini Me looked her age, dinosaurish, and Magnolia matched, but only to her chin.

The disparity between Magnolia's neck and chin was at least three decades. I know I'll get to facelift age myself, so I don't want to be too critical, never say never, but I hope if I ever ask a doctor to cut my face off and sew it back on, advancements in the overall process will have been made to include the clock rolling back on the rest of me—hands, butt, knees—so it won't just be my face that's tight as a tick. Everything on Magnolia and Mini Me was racing toward their thick ankles. Except Magnolia's rock-hard face.

"I feel certain, Mrs. Thibodeaux, this is what you've been looking for in my home."

Her hand shot up. "Oh no." She wagged a thick finger. "No, no, young lady. That is *my* home. Those are *my* things. And this is *mine*." She displayed the platinum coin, then put it where the sun don't shine, inside whatever manner of industrial bra she was wearing beneath her Lily Pulitzer yellow palm polo. "*You* are just an interloper."

"Interloper." (Mini Me, who lunged with every word.)

"I'm here to save you some time, Magnolia," I said. "I found the platinum you've been looking for, and it's fake." I watched the blood drain from her facelift. "Check it out." I waggled a finger at her industrial breasts. "Fake. Every single bit of it. So you can stop looking."

"I don't know how in the hell you think that's saving me time."

"How the hell is that saving us time?" (Mini Me.)

"And I have no idea what you're talking about." She reached in, pulled out the platinum coin, and passed it to Mini Me. "See if this is fake." Mini Me took the coin, cocked her head, opened her mouth, and bit down on it. "Is it fake?"

Mini Me moved it to the other side of her mouth, as if those teeth were better at detecting genuine precious metal.

"I don't know," she said. "It sure tastes real."

"Is this what you've been looking for, Magnolia?"

"I'm not looking for anything from you, young lady."

"Not looking." (Mini Me, who was trying to tuck the platinum back in Magnolia's industrial bra until she was slapped off.)

Fantasy, who had no intention of putting her dog in this fight—she had problems of her own—polished off her mint julep, then placed her empty silver cup on the tray.

"Say," she said. "Not that this isn't fascinating, but do you mind if I use the ladies' room?"

Magnolia, her sights set on me, waved permission.

Mini Me waved too.

"Talk to me, Magnolia." I crossed my legs and leaned in, just me and this dingbat, getting real. "If this is what you've been looking for, you can stop, because I found it and it's fake. Every bit of it."

Her hand rose to her mouth and she began to violently chew the side of her thumb. I could hear her teeth clacking.

Mini Me stared intently, her own fist slowly rising to her face, and her teeth snapping in imitation. Magnolia wasn't about to confess she'd been looking for the platinum, but I needed to keep her busy while Fantasy snooped around upstairs.

"Or are you looking for something else?" I asked. "Jewelry? Family heirlooms? Photographs?" I hoped she wouldn't gnaw off her own thumb with me as witness. "Trinkets? Knickknacks? Art?"

Chomp, chomp.

I waited a beat, then softened my delivery.

"Did you leave memories there, Magnolia?"

Her eyes, ice cubes, met mine.

"Ha."

"Ha!" (Mini Me.)

"Cash?"

She shifted her substantial weight so fast, she almost toppled off her throne. So she was looking for money too. Her husband hid platinum *and* cash in my home, didn't, or couldn't, take it with him, and hasn't, or can't, come back for it.

There was a stash of cash in my home too, and Magnolia was after it.

I. Am. Moving.

Fantasy sliced through the tension when she reclaimed her seat, then reached for my mint julep. I looked at her.

"What? I'm not driving."

"If you're finished hurling accusations at me, and your friend here is finished day drinking, get the hell out of my house," Magnolia said. "I'm very busy."

"Very. Busy." (Mini Me may have found a love bug.) (Her arms shot out in quick succession and she snatched at thin air, her head rolling around as she tracked something the rest of us couldn't see.)

Fantasy held up a finger, knocked back the julep, and stood. "Thank you for your hospitality, ladies."

"You're both crazy."

"You're crazy." (Mini Me.) (Still looking for the love bug.)

"I've said what I came to say, Magnolia." I stood, she stood, Mini Me tried to stand until she realized she was already standing. "Next time you want to chase your tail around my house, *Davis*, you call first."

"Call first." (Mini Me.)

"And let me save you a trip. I won't be in."

"Not in." (Mini Me.)

I turned at the door.

"Like you call me before you come to my house?"

"You know?" Magnolia was gathering the ire she'd lost. "I'm calling Jeremy about you."

"I'll dial the number for you, Magnolia."

Fantasy won the race to the front door, I was two steps behind, and Magnolia lumbered along. Mini Me, closer to the ground, still had a little pep in her step and threatened to overtake her fearless leader, so she was two steps forward, one step back.

"I don't appreciate you coming here accusing me of breaking into your house, calling me a thief and a liar."

"Thief! Liar!" (Mini Me.)

"It isn't even a house. It's a casino, young lady." She opened the front door, hoping to usher me out of it quickly. "A casino."

"A casino." (Mini Me.)

"And let me tell you something else." Her beady gray eyes bore into mine. "If you care anything about your marriage, you'll get your husband out of there while the gettin's good. There's too much temptation for a man in that place, especially married to a little wimp like you."

"Little wimp!" (Mini Me.)

A chill passed through me, straight to wind chimes somewhere, because just then, a heavenly tinkle tune rode in on a blanket of sun. It hit Magnolia square in the face and she squinted, tugging her visor down. She held out her hand to Mini Me, presumably for sunglasses, and Mini Me shot off.

I had a foot out of the house and Fantasy had a hand on the car door at the street. It was just me and Mrs. Mardi Gras.

"Where is Christopher Hall?"

Her eyes narrowed to snake slits and she spoke through clenched teeth. "Even if I knew, I'd never tell you."

I reached into my purse and pulled out one of the hundred-dollar bills Fantasy and I found in a bathtub. She snatched it from me. "Take it to any bank, Magnolia, and they'll tell you it's counterfeit."

The money shook in her hand.

"It's over, Magnolia. Done. I found the platinum and I found the money. All fake. So stop looking." Her knees buckled with the (lies) news. She grabbed for the door to hold herself up, and the hundred-dollar bill, slipping from her hand and surfing a wave of July sun, blew away. "Set foot on Bellissimo property one more time, and you're going down."

"Don't come back here."

"Don't make me."

SEVENTEEN

"What was that about?" Fantasy, knowing I'd held back to say something to Magnolia privately, wanted to catch me off my game. When it comes to work, Fantasy and I don't do private, but these weren't the best of times. She waited to ask until I was in a terrible fight with the car to stay in only two lanes, while taking a right onto Earhart Expressway. "You were right behind me, then you stopped to whisper something to Dingbat."

I let go of the steering wheel with my left hand long enough to swipe the space between my eyebrows, what I do when I lie. "I told her the next time I catch her in my house, I'm calling the police." Which wasn't exactly a lie, but nowhere near the whole truth. "How'd you do?"

"I didn't find Holder Darby or Christopher Hall tied up in the attic," Fantasy said. "But I did find Ty."

"What kind of shape is he in?"

"Well, I don't know, Davis. Maybe I'll just keep it to myself."

The mood in the car went dark. Very dark. Instead of taking the interstate ramp to I-10, I pulled into a fast-food parking lot and threw the big nasty Cadillac boat in park. We sat there, tugging on gloves. Getting ready to duke it out in the cheating ring.

"Who eats Burger King?" Fantasy leaned back and closed her eyes. She wasn't quite ready to fight. "How are they still in business?"

"I don't know."

I have a husband, parents, a sister, and I have a partner. My relationship with Fantasy is unlike any of the others, because

Fantasy and I trusted each other with our lives. It's not like we're in the trenches, walking a beat in West Chicago, but we counted on each other nonetheless. And we have our West Chicago moments.

"I shouldn't have told you," she said.

"I already knew."

"Well, I shouldn't have admitted it."

I bounced the side of my fist off her knee. "How can I help you get it together, Fantasy? You need to take care of this, because I need you."

She turned to me with bright eyes.

Fantasy doesn't do bright eyes, because Fantasy isn't a crier. But when her chin began quivering, I changed my mind. Maybe she is a crier. A tear spilled and sparkled down her dark cheek, and now I was two-for-two. I'd made Bianca, who doesn't cry, cry, and now I've made Fantasy, who doesn't cry, cry. I'm the crier. I cry when we're watching "The Price is Right" and a player spins a dollar on the wheel. I cry every time No Hair leaves for Tunica. At times, with my husband, when out of absolutely nowhere, and crying is the very last thing I should be doing, I collapse in a heart-too-full puddle, and he thinks he's hurt me.

I reached out for my friend, and her head hit my shoulder. "Oh, Davis. Holy shit."

I held her until the waterworks stopped.

* * *

One thing's for sure: People don't go to Burger King for the coffee. Sludge. Mulch-based. Delicate nuances of swamp. One rancid sip and Fantasy was her old self.

"I burned the whole roof of my mouth on this nasty coffee, it ruined the julep thing I had going, and do you think if we put the top down on this car, it would stink less?" She had an arm out the open window, catching the wind. "It's our secret, Davis."

It took her five miles to catch enough wind to start talking.

"I have no intention of leaving Reggie, so I can't tell him. He'll want a divorce, then I'll have to go through six months of groveling, and I don't have six months of grovel in me. I don't have six minutes. Can you imagine?"

I couldn't.

"Once we agreed to stay together, which would be when he got his shattered ego in check, he'd cheat on me so we'd be even. And there's another six months down the drain while I chase down some random whore and yank out her hair." I noticed her looking at her coffee cup like she might give it another go. She changed her mind. "If I confess, it will take a year for us to get back on track. If not longer."

"Clearly, you don't like the track you're on, Fantasy."

"I do," she said. "It's my track. My life. My world. And I don't want to disrupt it."

I stayed quiet.

"It was one hundred percent personal," she said, "what happened with Miles."

There she went again, singing his name.

"It was my deal, my thing, my moment, all for me, and I'm better for it. My batteries are charged. I needed it and Reggie and I will be better for it."

I couldn't wait to hear this.

"I honestly don't think it's any of Reggie's business."

I turned to her. "And you wonder why I hesitate to talk to you about work right now? Have you lost your marbles?"

A truck lost its tire. Not just then. Sometime earlier. The tire was on the shoulder, just barely over the white line, but I didn't have my eyes anywhere near the road. I was looking at Fantasy, who said having sex with a total stranger, repeatedly, six times yesterday, six, (s-i-x), was none of her husband's business. I didn't see the logic and I certainly didn't see the tire. I couldn't swerve the boat in time to miss it.

I clipped the edge just right, the tire arced through the air to the median, and the Cadillac, after a full donut spanning two lanes, followed. We came to a stop in the grassy median with the tire rolling in front of us. The tire rolled one more time, then gave up.

"Jesus! Shit! I hate this car!"

I thought it best we sit a minute.

"It's that Burger King coffee," I said.

"No doubt."

We sat quietly while the officer who'd roared in behind us did his thing.

"Is your gun loaded?" she asked.

"Why? Do you want me to shoot this guy?"

"No. I'm just wondering how much trouble we're in."

"I have my permit."

"I don't have mine."

Great.

"What's taking him so long?"

The answer came from all sides. The officer had called for backup. Now we were surrounded. They came at us slowly, weapons drawn. We knew the drill; we let them see our hands. We slowly exited the vehicle when they said slowly exit the vehicle. We turned, laced our fingers on top of our heads when they said turn and lace our fingers on top of our heads. Finally, they told us what we'd done wrong, other than reckless chasing of a rolling tire into the median. We were driving a stolen car.

One of them popped the trunk. All of us jumped back ten feet. It was full of fresh raccoon skins and a million dollars of counterfeit money. Baylor had better hit his knees and confess all his sins, call his grandmothers and say bye-bye, because he was going down. Hard.

"Did something happen at home, Fantasy?" We were in the backseat of a sheriff's deputy car, cuffed and on our way to jail.

"Not a thing. Not a damn thing. Nothing happened at home. Nothing ever happens at home."

Quiet mouse.

"And it's not that I don't love Reggie, Davis. I do. Of course, I do. He's the father of my children."

No squeaks from me.

"I'm not looking for a way out of my marriage. Reggie and I are a machine. It takes both of us to keep it running. I'll get over myself. I'm already over myself. It's done. I did it. One stupid night. One stupid day and one stupid night. And a little of the next day. No looking back. No regrets."

Worse things have happened post Pine Apple moonshine.

Still.

There must be thirty Waffle Houses between where we'd been taken into custody and the St. Tammany Parish jail, where we were headed. Fantasy blurted out bulletins every time we passed a Waffle House.

"It's not the end of the world."

(True.)

"There's not a doubt in my mind Reggie has cheated on me once or twice."

(I didn't know about that.)

"I think Magnolia is doping ol' Ty. That old man is totally out of it. I found him in the last bedroom in a hospital bed."

"Did you talk to him?"

"Davis," she rattled her handcuffs, "the man was drooling."

We sat quietly. Two more Waffle Houses.

"It was an apology for the chandelier almost killing him that got all the way to naked. So, really, it's your fault."

(Six apologies? I've never been that sorry in my life.) (And this is *my* fault?)

"Ty Thibodeaux has one foot in the grave and the other on a banana peel."

(Banana peels. Banana milkshakes. I'll call Calinda and get her to bust us out.)

"I don't want to go home."

(I wonder why.)

"You're not going home anytime soon, lady."

"Hey!" She lunged at the cage separating us from Deputy Barney Fife. "Mind your own business."

We turned down a two-lane that looked Waffle House free.

"You were right about Magnolia, Davis. All day long, you were right."

"I'm right about Paragon too."

We pulled to a stop at the St. Tammary Parish Sherriff's office.

"Now that," the car doors flew open and we were assisted out, "you're not right about."

"How was he?" I asked over the hood.

"Oh, dear God," she said.

And then we went to jail.

EIGHTEEN

One phone call is never enough.

"I had a small errand to run and what did I find in my parking place? Eddie the Idiot's mobile taxidermy. I swear, No Hair, I will never be the same after driving around with dead raccoons."

"He says they died of natural causes, Davis, and all he did was skin them."

"Since when is buckshot a natural cause?"

"Why didn't you drive Fantasy's car?"

"Someone slashed her tires."

"Days ago," he said. "What's she been doing she couldn't call someone in transportation and get new tires?"

"What?"

"Davis," No Hair said, "move on. Next subject."

"They're holding us on driving a stolen vehicle, reckless driving, criminal possession, carrying concealed without a permit, destruction of government property, and animal abuse."

"What did you destroy?"

"An exit sign and a bunch of guard rail."

"What's the criminal possession?"

"A bunch of counterfeit money," I said. "A bunch." I took a peek around the corner. I had a huge audience, so I covered the mouthpiece of the phone, a desk phone, formerly Greg and Marcia Brady's desk phone, with my hand. "You tell Baylor I'm going to kick his ass."

"Davis," No Hair said, "you're in jail, and you're not going to kick anyone's ass. Why you're calling me is what I want to know. I'm a five-hour drive away."

"I tried Calinda. She didn't answer."

"That's because she's busy doing your job while you're out rubbing Magnolia's nose in it, and I swear, Davis," I could hear him huffing and puffing, "if you don't get your act together, *I'm* coming home and kicking *your* ass."

Pfffffft. "This is all Baylor's fault, No Hair. If he'd have swapped cars yesterday like I told him to, I wouldn't be in jail."

"I wish you could hear yourself."

"Did you see Baylor when he was there? Do you know what happened?"

Nothing but static.

"No Hair?"

"We're going to talk cars later, if that's okay with you."

Dammit. What had Eddie the Ass done with my car?

"Let's slow down and talk about work for a second."

"First, tell me how I'm supposed to get out of jail."

"Call your husband."

"I'm not calling him."

"Call Fantasy's husband. He has all kinds of Louisiana connections."

Under the circumstances—she sat cross-legged on a cot behind me, her head resting on painted cinderblocks, her eyes closed, it was all very Zen—that probably wasn't a great idea. "He's out of town."

"Right," No Hair said. "I can't keep up with her."

"Get in line."

I was in a front corner of the cell, lacing my fingers around the coils of the phone cord and trying to talk No Hair into busting us out. And he wanted to talk about work. Like I could work from jail.

"I heard back from the warden at Pollock, by the way. Christopher Hall didn't break out of prison. He's in the last stages of liver failure. Cirrhosis. It was a compassion release two weeks ago, so he could die on the outside."

"First, I'm sorry to hear that. Next, they should have kept him in, because the first thing he did was rain hell on me by bringing counterfeit money to the Bellissimo."

"I don't know why he'd want to spend the last few days of his life pulling a con."

"I don't think it was a con, No Hair. I think it was a payout."

"To whom?"

"Magnolia."

"For what?"

"I haven't gotten that far."

"You might be right on the payout end of things," No Hair said, "but you're dead wrong about Magnolia. Christopher Hall has no reason to want Magnolia Thibodeaux in federal prison. Where you're headed."

(Pffffft.)

"He and Holder Darby were an item back in the day, No Hair."

"I think I knew that."

"So maybe he just wanted to be with her again before, you know, the end," I said, "which is sweet. Until they told Magnolia my house was full of money and platinum."

"I don't believe for a second you could live there with a stash of cash right under your nose and not find it by now. The platinum was there, yes, but that doesn't mean there's millions of dollars there too."

I turned to check on Fantasy, who was now stretched out on the cot like it was a fluffy day bed, singing to herself. An old song, an old Dionne Warwick song, about never falling in love again.

"Magnolia Thibodeaux sure thinks there is."

"Here's an idea, Davis. Get yourself out of jail, go home, and find it. Lock yourself in there and find the money you insist is there."

"If Paragon doesn't already have it," I said. "My new theory is Paragon is behind everything. They're the ones who nabbed Holder and Christopher with the bad liver."

"When did you come up with that theory?"

"Just now."

"And you think that why?"

"Because I no longer think Magnolia nabbed them."

"And why would they bother kidnapping a special events coordinator and a dying convict?"

"Because Holder Darby and Christopher Hall know where the real money and platinum is."

"Obviously they don't, Davis."

"What?"

"*You* found the platinum."

No Hair had a bad habit of taking the wind out of my sails.

"*Someone* is behind all this, No Hair, and if it's not Magnolia, it's Paragon."

The square base of the retro telephone was in the floor outside the jail cell. I only had the clunky receiver. A deputy walked up and tapped his watch, then leaned over to disconnect the call. "No! No! Please! Two more minutes!" He held up a finger. One more minute.

"Here we go again. Paragon is not behind this and Conner Hughes isn't the bad guy. Have you even met him? He's too boring to be a bad guy. He's an honest man, Davis. Get that through your thick skull. You saved the day finding the platinum, you were right about Magnolia sneaking around looking for it, but you're wrong about Paragon. I want you off that dead-end road. Conner Hughes is not a thief or a kidnapper, and if you ever manage to get out of jail, you should probably look for Holder Darby and Christopher Hall at a hospital. I don't know what happened, but I strongly suspect it was related to his health, not our valued business partner."

Christopher Hall's liver did put a whole new spin on things.

"You do know Paragon has three convicted criminals on the payroll, don't you, No Hair?"

"Yes, Davis. I'm aware. And so does the Bellissimo."

"Who?"

"YOU!"

He had me there.

"I'm getting ready to say something, Davis, and you listen up."
(As if I hadn't been listening.)

"If I hear you say Paragon Protection one more time, we're going to have a more serious talk than this one. We're going to have a come to Jesus talk."

"I know for a fact their game is rigged, No Hair. They've already chosen the winners."

"It's their game, Davis, and as long as they keep it in that room and don't violate the agreement they made with the Gaming Commission, I couldn't care less."

The deputy came back. I squeezed my eyes closed, cradled the phone receiver between my ear and shoulder, clasped my hands in prayer, and had my own come to Jesus talk. "If you'll forgive me of all my sins, Lord, all of them..."

"What?" (No Hair.)

"Oh, holy night. Praise be thine name."

"Who?" (No Hair.)

"Amen and amen."

I peeked. The deputy was gone.

"DAVIS!" (NO HAIR.)

"WHAT?" (ME.)

"Let's wind this up," he said. "You're wearing me out."

"When are you coming home, No Hair?"

"In two weeks," he said. "Five minutes after the grand opening."

"That's too far away."

"Did you tell Bianca she had menopause?"

"Uh, not in those words," I said. And I'm missing her gyno appointment right now. "Are you going to call the governor and bust us out before Bradley finds out about this?"

"No," he said. "I'm not. But Baylor is on his way."

"What's he going to do? Flirt us out of here?" I asked. "We need a presidential pardon, No Hair, or Michael Bublé. They've got a million pieces of evidence against us."

"They've got nothing," No Hair said. "Cop a plea to the car

theft. Tell them you found it on the side of the road with the keys in it and knew nothing about the contents."

"I would have gladly told them that an hour ago, No Hair, but there's a small problem." It was Eddie the Ass's car. I'd never hear the end of it if I let Eddie go down on the counterfeit possession charges. He'd be in prison for the rest of his life. Not a bad place for him, but still, probably not the right thing to do.

"He never registered the car, Davis. And he paid cash for it to a drug dealer. Let St. Tammany keep the car and the counterfeit money. Chasing down the owner will give them something to do for the next six months. They can't charge you or Eddie."

A light at the end of this dark dark tunnel.

"Please tell me you're not joking, No Hair."

"A bondsman should be walking in the door any minute, and Baylor is on his way to pick you up."

Good. When he gets here, I'm going to rip him to shreds over this car business. Then I'm going to find the absolute nastiest job in the three million square feet of Bellissimo property and give it to him. Permanently. While I hole up at my computer and nail Paragon. They have Mint Condition rigged for a reason, and I'm going to find the reason. I thought it best to keep it to myself until I found something concrete—I couldn't tell Fantasy anyway, because she was asleep, napping away the infidelity—lest I be accused of harassing our Valued Business Partner again. I stretched out on my cot and stared at the cracks in the ceiling. Something was going down. I could feel it. I didn't know what, but something.

* * *

Stepping off the elevator a free woman, I saw my new neighbors. In the seven hours I'd been gone on Wednesday, to New Orleans and to jail, Jay Leno's place had been dehydrated, because there was a flurry of activity down the hall. I spotted Lover Boy Miles standing off from the group; he pretended he didn't spot me. I probably should have shot him in the elevator that first day.

Not only was Jay's place in working order, Bradley and I had a new chandelier, a normal chandelier, above our new front doors, normal front doors made of solid wood, and best of all we had a new doorbell, one I was sure didn't sing about saints. I couldn't get in the new front doors (and neither could Magnolia), so I rang the doorbell.

Ding. Dong.

It was a miracle.

Sears opened the door wearing Bellissimo coveralls.

"Hey, there."

"How's it going, Sears?"

"Pretty good." Behind him, a piecemeal trail of canvas tarp covered the floor coming out of the secret door in the fleur-de-lis wallpaper and across half the foyer. New to the foyer, and hugging the east wall, were four metal mountains. "I'm breaking the machines down to the nuts and bolts, rolling the scrap out here, then packing it on pallets." He pointed to the mountains. I had the world's most beautiful foyer: a fake magnolia tree in a cast iron tub, an Igloo refrigerator, and now a scrap-metal junk display on pallets. "Mr. Cole wants to recycle all this. Say," he said, "have you been back there?" He threw a thumb in the direction of the Bourbon Street Bank.

"No."

"Huh." He scratched his neck. "Pretty interesting."

"Keep dismantling it, Sears. Everything you see. Bust it into a million pieces."

"You got it."

"And not a word to anyone." He zipped his lips. I hiked my spy bag a little higher on my shoulder. "By any chance, would you like a big cooler?"

He eyed the Igloo refrigerator. "Sure."

"Have you seen the cat?"

"Not so much," he said, "but your lady doctor is here."

I'd missed Bianca's gyno appointment. By a mile. "Where is she?"

Sears pointed in the general direction of Who Dat Hooters.

* * *

Dr. Paisley Caden, board certified doctor of obstetrics and gynecology, had offices on Prytania Street in New Orleans that made Jay Leno's place look like subsidized housing, but she mostly worked out of her six-room suite at the Hotel Monteleone on Royal Street in the French Quarter.

She had one of the rooms set up for brain transplants. Very medical. Very discreet. Her patients were rich, famous, and paid her a fortune to cover up their Big Easy indiscretions before they went home to their husbands in LA, DC, and HC. (Hot Coffee. It's in Mississippi. A real place, a hundred miles from Biloxi, just northwest of Hattiesburg.) Paisley is five feet tall, of Chinese lineage, but having been adopted by a Louisiana husband and wife cardiology team when she was three months old, was an All-American Girl. Proof? I found her with her Jimmy Choos propped up on my grave marker coffee table, eating popcorn, and watching the Bravo Channel. I plopped down beside her.

"Do you watch this show?" she asked.

"Never. I don't know who these people are."

She passed the popcorn, her eyes glued to the big screen. "Fascinating," she said. "I can't figure out what they're famous for, other than their decadent lifestyles and willingness to let cameras follow them into the bathroom."

"How long have you been waiting on me?"

"Four episodes," she said. "I'm trying to figure out who their vagineer is."

"That," I said, "is gross. Is that what you call yourself?"

"I call myself a genius," she said. "You should see my portfolio. I'm up seventeen percent in this ridiculously depressed economy." She ate popcorn. "Where have you been?"

"Jail."

"That sucks."

She took a slurp of something red. "What is that?"

"A cranberry smoothie. It's very good for your girl parts."

"Good to know."

"And great with a shot of vodka."

"Better to know," I said. "Did you meet Sears?"

"Your new handyman? Yes. And I met your cat."

"Not my cat, Paisley."

"You do know the cat needs to be checked for toxoplasmosis before you get pregnant, right?"

"You can remind me of that if I ever see my husband again."

Five minutes of junk TV and popcorn later, she asked, "How's Baylor?"

Paisley was several years older than Baylor, but looked several years younger. She, along with the rest of the female population, wasn't immune to his dimple, and the two had been friends with benefits since the day Baylor drove to New Orleans to hand deliver a lock of Bianca's hair. Bianca wanted Paisley to report back on her iron level and gum health based on the fair-hair sample. Bianca demanded Baylor wait on the results, which apparently took three days. Paisley tossed the hair, and her clothes, charged Bianca ten thousand dollars for the all's well report on her gums, then examined Baylor for three days.

"He's okay," I said. "He'll never change."

"I hope not." Her whisper eyebrows danced.

"I'm not talking about his looks, Paisley. I give him a simple job, he screws it all the way up, then I ask him to do the near impossible and he saves the day. I wish he had some middle ground."

"Oh, he has fantastic middle ground, Davis." She opened her mouth to tell me all about it and I raised my hand in a stop sign. Don't need to know.

"Where is he?" she asked.

"I sent him on an errand."

"But he's around?"

"He'd better be."

She picked her phone up from her lap and her thumbs flew as she shot out a text message. Most probably to Baylor. The popcorn bowl was nothing but a layer of brown kernels when Paisley asked, "So what's going on with Bianca?"

I let my head rest on the back of the magnolia sofa and stared at the gilded ceiling. "Hot flashes and weight gain."

"Oh, shit."

"You have no idea."

"Has anyone given her the good news?"

"Her Johns Hopkins team," I said, "and me."

"You're lucky you're still alive."

"Tell me about it."

Paisley shook the popcorn bowl, which sounded like rocks in a tin can when factoring in Who Dat Hooters acoustics, just as the cat snuck up behind us. The sudden noise scared it out of its fur. It shot straight up and hooked a paw on one of the fake balconies, then began singing its cat scream song.

"God, that cat is ugly, Davis."

Oddly enough, I was a little offended.

I walked to the balcony and stood under the cat. "Come on, Cat." It weighed its options, found only me, then dropped into and ran its claws down my sleeves before it shot off. I rubbed my arms.

"Speaking of ugly," Paisley said, "have you seen your kitchen?"

Between Magnolia and jail, I'd forgotten all about the kitchen. Which reminded me. I told Paisley I'd be right back, then stepped into the kitchen and retrieved Bianca's Valentino calendar.

I heard a low hum from the refrigerator. I opened one of the four doors, placed my hand on a shelf, and felt the cold. Another miracle. The kitchen was a war zone, but still a miracle to have lived without a working refrigerator for nine months and then have one.

"I don't guess you tried to see Bianca?"

I fell back into the sofa beside Paisley, passing her the calendar.

"I sent my vampire up there to draw her blood and didn't even try. What does it matter, anyway? She puts as much stock in my

medical opinion as she would that of a burrito boy's at Taco Bell."
She paused. "Does Baylor still love Taco Bell?"

"Every single day."

"God, it's all so hot."

"What's so hot about Taco Bell?"

"You know I'm not talking about Taco Bell." She flipped through Valentino. "I'll run her labs. I'd say she's a hormonal mess and needs replacement therapy."

"She needs therapy, alright."

"She's probably perimenopausal, needs to be on something to stave off osteoporosis, plus a little something to boost her metabolism, and probably something for anxiety."

"She needs something for meanness."

"Perimenopause goes on for years, Davis. You'd better brace yourself. Is she exercising? She needs a good yogi."

"She needs a good muzzle."

At the end of the fifth episode of "Socialites Screaming," Paisley stood and stretched. She reached out a hand and pulled me up. We slowly made our way to the King Cake room on our way to the new front doors. Sears, dumping a wheelbarrow stuffed full of sprockets and springs onto a pallet, making enough of a racket to scare every cat in Harrison County, tipped his invisible cap at Paisley as we stepped into the foyer. He and his wheelbarrow disappeared through the hidden door.

"Where's that guy going?" Paisley asked. "What's back there?"

"You don't want to know."

At the new doors, she put a hand on my arm. "And you don't want an only child, Davis. I'm an only child and it's crazy. My mother calls me fifty times a day," she said. "If I had even one sibling, it would be twenty-five. If I had two, it would be twelve and a half, which would be somewhat manageable. If I had three, it would be once a day. You and Bradley need to get going. You don't want to be preggers in your forties."

"I thought my generation could have babies well into their forties."

"You can. But why would you want to?"

Good point.

"Get going," she said. "Have several babies in a row. Boom, boom, boom. Get it over with."

"Soon," I said. "Very soon."

* * *

When Bradley finally made it in from work at one fifteen in the morning, I was still wide awake. I'd been in bed for an hour, the cat had been snoring for three, but sleep wouldn't come.

We met in the middle.

"It's done."

My mouse persona.

"The vault contents are back in the vault. The platinum is in the vault. The bank transfers are being received. It's over."

I would ask why he hadn't told me, but I didn't need to. He didn't tell me because he thought I couldn't handle it, knowing. He thought I'd show up and shoot Conner Hughes and his three thugs.

Bradley waited for me to process the news.

"What'd you do after you recovered four million dollars in platinum this morning?" He pushed my hair from my face.

"Not much."

NINETEEN

Between me, Fantasy, and Baylor, there might be one day a month when we all show up to work on time. On time for us might be four in the morning on a Tuesday, because we're (half asleep) playing slots while watching the drop crew (people in coveralls with lots of keys who gather the cash boxes from inside the machines) when the soft count keeps coming up short. On time for us might be midnight on a Sunday, because we're (half asleep) keeping an eye on the shift change after surveillance reported a week of unusual activity between pit bosses—a ten-minute paperwork handoff taking more than an hour. It took us way less than an hour to find their activity not all that unusual. It was your basic shift-change hookup.

When we didn't have anything pressing, which had been all summer long until this nightmare week, we staggered in to 3B whenever. Usually before lunch. We didn't punch a clock because we worked crazy hours. I'll tell you someone who did work straight hours and showed up right on time, and that's Sears. At eight o'clock on the nose Friday morning, I thought he was outside my bedroom door with four leaf blowers and a jackhammer. The problem was the cavernous foyer of the Big Easy Flea Market, from which every other room of Crazy Creole House stemmed. The slightest noise in the foyer bounced off the cast iron swimming pool that's home to the twelve-foot magnolia tree, up to the domed copper ceiling, down the fleur-de-lis walls, then amplified as it echoed through the rest of Cajun City. And with more gusto now that the refrigerator didn't override all other noises. Sears banging around in the foyer woke up the cat too, who thinks it needs to eat its toxic-waste food the minute it opens its cat eyes.

When I'd shaken off enough sleep to remember (I was married to Bradley) the bankers would only be here for twenty-four more hours, I found a little energy. I couldn't wait for all these people to check out tomorrow morning. Granted, today was packed, but there was hope. And too much commotion to sleep another half hour. I threw back the covers and my feet hit the floor.

On today's itinerary, in no particular order: The Convicted Criminal Paragon tech crew, having completed all the vault tunnel repairs on this end, would move to the Wells Fargo end for a half-day of inspection/maintenance; Dionne Warwick would arrive; and the bankers would play their semifinal and final rounds in the Mint Condition tournament.

Not on today's itinerary, but expected, in no particular order: I'd try to sneak into Event Hall B to satisfy my curiosity about the rigged Mint Condition game and get caught; I'd look for, but not locate, Holder Darby and Christopher Hall; and I'd have some manner of altercation with Bianca Sanders.

Padding across the bedroom floor and turning the corner to the his-and-hers vanity, I thought about my wedding vows. Bradley and I'd had an impromptu wedding last October and, try as I might, I only remember snips.

I know we exchanged quick vows, but I only remember that it felt like we were flying. I don't remember us saying the actual words, which were the standard "till death do us part," but somewhere in there, Bradley promised to make me coffee. And he has. Every day since "I do."

Before he left for work hours ago, he went to the war zone kitchen, rescued the coffee pot, tiptoed through the dark bedroom with it so he wouldn't wake me, set it between the his-and-hers speckled trout sinks with the tropical kingbird fixtures, and this morning, like every morning, all I had to do was push the button. The cat turned in circles, wailing its cat lungs out, whipping its big tail around, because it couldn't find its coffee. We knew it was here, cat and I both could smell it, but it wasn't on the countertop where the spoiled-rotten cat wanted to eat. We followed the lethal fumes and found that Bradley had moved the cat into his closet. Cat's bowl of noxious food was on a shelf Bradley had cleared. On the carpeted floor, beside the bed Cat made yesterday, sat a bowl of water and a food dispenser. The cat could slap a lever with its paw and be rewarded with fish-shaped treats.

I didn't stick around and keep the cat company while it ate its smelly breakfast. I hit the shower. Olivia Abbott needed to make a conference appearance, Collateral Chicken Cordon Bleu and all, and Davis Way Cole needed to get into Event Hall B and catch Paragon. Doing something. Anything.

I was all the way to lipstick and earrings when I heard a knock on the bedroom door. On my way to answer it, I glanced in Bradley's closet to see that the cat had remodeled. Somehow it had managed to open and empty Bradley's sock drawer. It piled the socks, Marcoliani cashmere, every pair, on its nest of Bradley's Armani and Brooks Brothers dress pants. Its eyes were closed and it was purring. I guess so, sleeping on cashmere.

I cracked the door an inch. Sears.

"Hey, Mrs. Cole. There's a man here who says you have his Cadillac."

My vision clouded and I heard a loud ringing in my ears. Like I might pass out.

"Holy Jesus, Davis!" He was yelling from the foyer, but he might as well have been in my ear with a megaphone. "I love this place."

*   *   *

My ex-ex-husband Eddie Crawford has the manners of a sewer rat, the morals of a grub worm, and the personality of a Chihuahua on crack. All that in a sleek, stealthy, swarthy, black panther package. I avoided him at all costs. And here he was.

"Can you tell him I'm not here? Tell him to leave."

"I can hear you, Davis!"

The sound system in Étouffée Estates went both ways.

"Get lost, Eddie!"

Sears clapped his hands over his ears.

"Sorry, Sears. I didn't mean to yell at you."

I stomped past Sears and down the hall to the foyer. I stopped cold and stared at my ex-ex-husband. He was Duck Dynasty. I hadn't seen Eddie Crawford in a long time, thank goodness, and apparently, since then, he'd given up all forms of grooming. A bushy beard trailed off his face, his hair was halfway down his back, and he was dressed in head-to-Army boots camouflage. It was ninety degrees out.

"Eddie. You look ridiculous."

"It's my job, Davis." He put great emphasis on the word job, as if it were breaking news to me that he was employed. "I have an earthy outdoor job. I'm one with the university."

I might be in an alternate university.

"This is one hell of a place you got here, Davis. No wonder you married the gay lawyer."

"Is Mr. Cole gay?"

I turned around.

"No, Sears. He's not."

"Don't listen to her," Eddie the Dumbass said. "She'll marry anything." Eddie head-rolled as he surveyed the French Quarter Flea Market. Hopefully he'd get dizzy, fall, and crack his head open. "Holy shit." Stroking his Brillo Pad beard, he poked his head in the door of the King Cake room, and got a peek at Who Dat Hooters, then back to me. "This place has my name written all over it. Any chance you have an extra room?"

"Where's my car, Eddie?"

"Where's *your* car?" He spun. "You got some nerve, Davis."

Sears, holding up a wall, was taking it all in.

"Did you drive my car, Eddie? Did you *touch* my car?"

"What's it to you?" he asked.

Sears, listening, listening.

"It's my car, you idiot. I want to know if it needs to be sent to the scrap yard."

"Yes, I drove your car, you airhead. What was I supposed to do? Hitchhike? You stole *my* car, Davis."

What was the best way out of this? Should I offer to buy his car from him? Money always worked with Eddie. Should I tell him where it is? St. Tammary Parrish would lock him up in a heartbeat. That would get him out of my hair for a few days. Should I march back down the hall and get my gun? Use him for target practice?

"Stay right there, Eddie." While I get my gun. "Watch him," I said to Sears.

*   *   *

I wasn't about to tell Eddie he'd never see his car again.

In the process of writing Eddie the rotten rotten rotten snake a check to get him off the Bellissimo property before my husband got wind of him, or equally disastrous, before Eddie knew Cooter Platt was here, because Cooter actually *liked* Eddie, I learned No Hair had given him three weeks off. Paid. Personal time, Eddie called it, to work out some issues, vehicular and health—to wit, the health risks associated with his demanding golf course grass duties that he believed, and his crazy mother, my ex-ex-mother-in-law Bea, confirmed, he was allergic to.

"To what, Eddie? What is it you're allergic to? Work?"

"Golf courses."

Then he went off on a tirade about how stupid golf was. What Jolie needed was a monster truck arena. That, he said, would bring in the business. When his paid personal leave was over, he was going to ask about a job in the casino, or follow his mother's sage advice and apply for disability, because he had a golf course rash that the ladies were afraid of. He started unbuttoning.

At which point, I promised him if he showed me anything at all on his physical person I'd shoot him right then and there and he'd never have another rash. Tearing off the check, made out to cash, I told him about a new casino in Philadelphia, where the blackjack dealers were girls in bikinis.

"Davis. I swear. You get dumb and dumber. You know good and well I don't have a passport."

God, help me.

"Philadelphia, *Mississippi*, Eddie. Right up the road."

"For real?"

Well, yes and no. I said it to get rid of him. He'd spend the next week looking for it. There is a Philadelphia, Mississippi, and there are casinos there, but I made up the bikini part.

"How am I supposed to get there if you're having my car detailed?" He thanked me, again, for my generosity. He marveled at the fact that I, so out of touch, knew how to treat a classic car and he asked if I'd started smoking pot, because it was an uncharacteristically friendly action on my part. He suggested I'd finally figured out how to get along with him. Or was it my way of flirting with him? But mostly, he wanted to know how he was supposed to get to bikini blackjack dealers if someone in a garage was scrubbing the gopher guts out of his upholstery.

My heart broke as I said, "Take my car." Take it all, Eddie. Just get out. Out of my haunted house, my marriage, my life.

He examined the check. I watched him count the zeroes on his fingers, making sure I wasn't pulling a fast one on him. On his way out, he told Sears, "Be chill, man."

From the war zone kitchen, to put off my commute to the office until my carsickness passed, I conducted message, email, and reality checks. Attagirls from Mr. Sanders and No Hair on finding the platinum. Calinda emailed Bradley's overloaded schedule for the day. Hot Deals from Amazon. A notice from the Regent Condominium Owners Association advising us to keep our clothes on next Wednesday because the exterior window washers would be there. Spam about my fantasies. J. Crew, bank statements, and my mother. She's making pot roast and a strawberry cake for Sunday dinner. We should come. I closed my laptop, inventoried my spy bag, and turned for 3B.

* * *

Fantasy was nowhere; Baylor was on a sofa. On the coffee table in front of him, a bakery: two white boxes packed three rows wide and five pastries deep with carrot cake and orange zest muffins, apple and cheese Danish, chocolate chip and raspberry croissants, and every variety of donut imaginable. He was halfway through a third box, washing all the sugar down with a giant Mountain Dew. He looked up and said, "Hey, Treasure Island."

It's hard for me to stay mad at Baylor.

"Hey, Sweet Tooth." I sat beside him rather than across from him, because I didn't want to watch him work his way through all three boxes. I helped myself to a cronut. "Have you ever read *Treasure Island*, Baylor?" I brushed sugar crystals off my shirt.

"I've been there."

"It's not a real place."

"It is too. It's in Vegas."

Right. "Well, the book is horrible," I said. "This poor little boy steals a treasure map and gets stuck on an island with a pirate named Long John Silver."

"Like the restaurant?"

Having gotten it all out of my system with my ex-ex-husband, I said, "Sure."

"I don't eat there. Maybe if they had fish tacos."

"My point is, the story doesn't necessarily have a happy ending."

"What happens?" He reached for more diabetes.

"The boy only gets a little piece of the treasure and ends up working in a hotel where everyone plays poker."

"Like us."

Exactly.

"But you found all the treasure," he said. "Your story has a happy ending."

I didn't find the platinum. It fell on me. Technical point. And I didn't believe for a minute it was all the treasure. That thought kept me awake last night and was still bothering me today, because something was definitely bothering me, aside from the fact Bradley withheld important information from me so I wouldn't shoot anyone. Maybe it was being arrested twice this week, which would bother anyone, especially if her husband didn't know. Yet. Or the loud steady beat of my baby clock ticking, maybe that's what it was. Maybe it was the love bugs or the fact that I'd never see my car again. It could be Bianca, or just the wear and tear of living in the Jazz Capital of the Bellissimo. The cat! It could be the cat!

It wasn't the cat.

My discontent was a direct result of being on the wrong track all week, which is to say my ego was bruised, which led to this: Did I want to be right so much so that I'd feel better right now if Magnolia Thibodeaux was in jail? Or if Paragon had robbed the Bellissimo vault? Or if they'd held Bradley at gunpoint last night and made off with the vault contents?

No. I wouldn't feel a bit better.

It was time for me to accept the fact that Paragon Protection wasn't here to steal from the Bellissimo, then move on with my life. Four million dollars tumbled out of the big red refrigerator, yay me, and I should, like everyone else, focus on that. I'd have to live with the fact that I'd never find Holder Darby, Christopher Hall, or Long John Silver. Magnolia Thibodeaux was a long list of undesirables, but she was no Long John Silver. And No Hair was right. Conner Hughes was too boring to be Long John Silver.

"Have you heard from Fantasy?"

Baylor swallowed a half gallon of Mountain Dew. "No."

I could give Fantasy credit for a chunk of the dark cloud following me around this morning. The choice she'd made, the long road she had in front of her if she got caught, if she confessed, or if neither of those happened and she simply had to live with herself and what she'd done. And then, because this was my mood: Could it be possible that Bradley and I ever got that far from each other?

"Where'd you get all this sugar, Baylor?"

"You sent me on a conference drive-by."

"Which is different than sending you out to rob a bakery."

"Megan." His mouth full. "Megan at the conference."

"Megan with the braces gave you all this?"

"She likes me."

Don't they all.

"That place is a ghost town," he said. "Megan said it's always this way on the last day and the bankers won't drag in until it's time to play the slot tournament. She said they'd show up for Diane Warwick tonight too."

"Dionne."

"What?"

"Never mind."

He finally got to the bottom of his white box and pushed it away with a groan.

"So how did you get all this?"

"It was in the conference dining room," he said, "a million donuts. They had fruit too."

"How'd you get into the dining room? How'd you get past security?"

"There wasn't any security," he said. "The security people were all in the event hall doing something with the game."

I'd tried to get through the doors seventy-seven times, and Baylor shows a girl his dimple, says he wants a donut, and breezes right in? "What were they doing with the game?"

"I have no idea."

At which point, finally, I barely cared what Paragon might be doing with their stupid game. I poked his distended stomach. "Look at you."

His chin dropped. "Why did I eat those last ten donuts?"

"Dopamine."

"I do get doped up on donuts. I need to stop."

"That's not what I meant. Sugar releases a chemical in your brain, Baylor. Dopamine." A tingle started at my toes. "It makes you keep eating the donuts after you've had plenty." The tingle kept going until it reached the top of my head. "Hop up, Baylor. You're going back to the conference."

"You want fruit?"

TWENTY

When stimulated, the circuitry in our brains making up the pleasure and reward center receives ten times the normal dose of the neurotransmitter dopamine, the happy hormone. Dopamine, the celebrity, the sexiest of our brain chemicals, rains euphoria on us when nudged—Christmas morning, a romantic wedding, a new car to replace the one we gave our ex-ex-husband. But dopamine can cause problems too, when it sends out happy-camper signals for risky activities, telling us to do them again and again, activities like drinking too much bourbon, eating too many conference donuts, having sex in the packed-out Bellissimo swimming pool at high noon (classy), and playing slot machines.

No one does dopamine better than a casino. We pass it out at the front door.

My first assignment at the Bellissimo three years ago had me wearing a wig in the middle of the casino. I hadn't been (on the payroll) at a slot machine ten minutes before I was drowning in dopamine—I could hear my own heart beating—and I distinctly remember how I reacted: I wanted more. I chased my initial win all over the place to feel it again. The surprise, the thrill, the bells and whistles, the *money*—it's, all of it, spectacular.

I caught on to the dopamine program fast.

Real fast.

At times I still play slots for work, when the job calls for it, or to pass the time, because I live and work in a building with four thousand of them, or just to blow off steam and leave the world behind. I enjoy being lulled by the setting, music, the spiked hot chocolate with whipped cream, the Calgon Take Me Away Triple Jackpot. (Who am I kidding? I play for one reason—because it's so much fun to win.)

When gamblers are on winning streaks, they lose track of time, place, obligations, their kids and their keys. They don't eat, sleep, or answer the phone. Find a gambler on a roll, in the win zone, flying high on dopamine, and he can barely tell you his mother's name. Seasoned gamblers learn to take the wins with the losses, which is to say they learn to deal with the dopamine quietly. If a slot machine has blown up, an envious crowd has gathered, and it takes the floor twenty minutes to verify the player's $200,000 win, yet the winner doesn't seem to be celebrating, in fact, he looks like he wants the payout over, so everyone will leave him alone and let him get back to his game—that's a dopamine pro.

On the other hand, let a casino virgin, a brand new twenty-one-year-old, or a banker at a conference who's never won a goldfish swimming in a sandwich bag at the carnival, win $200K, and that person is on the *floor*. We call it Jackpot Party, it comes in many animated versions. It too can be seen in all four corners of the casino, and the player hosting the Jackpot Party is so full of dopamine she has only two words left in her vocabulary: "I won! I won! I *won*! I won!"

It's the rare player who takes the money and runs. Most doped up gamblers won't stop playing until they crash. The real world fades away; it's just the player, the dopamine, and the game. They will play until they're emotionally, physically, and financially exhausted, giving every penny back to the casino, and then some.

It's like my husband, Mr. Sanders, and No Hair had been telling me all week—Paragon Protection meant us no harm. They were busy harming the bankers. Why?

* * *

Fantasy can't read my mind. She had no way of knowing I needed her. In our years of working together, I couldn't remember a time either of us, any of us for that matter, completely disabled our phones. Not only did she not answer, I couldn't ping a location on her. I called Mrs. Hello Kitty's room, nothing. I called Jay Leno's place and asked for Miles and the woman who answered held the phone away and called out, "Miles? Anyone here named Miles?"

Nothing.

It was easy for Fantasy to assume, platinum secured, we had an easy day, it being Friday and all. It's her two weeks of no laundry, blah blah. I knew good and well what she was doing and she could have at least run it by me. She could have shot me an email, text, or left a message. Her going totally off the grid was something we would have a serious chat about. Given the amount of time I didn't have, I couldn't put my cyber hunting dog skills to work; I'd have to worry about her later.

"It's me and you, Baylor."

We fist bumped.

"Work your magic and get past Megan." His back pockets were full of coiled fiber optic cable and the front pockets of his jeans each held a receiver, both about the size of cell phones and loaded with fresh lithium button batteries. "You have to get in the air ducts, Baylor. Start as close to the event hall as you can. Try the rooms on either side. If they're empty, get to the air ducts there. If that doesn't work, go to the dining hall. Hop up through a vent, scoot down the ducts till you're over the event hall, then place the cameras."

"You say that like I didn't just eat forty donuts."

I patted his cheek. "You can do it." I checked my watch. "Get going."

Then I got going. The conference attendees would rally for the semifinal round of the slot tournament soon and we needed the video in place before it started. I wanted a bird's eye view of the Mint Condition slot machines. And the winners.

Baylor on his way, I stepped into Control Central and woke everyone up—Toshiba, Hewlett-Packard, and Lenovo—and got busy with a chore I would have tackled days ago had I not been keeping a cat company, in and out of central booking, hunting Magnolia, chasing Fantasy, giving my car away, trying to protect the Bellissimo's and my own better-half assets, and consulting with Bianca's gyno.

I hoped I wasn't too late.

* * *

"Hey, you."

"Wife."

I clicked across the keyboards as I returned the two calls from my husband I'd missed while stuffing Baylor's pockets with electronics.

"Are you busy?" he asked.

"So-so. Human Resources sent a stack of applicants for the Special Events Coordinator job." (True.) "They want me to run backgrounds." (Also true.) "You?"

"I need a favor."

"Anything."

I had Paragon Protection's website up on three screens.

"Richard called. This weekend is Jolie's soft opening," he said. "He and Jeremy are swamped with VIPs."

"Am I supposed to be there?" Panic shot through me. It'd be just like Bianca to schedule me to be the face of Jolie, to rub elbows with the Vegas big shots who'd flown in to see the new casino, plus Tunica's mayor, dog catcher, and Corncob Queen, then not mention it.

"No," Bradley said, "but he did say Bianca hasn't left her bedroom in two days. Would you look in on her?"

My hands slid from the keyboards to my lap. The last thing I wanted to do. "Yes," I said. "I will."

"One more thing," he said. "Did you withdraw five thousand dollars from our checking account in Louisiana on Wednesday?"

Uh-oh.

"Yes."

"Why?"

"Bail money."

Awkward silence.

"We'll talk about it later, Davis."

✳ ✳ ✳

Control Central's three computers were full of Paragon Protection, so I dug my laptop from my spy bag and said hello, then connected to the video feed from Event Hall B. I plugged into five different camera angles, one wobbly, so Baylor was still placing them. The cables were spaghetti thin with pinpoint cameras on the tips, very cool. (Amazon.) He may have seriously screwed up the car deal and let me drive around with counterfeit money, but he'd busted us out of jail, he'd shown up for work this morning, and he was doing a fine job of crawling around the air ducts, giving me an aerial view of what our valued business partner was up to.

"Baylor." Earpiece to earpiece. "Can you hear me?"

"Hold on."

He could hear me.

"Yes."

"How long have you been up there?"

"Forever."

Forever might be, on the outside, fifteen minutes.

"Is anyone in the room?"

"The guards," Baylor whispered. "But they're half asleep."

"You have every one of the cameras pointed at a blank wall or the floor," I whispered back. "Can you adjust them?"

"What do you want to see?"

"Point four of the cameras on the Mint Condition machines and the other one on the door."

"Which door?"

"There's only one set of doors."

All five feeds wiggled, giving me serious vertigo.

"Baylor. Be still."

The five feeds settled down on my laptop screen.

"I can't breathe up here," he whispered.

"You're fine."

I turned down the volume on my earpiece. The soundtrack of Baylor navigating the air duct was atrocious. "The camera you have on the door, scoot it left. More left." I don't know why I was whispering. "A little more left. Okay, zoom out."

"Can I go now?"

"In a minute."

Before I could ask him to adjust any of the other camera views, the front doors opened and Conner Hughes walked in. His three convicted criminal companions followed him into Event Hall B.

This again.

I tapped out a message on my phone: *Baylor, stop breathing. Stay where you are. Don't even blink.*

Baylor: *I think there's a mouse up here.*

Me:

Baylor: *Davis?*

Me:

Baylor: *Davis?*

One of the men in black raised an arm and made a big finger circle in the air. The guards, who knew the drill well at the end of the week, filed out. The same man pointed to a chair. Conner Hughes walked to it and collapsed. As if he was being told where to sit. As if he wasn't in charge of his team. The criminals he trusts. And doesn't make a move without.

Two of the men in black held back, one took a step in Conner Hughes's direction, placing himself between our valued business partner and the doors, while the one directing traffic toured the Mint Condition machines.

Can you point a camera at the man in the chair?

The banker man?

There are four men in the room, Baylor. How many are in chairs? Yes. The banker man.

I'd seen Conner Hughes in this very room on Tuesday when he walked in with Bradley, but at the time I hadn't paid attention, because I'd been busy dropping my phone. I'd seen him on surveillance video, but mostly his slumped shoulders. Or his knees. This was the first time I'd gotten a good look at him. Conner Hughes was one color from head to toe, a dull yellow, the color of straw. He had a thick flat nose under wide-set eyes. His sandy suit swallowed him, and he had the demeanor of a death-row inmate waiting his turn. His long yellow fingers clawed at the arms of the chair and he stared at the double doors as if he wanted to dart through them. The expression on his face mirrored the one I'd been wearing all week, that of confusion, frustration, and exhaustion.

Something about his uneasy mannerisms struck a familiar chord, but before I could put my finger on it, act two of the rigged slot machine show started.

The men in black sat down at three chosen slot machines, opened the cabinets, and dove in. With a much better view today, I could clearly see one of the techs remove, then replace, the computer chip in the machine.

Baylor: *Davis?*

Me: *Baylor, shut up and be still.*

Baylor: *I'm not talking. I'm texting.*

Me: *Shut up anyway.*

Why were they going to all this trouble? Because they assigned seats at the Mint Condition tournament, a common tournament practice. They switched out the software so the players wouldn't know the game was rigged.

If the same winners were assigned the same seats for every round of play, and kept winning, there'd be mutiny. Like Treasure Island. So they moved the winners around. To move the winners around, they had to move the winning machines around by changing the internal programming from a slot machine with a normal payout to a super payout slot machine. What was so special about the three bankers who would sit at the winning Mint Condition machines? It was the stone left unturned that I'd tripped

over all week. What was the endgame of handpicking the winners?
Dopamine.

Paragon wanted the three winning bankers' minds on this game and off everything else. Distracted. Sidetracked. Not thinking clearly. With dopamine levels through the Bellissimo roof and money, money, money, falling into their laps.

Conner Hughes wasn't part of the problem.

He was a pawn.

* * *

Minimizing the Event Hall B video feed, cloaked under the privacy of a severely scrambled IP address, I turned back to my computers and hacked Paragon Protection's website. I slipped into their internal server via a loose security patch, where I was asked to login. A bit tricky, since I didn't want to take the time to make myself a potential client and log in legitimately after they approved me and gave me a password sometime next month.

What I should do is shut down the computers, let Baylor crawl out of the ceiling, then tell my husband his valued business partner was in trouble and let him take it from there. Or I could nose around Paragon one more minute.

Click.

When I bullied past the login, I was met with millions of lines of virtually impenetrable code. I stared at it, astounded by the exceptional programming behind this website. The FBI's website wasn't nearly as secure as Paragon Protection's.

Here's where they kept the secrets; I'd better take a peek. I wiggled my fingers above the keyboard—let the magic begin—and for the next twenty minutes, I tried to get in the front door of Paragon's system, my phone going nuts the whole time.

I'd forgotten Baylor.

Him: *I'm going to pass out. I'm thirsty.*

Me: *Has the room cleared yet?*

Him: *No.*

Me: *Wait.*

Him: *How long?*

Me: *Ten more minutes, you big baby.*

Him: *I'm hot.*

Me:

Him: *Davis?*

Then Bradley.

Him: *Davis? Someone just walked into the bank and cashed a $5,000 check drawn off our personal account. Did you write it?*

Me: *Yes.*

Him: *Why?*

Me: *I bought a Cadillac.*

Him: *A $5,000 Cadillac? Where is it?*

Me: *Impound in Covington, Louisiana.*

Him: *We'll talk about this when I get home.*

Baylor: *I'm getting hungry.*

Me: *You could not possibly be hungry.*

Baylor: *I am.*

Me:

Baylor: *Davis?*

When it was obvious there was no sneaking into Paragon's website, I changed my strategy and shot my way in. I injected a rogue code in the form of SQL (Structured Query Language) (you can keep this from happening by always using parameterized queries, so hackers can't ask your system random questions and get direct answers) and asked the software for a list of conference clients.

It looked like this:

```
"SELECT * FROM table CLIENT LIST = ALABAMA
+ conference + column = LIST " OR '1'='1';"
```

Boom. It answered me with a list of Paragon's Alabama clients.

Next and last query, because alarms were surely sounding all over Paragon's system that the website had been breached:

"SELECT * FROM table MINT CONDITION WINNERS = LIST + column = LIST " OR '1'='1';"

It came back with three names. Including Cooter Platt's.

Then, as often happens during a covert cyber romp, Paragon's system caught me, locked down, and I got the blue screen of death. I had my computers set up to implode rather than give up my location or identity.

I'm hard on computers.

I still had my laptop. I turned to it and pulled up the video feed from Event Hall B, which I'd completely forgotten while I was hacking. There was no video feed. The five camera feeds Baylor had crawled through the air ducts to place had been cut. Baylor did not answer his phone. It, too, had been disconnected.

Paragon had Baylor.

TWENTY-ONE

The last thing I cared about at the moment was food. I thought of lunch only when I looked at my watch and realized I'd hacked straight through it, leaving Baylor in the ceiling. Time slips away when you're paralyzing a remote operating system. I think it flew through my brain that Baylor hadn't checked in, but I wrote it off to him falling asleep.

He'd fallen, but not asleep.

I ran.

When I made it home to the Mardi Gras Mansion, I still didn't have a new key, and it took longer for Sears to answer the door than it had for me to get there from 3B. When he did open the door, I brushed by him and saw socks—Bradley's Marcoliani cashmere socks—dangling from the fake magnolia tree.

"Hey there, Mrs. Cole?"

"Not now, Sears."

I ran down the hall, dodging stray socks, until I reached my closet, quickly changed into a boring suit, sprayed my hair mop-water brown, and ran more.

"Hey, Mrs. Cole?"

"Later, Sears."

There was activity at Jay Leno's place, but I was too busy calling the elevator—poke poke poke—to take the time to avert my eyes and possibly get a glimpse of Dionne Warwick. I wouldn't have looked down the hall to see Elvis right then.

I raced through the casino, took the escalator steps three at a time, and couldn't get past the gold furniture and to Megan with the braces fast enough, who I found bent over her phone double-tapping Instagram pictures of baby polar bears.

"Whoa!" She grabbed the sides of her gilded desk.

"I'm with the Gaming Commission." I waved my fake badge. "Let me in."

She eyed me suspiciously, recognition dawning all over her face, and she opened her mouth to argue. I didn't want to shoot this girl; I was in enough trouble. So I ignored her protests and pushed through the double doors without permission, while she objected behind me. Two Paragon guards, at their posts, snapped to attention and blocked my way. I showed them my identification. "Gaming Commission. You have my man."

They eyed each other, then me. One of them said, "Stay here."

They stepped away, turned their backs, spoke quietly, then one pulled up a shoulder and talked into his radio. Back to me.

"You can check with the casino's general manager about the man you're looking for."

They turned Baylor over to Bradley. Which was much better than shooting him. This was going to be ugly. I ran.

Calinda raised a cautionary eyebrow, then waved me in.

I couldn't catch my breath for anything.

My husband was not happy to see me. Not the least bit happy to see me.

Baylor was in a chair across from Bradley, blood everywhere, an icepack on his face. He pulled it away and smiled his goofy Baylor smile. His nose was broken and his upper lip was swollen, purple-black, and split.

"Oh God, Baylor." I reached out and grabbed something furniture to hold me upright. "I am so sorry."

"Ith's cool. Third thime."

I touched my nose. Which has been broken no times.

"I'm so very deeply profoundly sorry, Baylor."

"The falling parth was cool," he said. I took a seat on the other side of him and placed a hand on his knee, not yet making eye contact with Bradley, who hadn't said a word. He would. He just hadn't yet. "Catching a sloth machine with my fathe wasn'th cool."

"Davis."

My world stopped spinning.

"Take Baylor and both of you go home. If you would, stay there until the conference is over. Home, Davis. Stay home." His words were measured, delivered verdict style. "Go upstairs and don't leave the residence, unless you're leaving the property, until our convention guests and vendors have checked out tomorrow."

"Bradley—"

"I don't want to hear it, Davis." He stood. "Not one word." His arm shot out and he showed us the door. "Don't call me twenty times and ask if I still love you. Of course I do. But today is the last day we'll work together."

* * *

There's crying, there's talking, and then there's cry-talking. When I called my father, I was off the chart cry-talking.

"Are you home, honey? Did you go home?"

"No." I gasped for air between bawling and sobbing. "Baylor wanted a *doooooonut*. How was I supposed to say *nooooo*? I broke his *noooooooose!*"

"Honey, you need a vacation. That's all. You've been working too hard—"

"I have *noooooot*, Daddy. I haven't worked all *suuuuummer* until *nooooooooow*, and it's been the worst week of my *liiiiiiiiife*."

I reached a whole new level of hysterical communiqué, on and on about platinum and Long John Silver, and I didn't stop until Baylor yelled at me from the bullpen.

"Dathis! Thake it thown a nohth! I can'th ethen eath my donuths!"

"You have to calm down," my father said. "I don't understand what you're saying, honey. You've been out of high school a long time and I'm not good at this anymore."

I scaled it back to a hiccupy drivel.

I used my sleeves to mop my face.

"Daddy, when you fired me, you still loved me, right?"

"Of course, Davis. Of course I did. And Bradley's not going to fire you. He just needs some time." He went on to tell me I was his sunshine, his only sunshine, and he promised me Bradley would love me for the rest of my life too, no matter how many legs Baylor broke.

"His nose, Daddy. He broke his *noooooose.*"

"There you go, Sweet Pea. It's not nearly as bad as it could've been."

"You didn't see Bradley's face, Daddy."

And here I had a little relapse, but I soon regained my composure. After Baylor screamed at me again. ("Shuth uff!")

"Daddy, can we talk about Cooter for a minute?"

(Sniff sniff.)

"Cooter Platt?"

My first truly comprehensible words since I'd dialed: "How many Cooters do we know?"

"I see your point," he said. "What about Cooter?"

"He's here."

"At the Bellissimo? I knew he was out of town. I'm keeping an eye on things at the bank for him, but he never said where he was going. You know how Cooter keeps to himself. Just part of banking, Sugar. He doesn't tell his or anyone else's business."

"Well, he's here. There are five hundred independent bankers from Alabama here."

"Davis, sweetie, there aren't five hundred independent bankers *in* Alabama."

A fact, having escaped me all week, that now had my full attention. He was right. If they weren't all Alabama bankers, who were they? Daddy interrupted me forming yet another conspiracy theory—alien bankers!—my new hobby.

"Cooter's at the Bellissimo. And?"

"I'm going to ask this gently, Daddy, because I've been so

wrong all week long, but is there any chance Cooter crossed over to the dark side?"

"Did I hear you right?" my father asked.

"Something's going on, Daddy, and Cooter's in the middle of it."

"Cooter isn't mixed up in anything criminal. He's as honest as the day is long."

And these have been some very long days.

"His was one of the three names I turned up on Paragon's website," I said. "Is there anything going on at the bank? Anything unusual? Strangers? Big deposits or withdrawals?"

"I wouldn't think so, honey, because Blanche hasn't said a word. I meet her there in the morning to unlock and I go back at five to help her lock it down."

Blanche Osborne. Pine Apple Savings and Loan's bank (and secret) teller. Insufficient funds at eleven in the morning, the whole town knew by lunch.

"Blanche hasn't said a word?"

"She complains about her hips and Earl." (Earl is Blanche's third husband. Not throwing stones, just sayin'.) "That's it."

Odd that Cooter's name would be on the short list I'd found, but having known Cooter all my life, I had to agree with my father.

"Be careful at the bank anyway, Daddy. The Paragon people are up to something. The chances of it having anything to do with the Pine Apple bank are—" I hated to admit it, but I had to—"slim, but it's Friday. Payday. And just be careful, Daddy."

"You too, Punkin."

"One last thing."

"Shoot."

"What's in Horn Hill, Alabama?"

I could hear my father thinking. "Nothing."

"That's what I thought. Would you mind nosing around anyway? Just take a peek at their tax records, real estate transfers, any unusual activity."

"Why?" Daddy asked. "What are you looking for, specifically?"

"This company, Paragon, has a recently acquired facility in Horn Hill."

"I don't know what they would've acquired. There's not a thing in Horn Hill but an old sock factory, Davis. They probably don't have more than two hundred people in the whole town." He said it as if Horn Hill wasn't even a dot on the map, while Pine Apple was the hot spot of Alabama. "But I'll look. I'll let you know if I turn up anything."

"Thank you, Daddy, and my last one last thing." I was beginning to feel like my old self again, my marriage probably in no better shape than Fantasy's, but at least I'd stopped blubbering. "Does anyone in Pine Apple have anything in the bank worth stealing?"

"Now, Davis."

"I know. I know. I'm not asking you to spill anyone's secrets. I'm just looking under every rock."

"Stop worrying about rocks," he said. "I have that covered."

*　*　*

Baylor, his face, particularly around his eyes, taking on a deep red hue in broad circles that went up to his eyebrows and dipped down on his cheeks, was asleep on the sofa. I pried the chocolate frosted donut from his sugar-coated hand, dropped it in a bakery box, then stacked the three boxes and threw them away. He'd go into a sugar coma if he woke up and found the donuts in front of him again.

At our little kitchenette smashing the boxes, the coffee pot spoke to me. It said, *Give Bradley some space. Save Conner Hughes quietly, and in doing so, you just may save yourself.* Then it said, *Make coffee.*

Baylor slept, with one little outburst requesting everyone leave his turkey shoes alone. I watched the coffee drip, poured myself a cup and sipped it slowly, putting (off my next chore) a plan of action in place. I wanted to curl up on the sofa across from him and take a nap myself, because we needed to be in top form tonight. It would be the three of us against the three Paragon techs. Because with one sip of caffeine it hit me, like a slot machine to the face, exactly where I could find Fantasy. She had a date. My partner, married with three kids, had a date, and she'd be at the Dionne Warwick concert along with everyone else, including my husband. I'd nab her from the concert, and somehow, someway, the three of us would extract our valued business partner, Conner Hughes, from the three men in black. And maybe then this feeling of impending doom, this cloud of apprehension I'd had following me since Monday, would lift.

If I'm wrong again, Bradley won't have to fire me. I'll quit.

I stepped into the dressing room while Baylor napped. I ditched the Gaming Commission outfit, shampooed back to red, and dressed to sell my soul to the devil. Or Bianca, as it were.

* * *

"I need to speak to you, Mrs. Sanders." I'd been talking to her bedroom door for ten minutes. "Please let me in."

"Go away, David."

"It's Davis."

"I don't care. Go away."

The two wet black button noses of Bianca's little dogs, Gianna and Ghita (they're of Yorkshire, England descent, but with Italian influences, because Bianca is so Italian, thus the ridiculous Italian names) peeked out and sniffed at the bottom of the door. They must not have known it was me, because there was no deep-throat growling, or it was possible they were distracted by the smell of the cat.

"I really need your help, Mrs. Sanders."

"Not my problem, David. Get your tall black girl to help you."

There was something so whack-a-mole about the dog noses under the door—one, then the other, then none, then both.

"That's who I need your help with."

The door flew open so suddenly I almost fell through it.

Recovering my balance, I wondered if I might've been interrupting a photo shoot for her Victoria's Secret Shape cover. Bianca stood there, tapping a feathered foot, arms crossed, dressed in a head-to-toe mint green silk pajama set. In the middle of the afternoon. Ruffled cami over short shorts, a floor-length matching silk jacket, and kitten-heeled slippers with feather pompoms at the toes. Her blonde hair was pulled back in a low ponytail and she looked pale under her perfect makeup.

Bianca was an exquisite woman who wore that dipped-in-money demeanor like skin, and with her it wasn't an act, but who she was. I felt a teeny tug on my heartstrings that she was wasting her forties worrying about her fifties, and I felt a deep-seated fear about how all our lives would change when Bianca heard the news that Paisley would soon deliver. And just like every time I let myself feel something for her, she opened her mouth and ruined it.

"Do you not understand your job? It's to help *me*. Under what circumstances would I help you?"

I leaned on the doorframe and sighed, a bone weary end-of-my-rope sigh. This was why I didn't waste too much time feeling sorry for Bianca. I was here for three reasons: One, it was my fault she'd locked herself in the bedroom; two, I told my husband I would and Lord knows I needed a few points with him; and three, I really did need her help. With all I do for her, you'd think she'd at least hear me out. "Five minutes, Mrs. Sanders? Just five minutes?"

"What, David? What?"

I followed her in, the dogs going for my feet.

"Can we sit down?"

"I can." And she did. On a creamy white upholstered chaise lounge. "You won't be here long enough to sit."

"I need you to go to the Dionne Warwick concert."

"Completely out of the question."

"All you have to do is walk in, get Fantasy, and leave. That's it."

"Absolutely not."

"Mrs. Sanders." Uninvited, I sat down across from her and dropped my spy bag at my feet. The dogs pounced. "I can't go to the concert." My husband will surely fire me on the spot, then file for a divorce. "But you can. I know Fantasy will be there, and I need you to get her for me. Just grab her. Drag her out of there."

She rolled her eyes. "David, you have gone completely mad. I can't pick her out in a public venue. I doubt I could find her if she were standing in this room."

"She'll be in the VIP section, probably in the front row." I fumbled for my phone. "She'll be with this man."

Out of the corner of her eye, she glanced. "Why is she with Dr. Holloway?"

"No," I said. "His name is Davenport. Miles Davenport. He's with Dionne Warwick."

"That man's name is Miles Holloway," she shook her finger at my phone, "and he's a renowned physician. Why is your tall black girl with Dr. Holloway?"

Bianca had so many employees—her medical team alone could staff a five-hundred-bed hospital—and she was probably mistaken. Not that I intended to point it out and die right now before I made things right with Bradley. And both men were named Miles, which was odd. "How do you know him, Mrs. Sanders?"

"My medical records don't concern you."

Said the woman who makes me go to the gynecologist for her.

She smoothed the lapels of her silk jacket. "Obviously, I know him because he's one of my physicians."

"What kind of physician?"

Bianca lunged at me and batted her eyes. She kept doing it. (Seizure, I guess.) "He's a transplant doctor, David. He did my eyelashes."

A transplant doctor.

A transplant doctor?

"With who?"

"*Whom*, David."

"*Whom*, Mrs. Sanders."

"Johns Hopkins."

I gently shooed her dogs off my spy bag they were so

interested in—they could smell the cat—because after the day I've had, I didn't want to get bit. By Bianca. I cracked open my laptop. Click click click, Johns Hopkins. Transplants. Physicians, no. Fantasy's boyfriend's pretty mug wasn't on the roster. Surgeons, no. Psychologists, no. Pharmacists, no. Anesthesiologists, again, no.

"Are you sure, Mrs. Sanders?"

"Do not question me, David."

Davis kept looking. Miles Holloway wasn't listed as a nutritionist, a social worker, or even a nurse. The last category I checked was where I found him. Administrative staff. Bianca was correct: He was with Johns Hopkins. This man, not with Dionne Warwick at all, and certainly not a doctor, was an assistant to the secretary of the director of the organ and tissue donation, and his name was Miles Davenport. I gave him the full screen of my laptop, then turned it for Bianca.

She glanced, barely interested. "That's Dr. Holloway."

"Miles Davenport." Then I read his job title aloud.

It took a minute for her feathered feet to hit the floor. She grabbed my laptop and saw for herself. When she looked up from the screen, her face was pasty white, her eyes darting everywhere, both absorbing the information and looking for a (weapon) way to blame it on me.

"He's Long John Silver," I said, more to myself than to her. "This man, Miles. He's Long John Silver."

"What, David? *What?*"

We stared at each other, both of us stunned and trying to process the information, when my phone buzzed beside me for the hundredth time.

Texts. All texts. All from Baylor.

I got porn on my phone.

I opened it.

It was spam about my fantasies.

But it's our Fantasy.

I have four.

She's more naked in every one.

Her legs are so damn long.
She's with that man. You know. THAT man.
It starts in the coffee shop downstairs.
Then she's next door to you in the Leno suite.
She's naked in those.
It's hard to believe Fantasy really has kids. She looks good.
Here comes another one. Cool.

I stared at my phone until it rang. The caller ID said Reggie Erb. Fantasy's husband was calling.

* * *

The switchboard connected (me) Bianca to Conner Hughes's guest room. He answered on the first ring, as if he'd been waiting on my call.

"Conner, this is Davis Cole. I'm—"

"I know exactly who you are. What do you want?"

He sounded angry, irritated, and desperate.

"Where is he? Is he watching you?"

After a long silence Conner Hughes sighed, an end-of-the-world sigh. "Yes."

"Can he hear you?"

"Yes."

"Can he *see* you?"

"Yes."

"Does he know who I am?"

"Oh, yes."

(Oh, no.)

"I'm on my way," I said. "I'm coming to arrest you."

The sigh again, the finish-line sigh. "Thank you."

(I) Bianca called for gorillas with Rugers. I doubted Miles Davenport would let me knock on Conner Hughes's door and walk off with him. I needed backup. While I waited, I called Cooter Platt. I told him it was good to see him again, say hi to Pine Apple for me, and asked how much money he'd won. In a rush of words, he told me he won ten thousand dollars during the semifinal round an hour earlier, bringing his total up to twenty-five thousand cash, and he was one of the three bankers who would play for the top prize tonight. If he won the platinum it would double his winnings. He told me it was good to hear from me, but he needed to scoot. He and his dopamine were on their way to the casino to warm up for the final round of Mint Condition.

Still waiting on the gorillas, Bianca in her dressing room trying to pull out her own eyelashes, I dialed Magnolia Thibodeaux. I shared snippets of my afternoon with her.

"If you don't want to be charged in any of this, Magnolia, you'll tell me."

"I'll answer your question," she said, "and then I don't ever want to hear your name again. I mean it. I don't want to see you, I don't want to think about you, and I sure don't want you anywhere near me. Ever."

"Done."

"Holder Darby showed up here. She said there was a million dollars in it for me if Ty would write a letter to the governor and get that crook Christopher Hall out of prison before he died. I wrote the letter and I still don't have my million dollars. Do you know where my million dollars is?"

I sure do. It's at the St. Tammary Parish Sherriff's office.

Bianca's butler, a man I'd never seen in my life, showed the gorillas in. I stepped into Bianca's dressing room to tell her I was leaving, and walked in on her tugging her extra seven pounds into black leggings and a sleeveless black silk tunic.

"David. Give me a gun."

*　*　*

I made a big show of pounding on the door of guest suite 2632. "Open up, Hughes." Two gorillas and their Rugers covered me.

Conner Hughes threw open the door. "What's all this about?" His fists shot out. *Cuff me, please.* "This is outrageous!" He feigned indignation and at the same time, gave a slight nod to the door across the hall. Guest suite 2631.

When we turned the corner for the elevators, he fell against a wall. "Lock me up. Throw me under the jail. For God's sake get me away from him and out of here."

I swept out an arm, after you, Mr. Hughes. When the elevator doors closed, I said, "We need to talk first."

One gorilla stayed back and out of sight with an eye on the door of room 2631. The other gorilla escorted us to the basement level, where we took the back roads and alleyways to the secure holding cells below the casino.

"Have you eaten?" We took seats across from each other in an interrogation room.

"I haven't eaten," he said, "because I can't eat. I can't eat; I can't sleep; I can't breathe."

I called Plates, the family-style restaurant in the casino, and ordered the house special—a bowl of white bean and ham soup beside an overflowing platter of fried chicken tenderloins, slaw, green beans, copper-penny carrots, mashed potatoes and gravy, buttered cornbread, with chocolate cake for dessert, plus his-and-hers pots of coffee.

He ate every crumb while I sat across from him with my laptop, delving deep into public records, going as far as the World Wide Web would let me, gathering information about Miles Davenport. Every few minutes I jotted a note, and every few minutes Conner Hughes groaned.

He'd licked his dishes clean at the same time I'd seen enough. I closed my computer. "Conner, I need to hear the story. The whole story, from the beginning." His eyes kept darting to the door where he could see the gorilla's back through the glass pane. "You're safe here," I said. "He can't get to you."

"You don't know this man," Conner said. "You have no idea who you're dealing with."

TWENTY-TWO

On a cold January night in 1915, Gilda Goddard gave birth to twin sons, Henry and Charlie, weighing in, according to the chicken scale, at just under four pounds each. The whole time her husband Mercy, in the next room, whose shift started at sunup, wished his wife would pipe down. The town obstetrician, Dr. Lawrence, buttoned his heavy overcoat and said, "Fine looking boys you have there, Mercy. They were in a hurry. Those boys will go places."

The Goddard's lived in one of the seven hundred cookie-cutter homes that made up Horn Hill, Alabama, built by Horn Hill's only employer, Alabama Coal & Iron. Rent was $8.05 a month, deducted in equal parts through the month from the miners' cash paydays on Fridays at noon, a penny extra on the last Friday of the month. Two months out of the year, because of how things fell on the calendar, no rent was deducted on the last Friday of the month. It was called Fifth Friday and the townspeople partied.

Other features of the lively town of 3,200 at the time of Henry and Charlie's birth: a company store, churches, parks, theaters, a medical clinic and schools, all built by Alabama Coal & Iron.

The twins were born into one of Alabama's most bustling industrial towns and they died within weeks of each other eighty-seven years later in the same town. Horn Hill population, recorded by the U.S. Census Bureau, at the time of their deaths was one hundred and eighteen. But no one believed it, unless the count included stray dogs.

Henry and Charlie, in their late teens, married sisters and

went on to produce, between them, seven children, including Henry Jr., the first Goddard to graduate from college with a degree in geology, and Little Charlie, who went into the textile business, and single-handedly saved Horn Hill when he put the town's out-of-work coal miners back to work in his yarn and finishing factory. Horn Hill made a quick transition from coal to socks. Things were looking up in the '40s and booming in the '50s, but Japan jumped into the sock business and Goddard's Textiles boarded up in 1959, owing the United States government more than a million dollars in back taxes. That was the last of Horn Hill.

Around the same time, Henry Jr., a science teacher at Horn Hill High, to take a break from the menstrual synchrony between his wife and three daughters that was driving him crazy, signed on for a year-long exploration dig looking for nickel and chromium in central Montana. Henry Jr. and sixteen other modern-day prospectors set up camp along the Smith River, a tributary of the Missouri running through central Montana. After six weeks, Henry Jr. received word from home that Goddard's Textiles, in spite of all of Horn Hill's and Little Charlie's efforts, had closed its doors. Horn Hill's population was splitting in half daily, the residents fleeing for (food) work.

At the end of six weeks, it was obvious to Henry Jr. and his fellow geologists there was neither nickel nor chromium in central Montana. They'd found a little copper and a lot of marijuana, but no metals. They kept looking, because if they threw in the towel, their next exploratory gig would be hard to come by, not to mention they'd all lose their grant opportunities and tenured jobs at the various universities and energy companies they represented. So they dug in to wait it out.

At the end of six months, the geologists were starved for female affections, stoned out of their minds, and expert fly fishermen. The whole time, Henry Jr., who had no use for funny cigarettes or fish, worked the exploratory grid alone.

At the end of the year when the team gave up, packed up, and returned home to shave their beards and resume life with running water, Henry Jr.'s trunks were loaded down with what he thought was silver.

Back in Horn Hill, he took to his basement lab and found that the rocks he'd lugged home weren't silver at all. They landed on number seventy-eight of the atomic scale. While the others had been getting high and perfecting their overhead casts, Henry had quietly stumbled upon what would, thirty years later, be named the world's richest known deposit of platinum.

He locked the front door, pulled the living room curtains, and sat down his three teenage daughters. He passed out the platinum and gave them this advice: "Do not marry a dreamer like your daddy, because you'll always be hungry. Do not marry an industrialist like your Uncle Charlie, because you'll always be looking over your shoulder. The only thing I can think of that will give you girls a comfortable life and a good night's sleep is money. Marry bankers."

And they did. The girls packed up their daddy's advice and their raw-platinum dowries and moved to Wilcox, Morgan, and Blount counties, where the men they married established financial institutions in the small Alabama cities of Pine Apple, Pumpkin Center, and Susan Moore. All three families still owned the small banks and all three banks still held the pure raw platinum—the size of a dinner plate, the weight of a grown man, with a combined street value upwards of twenty million dollars—in their vaults.

Aside from trusted family members and a combined handful of local law enforcement officials, the only other people who knew the platinum existed in the small Alabama banks were the few people left from Horn Hill who were old enough to remember, including Holder Darby, and the president of the company who built the vault drawers still containing the precious metals. The man sitting across from me. Conner Hughes.

"Do you know what a perfect storm is?" he asked.

"In meteorological terms?"

"In general." Conner Hughes's eyes were bloodshot and bleary. "Miles Davenport was in the right place at the right time to learn of me, Paragon Protection, and this conference on the same day Holder Darby received devastating personal news. All three events. At the same time."

"And this created a perfect storm?"

"We're living it," he said. "We're in the middle of a perfect storm."

Yes, we are.

"Who approached you first, Conner?"

"She did. Holder Darby. In her office." He pointed skyward in the general direction of the executive offices. "I was here to sign the final paperwork on the conference when she broke the news."

"So she'd already offered you up to Miles Davenport?"

"Me, you, some crazy bat in New Orleans, your husband," Conner said, "three Alabama banks, and the black girl."

Fantasy.

"Holder Darby shoved him straight down all our throats."

"What did she say would happen if you didn't cooperate?" I asked.

"She said they'd go after my biggest client."

"In what capacity?"

"Miles Davenport would wipe them out."

"Their vault?"

"The bank, the vault, everything," he said. "It was my choice. Contain it to this week, this conference, your little vault and three insignificant Alabama banks, or help them rob First American in downtown Chicago."

"Why?" My hands were in the air. "*Why?*"

"For a liver."

*   *   *

Miles W. Davenport, MD, had his medical license yanked by the Maryland Board of Physicians when two of his post-op kidney transplant patients died after he switched the donor kidneys, giving Patient A Patient B's kidney and Patient B Patient A's kidney, and didn't even know it, because fifteen minutes after he changed out of his scrubs, he was backing his Jaguar out of his reserved parking space. Post-op was for interns. They located him that night, floating around Lake Montebello on his fifty-foot Bruckmann yacht with three hookers and a blood alcohol level of .14.

After the trial, and as part of his malpractice and gross negligence plea bargain with the state, he was admitted to the Rosewood Center, formerly the Asylum and Training School for the Feeble-Minded, in Ownings Mills, Maryland, where he lived for the next three years being treated for alcoholism, prescription drug abuse, depression, antisocial personality and obsessive-compulsive disorders.

When he was released from Rosewood, he moved back to Baltimore to serve out the next five years of his sentence, fetching lunch and dry cleaning for the doctors who made up the Comprehensive Transplant Team at Johns Hopkins Bayview Medical Center. His job paid minimum wage, barely covered the rent on his efficiency apartment, and was all the way around humiliating.

Dr. Randal Holloway, who would bank a hundred thousand cash to transplant some crazy Southern casino woman's eyelashes, plus get a badly-needed week off, sent the office errand boy Miles Davenport to the Bellissimo Resort and Casino in Biloxi, Mississippi on a pre-op fact-finding mission, where Holder Darby, who was to escort the crazy Southern casino woman's organ transplant representative, met him at the front door. Because Holder needed an organ transplant. For Christopher Hall. And she was willing to do whatever it took.

"What did she offer him?" I asked.

"I don't know exactly how it went down," Conner Hughes said, "and I don't even care, but his first payday was when she arranged for him to do the eyelash surgery. They used that money to set up everything else. In exchange for the liver transplant, she agreed to help him rob the Bellissimo vault."

"Which is where you came in."

"Exactly. Lucky me. I had to show him how to rob the vault."

"I've been waiting for the vault to be robbed all week, Conner."

"Oh, I know." He drummed his fingers on the table. "We all know. You're lucky he hasn't killed you *and* your husband. You'll be very lucky if your friend makes it out of this with her life." I felt a jolt of electricity course through my body.

"Keep talking," I said. "I need to know everything. When will he attempt to breach the vault again? Tonight?"

"Oh, no," he said, "they've given up on the vault. They had to call off the first attempt because your husband had emptied it. They regrouped. The plan was to hold a gun to your husband's head and have him hand over the contents, but when they got him in the vault alone *you* showed up. And all hell broke loose." He leaned across the table. "Do you have any idea how much trouble you've caused?" he asked. "Do you have *any* idea?"

I've heard one or another version of these particular words my whole life. It got old.

"Who is *they*?" I asked. "The techs who work for you?"

"They don't work for Paragon." He was quick to correct me. "Those thugs are straight out of prison. They're Davenport's men." He ran a hand through his thick gold mane of hair. "But all they have left now is my money and the platinum in the Alabama banks."

"Your money?"

"Mint Condition. I supplied the money for the game."

"And he plans on walking off with it? How? And when?" I began gathering my things.

"Tonight. As soon as the tournament is over, when everyone in this building, including him, is at the Dionne Warwick concert and while his crew is robbing the Alabama banks."

"How is his crew going to be here to empty the machines and hit three Alabama banks at the same time?"

"*I'm* supposed to empty the machines." He reached into his pocket and pulled out a lone key. It was short, squat, silver, and it opened slot machines. "And deliver the money to his room."

I held my hand out, then wrapped it around the key he placed in the middle of my palm.

"You have me," Conner shrugged, "so all he has left are the banks."

"Write them down, the banks." I pushed a sheet of paper and a pen. He scribbled, then pushed back. *Pumpkin Center, Susan Moore, Pine Apple.*

My father.

"How?"

"The black woman. Your friend. She's breaking into the banks."

While we talked, messages had stacked up on my phone.

From No Hair: There'd been some kind of a hellacious mix-up. The Bellissimo had Josh Groban, who was supposed to headline at Jolie tonight, and the Jolie had Dionne Warwick, who was supposed to be here.

From Sears: Something is going on with the cat. It dragged a pair of Mr. Cole's dress pants to the tree in the foyer. If it were him, he'd call a veterinarian.

From Baylor: His nose started bleeding again and he called Dr. Paisley. She's here and making him hang his head off the sofa, she needs to talk to me, and he thinks he might sneeze.

From Fantasy's husband: What the hell is going on? He has received two pictures of his wife, one at five, another at six, neither one of which he thinks very highly of, and she's not answering her phone.

From my father: Activity in Horn Hill, check. Six weeks of construction on the interior of one of the abandoned sock warehouses and, judging by what shipped in, all from one company, MedQuip, which sold nothing but medical equipment. It looked like someone built a small hospital inside a ramshackle warehouse.

And from my husband: Help.

His was the only message I responded to: *On the way.*

When I looked up from my phone, Conner Hughes was staring

at me, beads of sweat on his brow, his breath coming and going in a thin pant, and he'd run his hands through his hair so many times it was somewhere between spiked, wrecked, and ready to jump off his head.

I sat on the edge of my seat, ready to leave this room. "Why didn't you tell us, Conner? We would have helped you."

"If I'd breathed a word," he looked me dead in the eye, "I promise you we'd all be dead."

The clock ticked, the hands lined up, it was six, straight up and down.

"I have one more question." My hand on the doorknob.

The weary man looked up.

"What's he got on you?"

"He has my cat."

TWENTY-THREE

In all my years of working on the right side of the law, seven as a police officer in Pine Apple and now more than three at the Bellissimo as a Super Secret Spy, I'd never come across a Miles Davenport, a master criminal, a man who had, right under my nose, used his strengths and others' weaknesses to orchestrate a con so elaborate—his tentacles reaching and wrapping around Holder Darby, Christopher Hall, Conner Hughes, Magnolia Thibodeaux, three unsuspecting small town Alabama banks, the Bellissimo, and my best friend—I felt (totally alone, with No Hair in Tunica, Baylor's face smashed in, and Fantasy in his grips) helpless to stop this runaway train. He'd had months to put it together; I had mere hours to take it apart. My only hope was to play the game the way he played it and find some faith.

When you do what I do, faith is something that can slip through your fingers: faith in the system, faith in justice, faith in people. When you see enough, you give up. When you see too much, you start worrying. When you think you've seen it all, a point I'd reached without knowing it, you freeze your life and the lives of those closest to you. You think even the mailman is out to hurt your husband. You think your father, who taught you everything you know, can't handle a simple bank robbery without you. You think your partner, a strong, brave, fearless woman, can't dig out of the ditch she threw herself into. You think you can't bring a child into this cruel broken world, because it's safer for the child to stay a dream than become a vulnerable reality. I'd lost my faith. It was time to find it.

* * *

I ran past Calinda.

He met me halfway between his desk and the door and I caved. We stayed there as long as we could. Three seconds. We sat across from each other in armless brown chairs, our knees touching, both of us wide-eyed, shocked by the events of the past two hours and panicked about what might happen in the next two.

"Where's Conner Hughes?"

"He's downstairs in one of the holding rooms, across from the drunk tank."

Bradley nodded.

"Where's Miles Davenport?"

"He's still in his suite unless he jumped out the window."

Bradley studied the carpet.

"Where is Bianca?" he asked.

"She's upstairs having an ophthalmologist cut off her eyelashes."

"Please tell me you're kidding."

"I wish."

Bradley pushed his sleeve cuff back and checked the time. "What's our next move?"

"My next move is Christopher Hall."

"And he's where?"

"Horn Hill."

I watched him think. We had to have Christopher Hall. And it was almost certain we'd find Holder Darby with him. We needed her too.

"How far is it?"

"In the Sikorsky, thirty-eight minutes," I said. "If I drive like a bat out of hell, it's three hours."

"Then the banks," Bradley said.

"Yes. They'll start hitting the banks as soon as it's dark, while we're supposed to be at the Mint Condition finals and the concert."

"So you plan to go to Pine Apple after Horn Hill?"

Without thinking, I raised my hand to my heart. "No, Bradley. I can't be in four places at once." I swallowed. Hard. "Daddy can handle it."

"How do you *know* it will be Pine Apple first?"

"Because he's OCD. He'll go in alphabetical order."

Bradley shook the information into his head.

"We'll take the helicopter." He summoned it with one text.

"You can't leave, Bradley."

"I won't let you go alone, Davis."

I opened my spy bag and only hesitated a little when I passed my husband a Remington 1911R1 Carry Commander and two extra magazines. He tucked the gun at his back and dropped the mags in the inside pocket of his jacket.

"Are you good, Bradley?" I grew up with guns. For me, carrying a gun was no different than carrying a purse.

"Davis," he said. "Have a little faith."

We took the private elevator behind Bradley's office to the roof where the helicopter was waiting and roaring. The second I stepped out, it tried to blow my clothes off. Bradley shielded his face with a hand against the prop blast and stepped in front of me to block it. I burrowed into him and raised my voice to tell my father that Fantasy was on her way to rob the Pine Apple Savings and Loan vault. "She's only after one thing, Daddy," I yelled. "The platinum. And she'll be there at exactly eight o'clock. She'll have muscle with her, so use your best judgment. Don't try to stop her, but somehow get a message to her that we'll be waiting for her at midnight at the First Bank of Susan Moore."

*　*　*

The Sikorsky is the delivery van of the Bellissimo fleet, used for short runs to pick up bluefin tuna, cuddlefish, and squid hitting New Orleans ports, and this for a resort already on the Gulf. Fresh seafood isn't good enough, go figure. (Sushi changed the whole world. And not necessarily for the better.) The helicopter had twin turbine engines, four-bladed main and tail rotors, leather seating for eight, and Sirius XM. It's sleek, black, and quiet after the doors close, but once you're locked in, it has a little bit of a fishy smell. Or maybe I imagined it. I sat in the copilot seat so I could use the radio. The cockpit dash looked like Christmas on Mars.

Up, up, and away.

It was a clear night, not a cloud on the weather radar or in the sky, and the pilot, Dewey, wearing a navy blue flight suit with Bellissimo Whirlybirds embroidered above his name, grinned from ear to ear and welcomed us aboard. He showed me how to switch the radio from navigation to communication. It was all so Buzz Lightyear.

The closest hospital was Andalusia Regional, fifteen miles from Horn Hill, and I radioed Andalusia Emergency Services first. The switchboard and I repeated the same lines several times.

"Yes, a liver transplant."

"In Horn Hill."

"*Yes!*"

"In a warehouse."

"*Yes!*"

She put me on hold and a man picked up. "This is Dr. Ingram."

I went through it again. Same questions.

"Is the surgical team with him?"

"I have no idea."

"Is someone monitoring his fluids, electrolytes, and kidney function?"

"I really don't know."

"Okay." This doctor had about had it with me. "What are the results of his last LFT?"

"What's an LFT?"

"Lady," Dr. Ingram said, "really. You say you have a transplant patient in the middle of nowhere, in a warehouse, and that's truly all you know?"

"Correct."

"I'll put a team together and meet you there, but I want you to know if I had so much as a kid with a bee sting in the emergency room right now, I'd hang up on you and try to forget you called." Beside me, Dewey the Whirlybird pilot, with the bearing of a man behind the wheel of his Roadster on a Sunday afternoon drive through the countryside, casually glanced across the colorful cockpit dash, checking this and that—altimeters, transponders, the Dow. All he needed was a driving cap, a cocktail, and a wicker picnic basket.

"You can't bust in, Dr. Ingram. It's a volatile situation," I said to the radio. "You have to wait on my team."

"When does 'your team' arrive?"

I looked at Dewey, chewing a toothpick and humming. "ETA twenty-two minutes."

"I heard him," Dr. Ingram said. "One more question. Do you know if the patient is on immunosuppressives?"

"I don't even know what immunosuppressives are."

"Do you even know which warehouse?" he asked. "There are four buildings in Horn Hill. One factory, three warehouses."

"Look for signs of recent traffic, activity, lights," I said. "I've truly told you all I know."

My next radio shout out was to Emergency Services of Covington County. I had as much credibility with them as I had with the good doctor. Same questions.

"A liver transplant?"

"Yes."

"In a warehouse?"

"Yes."

"In Horn Hill."

"Yes."

"Ma'am, you do know that filing a false report is at best a misdemeanor and at worst a federal offense."

"I'm well aware." My cell phone was in my lap. At the altitude we were flying—we were probably grazing treetops—I still had good cell service. It was six minutes after seven. I twisted in my seat to give Bradley a glance, who looked up from his phone and shook his head. Reggie hadn't contacted me or Bradley and we could only assume that meant he hadn't received a seven o'clock picture of his wife with her long legs in the air. Taking it from there, we could only assume Fantasy was cooperating.

"We'll meet you at the junction of Eighty-four and Three thirty-one," the man said, "and be ready to go to jail if we don't find a guy with a new liver in a warehouse."

No, thank you. I'd had enough of that this week.

"Ask him where I can put down." (Dewey the jaunty Whirlybird pilot.)

The Covington County dispatcher heard him. "Anywhere," he said. "It's no-man's land. Wide open."

Dewey sat it down seven minutes later in an empty field. Several cars were waiting, and by the time we'd untangled ourselves and stepped onto solid ground, the slicing blades above our heads slowing and quieting, patrol cars from Opp, Gnatt, Babbie, and Onycha had arrived.

Who named Alabama? Really, who came up with all this? It's embarrassing.

The officer in charge quickstepped to meet us, two deputies on his heels, the rest standing back and admiring the Sikorsky. The front man took a look at us—big burly pilot wearing a uniform, six-foot-tall two-hundred pound blonde man in a power suit, and me, all of five-foot-two, red hair pulled back in a ponytail, jeans, white t-shirt, red flip-flops, pink toenails—and asked who was in charge. I raised my hand.

"You're kidding, right?"

Bradley whipped out his business card and we were awarded instant credibility.

"What's going on?" Front Man asked.

I started with the SparkNotes, but boggled his brain at the eyelash transplant. He held up a stop sign. "Okay," he said. "That'll do."

The medical team, Front Man said, was on the other side of Horn Hill.

"How far?" I asked.

He turned and pointed. "Over that hill. You've never been to Alabama, have you?"

"I have," I said. "Yes, I have."

We caravanned to the collection of dilapidated warehouses, the ambulance and a white SUV bringing up the rear. We approached from the south, and went dark when we got within shooting distance. We had the cover of late dusk, a clear sky, and a rising crescent moon to sneak in by. Front Man put it in park, pulled night vision binoculars from his console of goodies, his crackling service radio the only noise in the car other than Bradley shuffling in the back seat of a police car, a place he didn't know well and I knew too well, when Front Man said, "There." The warehouses formed a sloppy U at the end of a road paved by the Romans. "We've got something." He pointed to the left of side by side buildings; both looked about thirty feet tall with close to two hundred thousand square feet of interior space.

"Looks like three levels in the building, and there's infrared coming from the second level."

"How many people?" I asked.

The binoculars fell to his lap and he turned to me. "Lady. We're a thousand yards away. I can't really take a headcount." Front Man's arm shot out of the driver window, and he issued hand-signal orders I couldn't see. We crept closer. I glanced in the rearview mirror to see every vehicle in the caravan behind us riding their brakes, glowing red, red, red. We looked like Amsterdam sneaking up on Armageddon. When we were within a few hundred yards of a receiving bay, Front Man's arm shot out the window again and the patrol cars behind us spread out. He turned to me. "Ready?"

I was locked and loaded.

Every single bit of me wanted to ask Bradley to stay in the car.

The grounds surrounding the building were spotty islands of pavement in wide cracked chunks, loose gravel, and weeds up to my knees. The area was littered with broken glass, trash, and saber tooth tigers. (Probably.) Night fell around us as we breached the building from the four original entrances and three unoriginal gaps in the metal siding large enough to drive cars through. We stepped into the pitch black interior.

I could barely hear the buzz of a distant generator over the blood rushing through my temples and roaring in my ears. We moved through the building stealthily, silently, communicating with head jerks and hand signals, and this, from a collection of rural Alabama cops whose biggest busts this year had no doubt been expired tags and teenagers drinking Jungle Juice.

As my eyes adjusted, I saw rusty factory equipment, weed gardens decorating them at intervals. We were coming from all directions of the building, our mutual destination a stairway made of steel in the middle of the room. Corrosion had eaten through the grate in places large enough for me to fall through and several rusted steps were completely gone.

We reached the top of the stairs and flanked the door, all guns drawn. Front Man checked for booby traps and didn't find any. We went in on Front Man's finger count, and once in, bumped into each other staring at the surreal scene in front of us. It was exactly what I expected and the shock of seeing something so totally unexpected took my breath away.

A ten by twelve sterile surgical suite covered with industrial plastic had been dropped into this ravaged building. Large generators on both sides gave it a glow and operated the ventilation system, a series of overhead cylinders wrapped in silver insulation that snaked to an exterior wall.

Front Man and I looked at each other curiously, as, clearly, the occupants of the room had to know we were there, yet there was no movement, aggressive or otherwise, inside the plastic clinic. He and I inched forward, found the break in the plastic and pushed through.

I found Holder Darby.

She was stretched out in the hospital bed beside Christopher Hall, who had a white sheet pulled up to his chin. His face was the color of a storm sky, his black lips parted, one eye open, one eye closed.

Front Man hit his radio. "I've got a four-one-nine in Horn Hill."

"What's that?" My husband whispered.

I stood on my tiptoes to get to his ear. "A corpse."

Holder Darby scanned the intruding faces and found mine. "You."

TWENTY-FOUR

Holder Darby was cuffed to the gurney in the back of the ambulance on her way to Andalusia Regional Hospital. I climbed in the back and sat on the EMT bench. She stared at me for a long minute, then turned the other way.

"I'm sorry for your loss, Holder."

She spoke to a defibrillator. "You have no idea."

"I do, Holder. I love my husband very much. I never want to lose him."

She turned back to look at me, her dark hair matted, her gray eyes dead, her pale lips dry and cracked. "I want you to know it was worth it to me to have the opportunity to say goodbye to him."

At the expense of so many.

The activity beyond the ambulance was more action than Horn Hill had seen in a long time and the town (of four) had gathered to watch. Bradley, standing with Front Man, raised his arms above his head and tapped his watch. I nodded.

"Holder," I said, "after you're released from the hospital, you'll return to Biloxi."

She heard me.

"Does he know?" she asked.

"Does who know what?"

"Does Miles Davenport know?"

"What?" I asked. "Does he know what?"

"That you caught him."

"I haven't caught him." Voices from outside the ambulance filtered in. "Does he know what's happened here?"

"I'm sure he does," she said. "He let it happen. He never

showed. He never intended to. This whole time. There was never a liver." She stopped. "What day is it?"

"It's Friday. Night."

"He was supposed to be here Wednesday. Or another day. I don't remember." She blocked the ambulance's interior lights from her eyes with a shaking hand; she couldn't piece it together and she didn't want to. "Is Conner Hughes still alive?"

"Yes. We have him."

"Is his cat still alive?"

"I think so." I hope so.

"What will they do with Christopher? Where is he now? Where will they take him?"

"He'll be with you." Which wasn't a lie; his body was being transported to Andalusia Medical, the closest hospital, and where she was headed. The news gave her some relief and me a window. A window I needed to jump through quickly. "Holder, did Christopher tell you where the money is in my house?"

"Money?"

"Yes. I think there's money hidden in my house."

"There is." Her head rocked against the pillow. "But Christopher didn't know where. There's platinum in there somewhere too."

"I found it."

"Ty hid the money and the platinum years ago. Before he lost his mind. I told Magnolia about it just to lure her in, and from that moment on, she's done nothing but try to get it out of him. And he's gone," her voice shook, "everyone's gone." She stared straight through me. "Good luck."

"You too, Holder."

She turned back to the defibrillator.

I ran into Dr. Ingram, as in full body slam, when I rounded the corner of the ambulance. "Put her on suicide watch." He gave me a two-finger salute.

On my way across the parking lot to my husband, I called Lady Man Helen Baldwin. I woke her up.

"Are you calling about that damn cat again?"
"Your sister is in the hospital in Andalusia, Alabama, Helen. Maybe you could get there."

* * *

Front Man flipped his head bar and siren; Bradley and I were back at the Sikorsky in four minutes. It was eight twenty. Bradley read messages on his phone while I stared at mine, willing my father to call. Fantasy and crew had to be in a hurry. Miles Davenport would want the robberies to take place on the hour, every two hours, and the thieves had to cover more than two hundred miles between Pine Apple and Pumpkin Center between robberies one and two. They'd had enough time to get in and out of Pine Apple. Daddy should have called.

"Hey-ho!" So many teeth on Dewey the Whirlybird pilot, or, so many teeth on He of Jolly Countenance in the Face of Death, Destruction, and Mayhem. "Who's ready for a night ride?"

Bradley made good use of the headrest. His lips were pressed together, his hands clenched in fists. He opened his eyes when I buckled up beside him. We talked and we didn't. It would take time for us to shake off Horn Hill, Alabama.

I dialed No Hair as we shot straight up from the ground.

"Whee!" (Dewey.)

"Davis," No Hair said. "I'm leaving now. I'll be at the Bellissimo in thirty-five minutes."

Thank God. I could handle Fantasy and the Alabama banks while No Hair took care of Miles Davenport and the Bellissimo. I told Bradley No Hair was on the way.

"Did you fill him in?"

"Go ahead." Then I closed my eyes.

The silence woke me up. That and our tour guide.

"Ladies and gentlemen," he twisted in his seat, "I'd like to welcome you to Absolutely Nowhere, Alabama." I woke to see (my husband) (unbelievable) we were hiding a nine-million-dollar helicopter behind a Walmart in Susan Moore, Alabama, a half mile south of First Bank. To my right, four sets of Alabama State Trooper headlights flashed a welcome. I grabbed for my phone to see I'd missed the call from my father.

"I talked to him, Davis. He's fine."

"Why'd you let me fall asleep?"

He tugged a lock of my hair.

* * *

The Walmart was of the Neighborhood Market variety: no tires, fine jewelry, or above-ground swimming pools filled to the brim with ninety-nine cent DVDs. One of the troopers called the manager, who walked over—the man lived two doors away from a Walmart—and let us in. We set up camp in canned goods. I stepped over to produce and called my father.

"Did I wake you, Daddy?"

"No, Sweet Pea." I was looking at sweet peas. "I'm still at the bank. We've got a mess here."

"How did she get in?"

"She popped the back door like she was cracking an egg. She blew the vault door with C-four, then she dripped nitroglycerin on the drawer holding the platinum."

"Damn."

"She's good," Daddy said.

"How many of them are there?"

"Four. Fantasy and three men. One kept a gun on her, the other two carried the platinum. They're in a black Chevrolet van. It's all on your phone. Photos, tag numbers, and a short clip of her I pulled off the bank video."

"How long were they there?"

"In and out in seven minutes."

"Did you get a message to her?"

"I left one in the vault drawer."

My heart stopped beating. "Daddy, if they saw a message you left for Fantasy, they'll kill her."

"Davis. Have a little faith. I put a strawberry in the vault drawer."

I was looking at strawberries.

The video on my phone showed a spherical interpretation of my best friend and partner, nose first, as she walked up to the black dot of the small vault's security camera and whispered, "There'll be a new millionaire at midnight," before she sprayed the lens black. The video ended with Fantasy being advised to shut up. I didn't see it and no one said it, but I know what it sounds like when someone takes a gut punch.

"What does that mean?" Bradley asked.

"I have no idea."

The radio beeped twice signaling Bellissimo air traffic chatter, confirming Mrs. Sanders was scheduled to depart from Million Air at midnight. Destination, BHM East, Atlantic Aviation, a private airstrip in Birmingham, Alabama. No additional flight plans had been filed.

"That's not right," Bradley said.

No, it's not. Bianca isn't going anywhere at midnight, and that's when I understood Fantasy's message. Miles Davenport would be the millionaire at midnight; he planned on leaving from Million Air airport at midnight. It was his exit strategy. His escape route was one of our airplanes. I had Dewey radio in and ask who'd booked the flight. The answer came back ambiguous: a man who identified himself as one of Mrs. Sanders's many butlers.

Surely to God Miles Davenport didn't plan on leaving the Bellissimo with Bianca Sanders.

I dialed the Bellissimo switchboard and asked the operator to connect me with the drunk tank supervisor, who put me through to Conner Hughes. "Does his plan include Bianca Sanders, Conner?"

"Who?" he asked. "The owner's wife? No. Her name hasn't come up once since the eyelashes."

Good Lord, Bianca's eyelashes.

Bradley was on his phone. He looked at me. "Found her."

I nodded. Bianca was safe. For now. "Where's the one place in the Bellissimo someone would be safe from him, Conner, other than where you are?"

"Where you live," he said. "The New Orleans place. He's superstitious. He hates where you live."

I texted No Hair: *The second you get there, find Bianca and get her to my place. Make her stay there.*

Right back: *10-4.*

*   *   *

While I'd napped across central Alabama, at ten on the nose, the Mint Condition slot machine tournament ended with three top-prize winners. McKenzie Martel from Susan Moore, Alabama, won $100,000 in cash and platinum. Cooter Platt from Pine Apple, Alabama, won $100,000 in cash and platinum. And Glendora Strand from Pumpkin Center, Alabama, won $100,000 in cash and platinum just as her bank, Third Bank of Bama in Pumpkin Center, was robbed. No cash was taken, just a slab of raw platinum. Badges from Five Points, Neel, Basham, and Speake (yes, all Alabama towns, humiliating) stood down as the black van cut through the night traveling east, and the only variation from the Pine Apple leg of the sting was this time one of the guns stayed with the van. In and out in sixteen minutes, with eighty miles of Alabama back roads to get to Susan Moore for the third and final heist.

After successfully knocking off the second bank, Miles Davenport, from his Bellissimo command center in room 2631, took a breath and called room service. Exactly the break we needed. He ordered a club sandwich on whole wheat, no bacon no mayo, two bottles of mineral water, and a seasonal fruit plate, hold the banana bread, and four bottles of Cristal Brut champagne. Chilled.

Counting his chickens.

No Hair, pushing a room service delivery cart, knuckled the door. "Room service."

"Leave it."

Ten minutes later, Miles Davenport pulled in the cart, checking the hall, right and left. The dime-sized camera, nestled between cut flowers in a square glass vase behind the club sandwich, gave us a perfect right-angle view of a wall and a slice of the closet door, but least we had audio.

No Hair heard him speak to the driver of the black getaway van, just as the van containing three men, two slabs of platinum, and one Fantasy, passed us on State Highway 75 on their way to Susan Moore. No Hair listened and relayed the Miles end of the conversation confirming the van's approach to First Bank, going over the exact timing of it all again and again.

Miles Davenport wanted the Chevy van driven onto the tarmac of Atlantic Aviation in Birmingham, the platinum transferred to his airplane, then the van was to be stashed in long-term parking. On his timeline. Drive to the airplane at exactly twelve forty-five. Exactly. Twelve forty-five or your head on a stick. Twelve forty-five. Have the van parked by one. One o'clock. Exactly. Wait with the van. Be with the van in the parking lot at one o'clock. When he'd repeated the instructions three hundred times, he briefly went over the First Bank exit strategy again, which is where we came in.

Two troopers stayed out of sight, but within a stone's throw of the bank. At the stroke of midnight, Fantasy breezed through the back door at First Bank of Susan Moore, like kicking open a gate, and twelve minutes later, the dozens of radios around me, five miles south, crackled. "Coming your way."

If we hadn't known they were carrying explosives, we'd have set up a simple road block. Since we knew they were, and none of us were in the mood to blow up, we set me up in a curve across both lanes of Alabama 75. I stood in front of a '97 gunmetal gray Subaru Outback Sport with a very flat tire. No shoulder and a reflective guardrail on one side of the curve, with a sharp drop-off on the other. Help thy neighbor aside, they couldn't get around me. I was ready to jump over the guardrail if they chose to knock the Subaru out of the way and keep going, but it was doubtful, as they probably weren't in much of a mood to blow up either. If, by some chance, they did get past me, we were waiting around the next curve with plan B. B is for Barricade.

My husband, standing back with the officers behind the cover of silver maple trees, didn't like the plan at all. I knew exactly how he felt. "This will be over in five minutes, Bradley."

He held my face in his hands. "I don't want this to be over in five minutes. I don't ever want this to be over."

I knew exactly how he felt.

As the van's headlights approached, I began waving and flailing. Help! My flip-flops slapped the pavement that still held the summer day's heat. The van slowed to a stop, and Fantasy's head popped out of the passenger window.

"What's the problem, lady?"

The driver said something.

Her arm shot out and she coldcocked him as troopers swarmed the back of the van.

Bradley came running.

Fantasy sat in the middle of the road with her head between her knees. I put an arm around her shoulders and gave her a squeeze. She turned her face to me and asked where her husband and sons were.

"I don't know, Fantasy."

"Where is *he*?"

"We were waiting for him at Million Air when he tried to leave."

She collapsed. We piled her in the Sikorsky.

"Hidey ho and welcome aboard!" (Dewey.)

I covered Fantasy with a blanket and poured her a shot of tequila, the only thing I could find. I texted Reggie. *We have her. She's safe.* He texted back. *Tell her I have a phone full of pictures of her. Tell her to get a lawyer.*

The platinum was removed from the Chevrolet van and when we took off, I could see it being escorted to a police station in Snead. (Around the corner.) Fantasy's three partners went the other way to be processed in Altoona. (At the fork, go left, then up the hill.) The Chevy van was towed to the Oneneta police station (just past Jimmy Irvine's mother's second husband's place), the only station around with a secure impound lot. At one o'clock, on the dot, when it was to have been in the airport long-term lot and full of Fantasy and platinum thieves, it blew sky high.

TWENTY-FIVE

The Bellissimo roof caught us by surprise, which is to say we dropped through the sky like a brick and slammed into a thirty-story building. Thud.

"Whoops." (Dewey.)

No Hair met us on the roof. He put his big arms around Fantasy and she stayed there a beat. She asked him if she could have a minute to (decide what to do with the rest of her life) shower and change before we sat down to talk. "We can wait until tomorrow, Fantasy." No Hair's tie was a bottle of Heinz ketchup. He wears distracting neckties so no one will notice he's bald. It doesn't work.

"No," she said. "I'll tell you what you need to know, then I'm going—" she stumbled, not at all sure of where to go from here.

"I've got her." I led her into the building.

We rode three different elevators down to 3B. By the time I swiped us in, it was so far into Saturday, if we kept it up much longer, we could catch the sunrise. And we weren't finished yet. We stumbled down the hall to the shower and she peeled off her burglar clothes along the way.

"Have you talked to Reggie?"

"Bradley has."

"So he knows?"

"Yes."

She stopped dead in her tracks. "Knows what?"

I opened my mouth, but no words came out.

"Does he know I'm okay?"

I pushed her into the shower. "Yes."

Thirty minutes later, we met in Event Hall B, where a Bellissimo drop crew was relieving the Mint Condition machines of cash and platinum, transferring it to a rolling cage. Two representatives from the Gaming Commission were there—this might get ugly—along with several Bellissimo attorneys who'd been dragged from their warm beds, plus two auditors from Hammond Stevenson Morris & Chase, also rudely awakened.

We found a corner conversation pit in Event Hall B with sofas and easy chairs, we found liquor, and we stared at one another. Fantasy was downright shell-shocked. I would have tucked her in and let her sleep it off, but I was too afraid to leave her alone and she was too afraid to be left alone. I activated a phone for her while she was in the shower, and after repeated attempts, her husband still wouldn't take her calls. Conner Hughes looked like someone had kicked him across the state of Mississippi and back. No Hair had been away so long he looked out of place, and Bradley looked like, well, Bradley looked like a man who'd dropped everything to be with his wife, bobbed around the entire state of Alabama for four hours, witnessed a gruesome death scene, and a multi-jurisdictional takedown with a six-foot-tall black woman having a meltdown in the middle of a two-lane Alabama highway. He hadn't given me the gun back.

In our loose circle, all the attention focused on Bradley. I'd have been looking at him anyway. Everyone else was looking to him for permission to go home, to bed, anywhere but here.

"Where is Dionne Warwick?" Bradley asked.

"She and her band loaded up two hours ago," No Hair said, "headed for New Orleans."

"Where is Josh Groban?"

"Gone," No Hair said, "on his way to California."

"Where's Baylor?" Bradley asked.

"Who's Baylor?" Conner Hughes asked.

"He's with us." I pointed. "He fell out of the ceiling."

Conner Hughes nodded.

"That boy took one in the face," No Hair said. "He's with Bianca's lady doctor."

"What happened to Baylor?" Fantasy asked.

I patted her leg. "Long story."

"It couldn't be too long if he's with Bianca's gynecologist."

"Where *is* Bianca?" Bradley took control of the conversation before it ran away.

It happens.

"I put her at your place," No Hair said. "She understood she was to stay put. She should be there."

If Bianca is in the Great Gumbo Getaway, someone pass me a blanket and I'll sleep here.

Bradley focused his attention on Conner Hughes and Fantasy. "The three men in custody in Alabama," he said, "the same three men who inspected and repaired the vault," he took a breath, "the same three men who were in charge of the Mint Condition machines—"

"The bad guys," I said. All heads turned my way.

"—is there anyone else, Conner? Fantasy?" Bradley asked. "Is there anyone else in this building who worked with, worked for, knew Miles Davenport, said boo to Miles Holloway, rode in the elevator with Miles Davenport—"

I raised my hand. "I rode in the elevator with him." All heads turned my way again.

"To the best of my knowledge," Conner Hughes said, "if you have him and if you have his three men, you have everyone."

"Right," No Hair spoke up. "We need him. Where is *he*? What's the plan?"

I heard a ringing in my ears, a clacking, then a siren.

No Hair scanned the faces of his very attentive and suddenly very awake audience. "Am I missing something?"

I could see the rapid rise and fall of Fantasy's chest out of the corner of my eye.

"Oh, hell no." Conner Hughes slowly turned his head from side to side. "No, hell, no. Oh, no. No. Hell no."

"I asked if there'd been any problems at the airport," Bradley said to No Hair.

"And I said no," No Hair said. "Because there weren't. Bianca didn't show up for her flight, I already had her at your place, and there were no problems."

"Miles Davenport not being taken down at the airport is a problem."

*   *   *

The long night got longer. The bar glasses disappeared and the coffee cups came out. It was three in the morning and we began furiously backpedaling.

Granted, too much had happened in a short amount of time, as evidenced by the fact that all of us looked like we'd been hit by a bus, three times, by three different buses, successively larger buses, and No Hair had been the last one onboard. Bradley thought I'd gone over it with No Hair and in all the Alabama activity, I thought he'd gone over it with No Hair.

As it turns out, neither of us had specifically instructed No Hair to lead the airport charge against Miles Davenport. So Miles Davenport not showing up at the airport didn't even register on No Hair's radar, because he knew nothing about it in the first place.

"I thought you had him, No Hair," I said. "This whole time we've been sitting here, I thought he was locked up."

"I never had him, Davis. I had confirmation that he'd tried to book a Bellissimo jet in Bianca's name."

"How did he even know enough about our internal operations to call transportation?"

A question I should have asked hours ago. In my defense, I'd been three hundred miles away and a little busy.

Fantasy found her voice. "You're forgetting he *knows* Bianca." Fantasy found her legs. "He replaced her eyelashes." Fantasy walks and taps her lips when she's thinking. The fingertips of her right hand were red and raw. Don't play with nitroglycerin. "Not to mention he's had our operating manual for months," she said, "because he's had Holder."

Conner Hughes raised and shook a me-too finger.

No one said, but it was the elephant, that Miles Davenport's ticket this week had been Fantasy. She'd played right into his (bed) hands. Holder Darby's life was ruined. Christopher Hall's life was over. It was yet to be seen if Conner Hughes would land on his feet after the dust cleared, but in the long run, I had a bad feeling the price Fantasy paid for being caught in Miles Davenport's web would be the highest.

* * *

We contacted surveillance and had them bring up whatever footage they could from the casino floor and all elevators that could be accessed from room 2631. I issued a property-wide APB on him with all of security, pit bosses, slot attendants, valet, the guy emptying ashtrays, and my favorite Friday night hooker in the main casino bar. (Sadie. She knows everyone.) I thought about calling Kinko's and having flyers printed. All in vain. No sightings, and the video showed only one item of interest: A woman wearing a black trench coat, a wide-brimmed black straw hat, and dark glasses knocking on the door of room 2631.

"Who is that?" Bradley asked.

My heart jumped to my throat when I answered. "It's Bianca."

"Surely not," No Hair said.

We ran the video feed forward and back, then again, and never saw anything but a woman in black knocking on the door.

I turned to No Hair. "You're sure she's upstairs at our place?"

"I'm positive."

"Call her," Bradley said.

I dialed. "Mrs. Sanders? Where are you?"

"I'm at your home, David, and it is atrocious. I need to speak to you immediately."

I hung up.

"She's fine."

We called transportation and waited to be patched through to the fleet supervisor. We crowded around the gold marble table where my phone, on speaker, was keeping company with coffee cups.

"Walk us through it."

"The call came in at nine o'clock," he said, "on the dot, from a man who identified himself as Mrs. Sanders's butler. He said she would take off at midnight. Exactly midnight. Forty-five minutes before the flight, we called to tell her the car was downstairs waiting to take her to the airport, but she didn't answer. And she never showed. We waited an hour, then pulled the plane back in the hangar. It's not the first time Mrs. Sanders has changed her mind or given us conflicting and confusing instructions. Several months ago, we landed in Denver and she said she meant Dallas, and expected us to know it, because she wasn't wearing her snow boots. She fired the entire crew."

That's our girl.

Miles Davenport could have walked out the front door, hailed a cab, and been on his way to Bangkok. Miles Davenport could have easily stolen or carjacked a vehicle and driven to Birmingham to meet up with his platinum. Miles Davenport might still be at the Bellissimo. Watching us right now.

"I know where he is." All heads turned my way. "He's at Jay Leno's place."

*　*　*

Except he wasn't.

I had sensory overload from being with too many people for too many hours and vertigo from the helicopter rides and lack of sleep. I was jittery from the two cups of coffee, and now I had déjà vu.

Inside Jay Leno's door, Dr. Paisley's clothes were in a trail to the sofa, a bright red bra dangled off a solid white lampshade, and

Baylor, naked from the waist up, his nose still very very broken, sat up from the sofa and pulled a gun on us. "Shith!"

Paisley, her hair styled Light Socket, also naked as far as we could see, rose up from the same sofa.

There's just no telling what all that sofa has seen.

I picked up Baylor's pants from the pile and threw them at him. "Get up."

"Davis," Paisley said. "I need to talk to you."

"Not now."

When they joined us in the hall five minutes later, neither Baylor's nose nor Paisley's hair in any better shape than it had been five minutes earlier, Bradley called it. "We're done. Everyone get some sleep. We'll meet again in the morning."

My nice warm bed was just steps away.

"Jeremy, if you would, escort Bianca home."

No Hair nodded.

"Fantasy, stay with us."

"I need to go home," she said.

Bradley didn't hesitate when he said, "That's not an option for you right now."

She paled. She swallowed. She studied the floor.

"Conner, stay here." He threw a thumb at Jay's door. "I'll post guards at the elevator and at the door."

Conner nodded. He was so beaten up, he'd have agreed to take the other end of the sofa from Baylor and Paisley.

It was a long walk home down the hall and around the corner. When we got there, neither I nor Bradley had a key.

"No one's given me a key, Bradley."

"How have you gotten in?"

"Sears," I said. "Sears has let me in and out."

"Stand back," my husband said. He pulled the gun from under his jacket and shot through the lock before any of us could stop him. I honestly didn't know how much more I could take. We looked at one another when we heard a loud thud and extreme crying from the other side of the door. Bianca.

Bradley, gun drawn, kicked the double doors open with his foot.

We stared into the foyer of the Big Easy Flea Market.

This one room.

If these fleur-de-lis walls could talk.

We were too stunned to move and the noise, obviously from the cat, was deafening. The cat's amplified cries bounced and echoed around the room, origin unknown. The magnolia tree in front of us had been decorated with wool streamers. The cat had shredded Bradley's Armani and Brooks Brothers dress pants and they hung from the tree in ribbons. Every sock Bradley owned was in the foyer, either in the tree or on the floor. The cries were coming *from* the tree. I ran. Something was so very wrong with the cat.

Bianca was against the back wall wearing my pink bathrobe and drag queen false eyelashes, two sets, tops and bottoms, none anywhere near straight. She blinked the big things and I swear the accompanying draft blew my hair from my face.

The cat was crying its cat heart out. I was at the base of the tree moving branches and magnolia leaves as fast as I could and I couldn't find it, I could only hear it. Changing positions, I caught a different view of Bianca through the tree limbs. She was standing between two chairs holding a taser gun.

"*Bianca?*" I heard Bradley's footsteps cross to her. "Where did you get the gun?"

"It's David's."

"What have you *done*?" he asked.

I couldn't see the cat, but I could see the scene from between the branches. Bound and gagged in one of the chairs was poor Sears, and his face was a maze of crisscrossed lines of dry blood: His eyes, his lips, and ears were slashed slices of inflamed flesh. He looked like he'd walked through a glass door, and he rocked in his prison chair, wild-eyed.

In a second chair, on the other side of Bianca, a chair that had tipped over on the floor, the thud we'd heard, was Miles Davenport. He too was bound and gagged and he'd been beaten to a pulp. One of his eyes was swollen completely shut, like he was wearing an eye patch, and when his chair tipped over and hit the ground, it trapped his bent leg. We were looking at a one-eyed one-legged master criminal.

Long John Silver.

Bianca, with her gargantuan crooked eyelashes, trained her taser gun on him. "Tell them what he did to me, David! Tell them!"

"They know, Bianca," I said from under the tree. "Tell us what *you* did to *him*."

Hands on hips, she spun my way and used the taser gun to mark her words. "I *never* gave you permission to call me by my first name."

"And you've never known mine."

The cat. The cat. I finally found a blur of yellow, but I couldn't catch it. The cat raced up and down the tree trunk from me to the sock nest, then back to me. When it got to me it put its cat nose almost against mine, cried, then raced back up the tree. I was helpless to slow it down, figure out what was wrong with it, stop the crying, or catch it.

"Something is wrong with your cat, David." I pulled my head out of the tree and found Bianca. She blinked several times, probably starting a typhoon in the Gulf.

"Did you *tase* it?"

The cat, realizing I wasn't under the tree with it, started crying again. I dove back in. I moved in the direction of the noise, directly in my ears now, it was so dark at the base of the tree. When I pulled my head out again to ask for a flashlight, I saw Bradley behind Sears, trying to remove his Marcoliani sock gag. I hoped he wouldn't go for his new favorite toy and shoot the sock off Sears's head.

"Why do you have Sears tied up, Bianca?" Did she know something we didn't? Was Sears in on this?

"That man," Bianca pointed to Sears with her taser gun, "obviously did something to your cat, David. He's an animal abuser."

Sears, finally free of his sock muzzle, made his presence known. "STAY AWAY FROM THE CAT! GET AWAY FROM THE CAT!"

I pulled my head out of the tree.

"What?" I asked Sears. "*What?*"

Sears hadn't walked through a glass door. The cat had attacked him. This was what he'd been trying to tell me.

No Hair had the barrel of his gun aimed between Miles Davenport's eyes. He didn't look away as he said, "Fantasy?"

Her slow march to where Miles Davenport's overturned chair bounced against the marble floor as he hopelessly struggled would have been the footsteps heard round the world had the cat not been going out of its cat mind.

"Trade places with me, Davis," Bradley said. "Get Sears untangled and let me find the cat."

I took another look at Sears's face and decided it wasn't a bad idea. I didn't want the cat to tear up my face too. Not that I wanted it to tear up Bradley's. Climbing out of the cast iron bucket I was halfway in, I caught a glimpse of Paisley who (had no pants on) I'd totally forgotten about, beside Baylor who (had no shirt on) I'd forgotten about too.

"Can you help a little, Baylor?"

"With *whath*?"

He had a point.

"How abouth I noth leth anyone elthe in, Dabith?"

That would work.

I almost ran into Bianca's eyelashes as Bradley and I switched places. My robe did not fit her. Words were pouring out of Sears as I approached him, including socks, refrigerator, stun gun, cat, nothing I could make any sense of until he said, "That woman with the eyelashes beat that black man within an inch of his *life!*"

"Bianca." I stopped everything. "Give me back my taser gun and quit with the weight lifting."

"Give it to her, Bianca," Bradley said.

Her eyelashes quivered at me, then at Bradley, the one below her left eye losing ground and headed south. "Why is everyone calling me Bianca?" she wailed. "When did I give *any* of you permission to call me Bianca?"

Bradley didn't get anywhere near under the tree to rescue the cat when he let out a yelp and was right back out. I whipped my head around to see a bright line of blood beading a diagonal line across his cheek. He didn't find the cat, but the cat sure found him.

"Back," I said. "Trade again. At least the cat isn't trying to kill me."

Fantasy had a black boot on Miles Davenport's bloody, busted up ear, an itchy gun on him, and she was posed, with her foot on his head, as if she'd reached Mount Everest. Miles Davenport, from under her boot, still bound to the chair and in the floor, had the fear of God in his eyes. Just like Monday, when I'd first seen him in the elevator, but this time he meant it.

"You know the difference between me and you, buddy?" He trembled. "I have faith. That's why I'm standing here with a gun on you and you've had your ass kicked on the way to prison. You have no faith. You should work on that."

The cat let out a war cry and I dove under the tree again, this time from a different approach. I was finally close enough to reach it when Bianca stopped traffic again.

"Someone get me a drink. You with the black eyes and broken nose. You're not busy. Get me a drink. Anything with alcohol in it. I'm exhausted with sobriety. David, climb down from that tree and get me a drink. Someone get me a drink."

"No!" From behind me, Dr. Paisley spoke up. "No, Bianca. You can't drink. You're pregnant."

The room grew deathly quiet, the cat and I blinked at each other, and the silence wasn't broken until Bianca passed out cold onto the floor.

I swallowed. Hard.

"Cat?" The cat stared at me with huge, sad, unblinking eyes. It looked up to the sock nest, whimpered, then back at me. "Show me, cat," I whispered. "Show me."

The noise all around me was that of Bianca being administered to.

"Who knocked Biacath upth?"

"Bianca. It's me. Dr. Paisley." Slap slap. "Someone get her water." Slap slap. "Can you hear me?"

"Davis! What in hell did you do to this kitchen?" (No Hair.)

"I'm what? I'm *what*?"

She's back.

"My weight gain! This is my weight gain! David! Where is David? I'm with child! Where is Richard? Where is my husband? David!"

Laughter cut through the tree branches. Fantasy. "Oh, my God! Bianca! You're pregnant. You're going to have a baby!"

"Everyone stop calling me Bianca!"

Fantasy tapped Miles Davenport's busted ear with her boot. "See there? Life goes on."

I would have so enjoyed every bit of this had I not been in the tree with the cat.

"How could I be *pregnant*? Does Richard know? David, get Richard on the phone this minute."

"How olth are you, Biancath?"

"Shut your mouth, young man, or I'll shut it for you."

"SHE WILL ZAP YOU!"

I'd forgotten Sears. I poked my head out of the tree and found him. "Are you okay?"

"I'll be fine, Mrs. Cole." He dabbed a wet magnolia hand towel around his injured face. "But we need to talk about my wages. I might need hazard duty pay."

"Sears," Cat pawed my hand. No claws, it just wanted me back under the tree. "Go out the front door, take a left, and keep going until you reach the Leno suite. Knock on the door and tell the man staying there we need him. His name is Conner. Tell him we have his cat."

"You got it, Mrs. Cole."

The cat mewled at me and swiped the fake grass around the

base of the tree. No more crying. I was finally where it wanted me. I inched my hands along the shredded raffia sprayed green to imitate grass, the cat's eyes on mine the whole time. It wanted me to help it dig in the grass. The cat begged me to help dig in the grass.

I felt my husband's warmth beside me. "Davis?"

"Bradley. Check the tree. Look in the sock bed the cat built."

He stayed beside me and said, "Baylor. Get up there and see what's in the tree."

"Here." My fingers were past the grass. I passed Bradley a banded stack of one hundred dollar bills. Then another. Then another. Then four more, then ten more, the cat quietly mewling the whole time. The room grew silent as I continued to pass money to Bradley. I kept my eyes on the cat's, and each time I pulled my arm away and held it out, my hand emptied a second later. I dug a money hole large enough for the cat to stick its head in, which it did, and cried. It raised its face and swatted at the hole, but it still couldn't get to what it wanted. I climbed farther into the cast iron tub that surely held millions upon millions of dollars until I found what the cat had been looking for. I cradled it in my hands and brought it out as gently as I could. It was the most beautiful thing I'd ever seen. The cat latched itself onto my arm and came out from the tree with me. The newborn kitten was solid white, with a dot of a pink nose and tiny pink eyelids. The cat crawled between my arms and cradled hands and began rubbing and warming the kitten with its smashed face.

From the sock bed above I heard, "Kittenths. Thwee kittenths."

From the open door behind I heard, "Princess Puffle Paws! Princess Puffle Paws! It's Daddy! It's your daddy!"

(Princess Puffle Paws? Really?)

I rocked back and my husband's strong arms caught me and eased me into a sitting position, money all around me, holding a mother cat in my lap and a baby kitten in my cupped hands. The room and everyone in it finally stilled. It was one of the most beautiful and peaceful moments I've ever known in my life. Until Bianca opened her mouth.

"David, you'll be the face of my pregnancy."

And how am I supposed to pull *that* off?

Gretchen Archer

Gretchen Archer is a Tennessee housewife who began writing when her daughters, seeking higher educations, ran off and left her. She lives on Lookout Mountain with her husband, son, and a Yorkie named Bently. *Double Whammy,* her first Davis Way Crime Caper, was a Daphne du Maurier Award finalist and hit the USA TODAY Bestsellers List. *Double Mint* is the fourth Davis Way crime caper. You can visit her at www.gretchenarcher.com.

Bently Yarnell

Bently Yarnell is a Lookout Mountain Yorkshire Terrier. He loves barking, sleeping late, and going bye-bye. He's a graduate of Woof Woof Obedience School and his favorite treat is Beggin' Littles.

In Case You Missed the 1st Book in the Series

DOUBLE WHAMMY

Gretchen Archer

A Davis Way Crime Caper (#1)

Davis Way thinks she's hit the jackpot when she lands a job as the fifth wheel on an elite security team at the fabulous Bellissimo Resort and Casino in Biloxi, Mississippi. But once there, she runs straight into her ex-ex husband, a rigged slot machine, her evil twin, and a trail of dead bodies. Davis learns the truth and it does not set her free—in fact, it lands her in the pokey.

Buried under a mistaken identity, unable to seek help from her family, her hot streak runs cold until her landlord Bradley Cole steps in. Make that her landlord, lawyer, and love interest. With his help, Davis must win this high stakes game before her luck runs out.

Available at booksellers nationwide and online

Visit www.henerypress.com for details

Don't Miss the 2nd Book in the Series

DOUBLE DIP

Gretchen Archer

A Davis Way Crime Caper (#2)

Davis Way's beginner's luck may have run out. Her professional life is dicey and she's on a losing streak at home. She can't find her gun, her evil twin's personal assistant has disappeared, Bellissimo's Master of Ceremonies won't leave her alone, and her boyfriend Bradley Cole thinks three's a crowd.

Meanwhile, she's following a slot tournament trail that leads to Beehive, Alabama, where the So Help Me God Pentecostal Church is swallowing up Bellissimo's high rollers. The worst? Davis doesn't feel so hot. It could be the banana pudding, but it might be the pending pitter patter of little feet.

DOUBLE DIP is a reckless ride in the fast lane, and Davis Way can't find the brakes.

Available at booksellers nationwide and online

Visit www.henerypress.com for details

Don't Miss the 3rd Book in the Series

DOUBLE STRIKE

Gretchen Archer

A Davis Way Crime Caper (#3)

Bellissimo Resort and Casino Super Spy Davis Way knows three
things: Cooking isn't a prerequisite for a happy marriage, don't
trust men who look like David Hasselhoff, and money doesn't grow
on Christmas trees. None of which help when a storm hits the Gulf
a week before the Bellissimo's Strike It Rich Sweepstakes. Securing
the guests, staff, and property might take a stray bullet. Or two.

Bellissimo Resort and Casino Super Spy Davis Way has three
problems: She's desperate to change her marital status, her new
boss speaks in hashtags, and Bianca Sanders has confiscated her
clothes. All of which bring on a headache hot enough to spark a fire.
Solving her problems means stealing a car. From a dingbat lawyer.

Bellissimo Resort and Casino Super Spy Davis Way has three goals:
Keep the Sanders family out of prison, regain her footing in her
relationship, and find the genius who wrote the software for
futureGaming. One of which, the manhunt one, is iffy. Because
when Alabama hides someone, they hide them good.

DOUBLE STRIKE. A VIP invitation to an extraordinary high-stakes
gaming event, as thieves, feds, dance instructors, shady bankers,
kidnappers, and gold waiters go all in. #Don'tMissIt.

Available at booksellers nationwide and online

Visit www.henerypress.com for details

Henery Press Mystery Books

And finally, before you go...
Here are a few other mysteries
you might enjoy:

PILLOW STALK

Diane Vallere

A Madison Night Mystery (#1)

Interior Decorator Madison Night might look like a throwback to the sixties, but as business owner and landlord, she proves that independent women can have it all. But when a killer targets women dressed in her signature style—estate sale vintage to play up her resemblance to fave actress Doris Day—what makes her unique might make her dead.

The local detective connects the new crime to a twenty-year old cold case, and Madison's long-trusted contractor emerges as the leading suspect. As the body count piles up, Madison uncovers a Soviet spy, a campaign to destroy all Doris Day movies, and six minutes of film that will change her life forever.

Available at booksellers nationwide and online

Visit www.henerypress.com for details

THE DEEP END

Julie Mulhern

A Country Club Murders Mystery

Swimming into the lifeless body of her husband's mistress tends to ruin a woman's day, but becoming a murder suspect can ruin her whole life.

It's 1974 and Ellison Russell's life revolves around her daughter and her art. She's long since stopped caring about her cheating husband, Henry, and the women with whom he entertains himself. That is, until she becomes a suspect in Madeline Harper's death. The murder forces Ellison to confront her husband's proclivities and his crimes—kinky sex, petty cruelties and blackmail.

As the body count approaches par on the seventh hole, Ellison knows she has to catch a killer. But with an interfering mother, an adoring father, a teenage daughter, and a cadre of well-meaning friends demanding her attention, can Ellison find the killer before he finds her?

Available at booksellers nationwide and online

Visit www.henerypress.com for details

DINERS, DIVES & DEAD ENDS

Terri L. Austin

A Rose Strickland Mystery (#1)

As a struggling waitress and part-time college student, Rose Strickland's life is stalled in the slow lane. But when her close friend, Axton, disappears, Rose suddenly finds herself serving up more than hot coffee and flapjacks. Now she's hashing it out with sexy bad guys and scrambling to find clues in a race to save Axton before his time runs out.

With her anime-loving bestie, her septuagenarian boss, and a pair of IT wise men along for the ride, Rose discovers political corruption, illegal gambling, and shady corporations. She's gone from zero to sixty and quickly learns when you're speeding down the fast lane, it's easy to crash and burn.

Available at booksellers nationwide and online

Visit www.henerypress.com for details

GIRL MEETS CLASS

Karin Gillespie

(from the Henery Press Chick Lit Collection)

The unspooling of Toni Lee Wells' Tiffany and Wild Turkey lifestyle begins with a trip to the Luckett County Jail drunk tank. An earlier wrist injury sidelined her pro tennis career, and now she's trading her tennis whites for wild nights roaming the streets of Rose Hill, Georgia.

Her wealthy family finally gets fed up with her shenanigans. They cut off her monthly allowance but also make her a sweetheart deal: Get a job, keep it for a year, and you'll receive an early inheritance. Act the fool or get fired, and you'll lose it for good.

Toni Lee signs up for a fast-track Teacher Corps program. She hopes for an easy teaching gig, but what she gets is an assignment to Harriet Hall, a high school that churns out more thugs than scholars.

What's a spoiled Southern belle to do when confronted with a bunch of street smart students who are determined to make her life as difficult as possible? Luckily, Carl, a handsome colleague, is willing to help her negotiate the rough teaching waters and keep her bed warm at night. But when Toni Lee gets involved with some dark dealings in the school system, she fears she might lose her new beau as well as her inheritance.

Available at booksellers nationwide and online

Visit www.henerypress.com for details

FINDING SKY

Susan O'Brien

A Nicki Valentine Mystery

Suburban widow and P.I. in training Nicki Valentine can barely keep track of her two kids, never mind anyone else. But when her best friend's adoption plan is jeopardized by the young birth mother's disappearance, Nicki is persuaded to help. Nearly everyone else believes the teenager ran away, but Nicki trusts her BFF's judgment, and the feeling is mutual.

The case leads where few moms go (teen parties, gang shootings) and places they can't avoid (preschool parties, OB-GYNs' offices). Nicki has everything to lose and much to gain — including the attention of her unnervingly hot P.I. instructor. Thankfully, Nicki is armed with her pesky conscience, occasional babysitters, a fully stocked minivan, and nature's best defense system: women's intuition.

Available at booksellers nationwide and online

Visit www.henerypress.com for details

ON THE ROAD WITH DEL & LOUISE

Art Taylor

A Novel in Short Stories

Del's a small time crook with a moral conscience—robbing convenience stores only for tuition and academic expenses. Brash and sassy Louise goes from being a holdup victim to Del's lover and accomplice. All they want is a fresh start, an honest life, and a chance to build a family together, but fate conspires to put ever-steeper challenges in their path—and escalating temptations, too.

A real estate scam in recession-blighted Southern California. A wine heist in Napa Valley. A Vegas wedding chapel holdup. A kidnapping in an oil-rich North Dakota boomtown. Can Del and Louise stay on the right side of the law? On one another's good side? And when they head back to Louise's hometown in North Carolina, what new trouble will prove the biggest: Louise's nagging mama or a hidden adversary seemingly intent on tearing the couple apart? Or could those be one and the same?

From screwball comedy to domestic drama, and from caper tale to traditional whodunit, these six stories offer suspense with a side of romance—and a little something for all tastes.

Available at booksellers nationwide and online

Visit www.henerypress.com for details

CPSIA information can be obtained
at www.ICGtesting.com
Printed in the USA
LVOW01s2011021016
506955LV00002B/190/P